One Crow, Two Crow

by VIRGINIA CHASE

author of "The Knight of the Golden Fleece," etc.

"One crow, two crow," begins an old Maine folk chant. From this chant Virginia Chase has drawn her story—a novel set on Maine's lonely "barrens," where the land itself, fertile only for scrub and wild blueberries, breeds into those who live there something of its strength, its storms, and its silences.

Here two young people, with differing tastes and ambitions, fall deeply in love and begin their married life, coping with the land's severity and relishing its wild beauties.

In the nearby village, deserted by most of the young for the cities, are vividly seen those who have stayed behind—earning their livings by farming or fishing, or even, during this Prohibition era, by rum-running from Canada along Maine's secluded coves and harbors.

ONE CROW, TWO CROW is a story stark, gentle, and free of sentimentality — a story of goodness, of struggle and courage, and, ultimately, of joy.

Books by Virginia Chase

ONE CROW,

TWO CROW

A novel by

VIRGINIA CHASE Perkins

The Vanguard Press, New York

C 1

Published simultaneously in Canada by the
Copp Clark Publishing Company, Ltd., Toronto

Manufactured in the United States of America by
H. Wolff Book Manufacturing Company, New York

Library of Congress Catalogue Card Number: 70-155663

SBN 8149-0691-5

Designer: Ernst Reichl

For my daughter

One crow sorrow,
two crow joy. . . .

From a Maine folk chant

PART ONE

1925

1

It was Friday afternoon. Laura Leighton sat on the steps of District School No. 3, her bookbag and satchel beside her. She was a good-looking girl, well-formed and solid, with light brown hair, fair skin that flushed easily, dark, earnest eyes, and a mouth that was both warm and resolute. She wore a white shirtwaist with a starched round collar, a navy blue pleated skirt, and a red pull-over sweater. The day was cool for April.

As she sat there, her hands clasping her knees, she looked above the stretch of smooth gray ledges on which the school stood to the road that followed the sea. On one side of it gulls hovered, circling like bits of drifting paper above the pewter-colored flats. On the other side was a line of gaunt, gray-budded alders. The road was empty. No car was on it. No buggy. No loitering schoolboy.

She lowered her head and mentally checked on her fingers the things she should have done inside. Washed boards. Put on the spelling words and the new motto, *Onward, Ever Onward.* Averaged ranks and recorded them. Pinned up maps for display. Checked desks for tidiness. Filled inkwells. Some of the older girls had offered to help her. Usually she accepted their offers, for she enjoyed their company and valued the reassurance they gave her. *Everybody likes you, Miss Leighton. . . . Everybody says you're fair.* But on Friday afternoons she put them off, as she had done today.

She looked at the road again, shading her eyes, for the sun was low in the sky. Nobody. Nothing. Then she looked at her watch, a plain gold wristwatch on a black ribbon band.

So much of life, she thought, was spent in waiting.

Her very first memory had been of waiting—waiting for the news of her father and mother, who had gone for an excursion on the launch *Lucy Bell.* They had planned to take her and Doris with them, but Doris, who was almost fifteen, had preferred the company of her own friends, and at the last minute Flora, who was twenty-two and just married to Luther, had made a suggestion. "Leave Laura with me," she urged. "She's sure to get seasick if there's a swell." And her mother, who always listened to Flora, had agreed.

It had been a fine September day when they started out. Her mother had been wearing a peanut straw hat, tied on with a veil. Her father had carried a picnic basket on one arm, a folded lap robe on the other, for there had been a breeze blowing. "Be good," her mother had told her. "Mind Flora. Do just what she says."

After dinner she had been sitting on one of the kitchen chairs (raised by the dictionary so that she could reach the table), cutting out paper dolls with the second-best scissors. As she sat there, feeling very sorry for herself, very cheated, she had heard the wind—the real wind—blowing. From the window she had seen the trees in the orchard bend, seen the apples drop heavily and the dead twigs snap. By four, the room was so

4

dark that Flora had made her put the scissors away. A few minutes later, when Doris came in, the rain had begun to fall. "Drenched to your skin, I suppose," Flora had scolded. As she lighted the lamp and set it on the table, the flame on the wick wavered, steadied an instant, then almost went out.

Luther had come at five, wearing his oilskins. "Looks like a reg'lar gale," he said. At supper nobody talked much, and when the dishes were done they had stayed on in the kitchen to be near the telephone.

Around seven Flora had begun walking the floor. "Early this morning," she said, "I had a premonition." Being not quite five, Laura had not known what a premonition was, but she knew that something was wrong, and though she was very sleepy, she had not dared to close her eyes, feeling it would be a disgrace. Finally the telephone had rung and Flora answered. "The launch capsized near the Point," she told them, turning. "They've found Mama and Papa."

Luther must have expected Laura to understand, for he had picked her up and held her face against his big shoulder. But she did not understand. Mama and Papa had been found, hadn't they? The thing that had impressed her most was that Flora and Doris were acting as though they really liked each other.

Yes, she had always been waiting for something. For the fog to lift on picnic days; for the library to open; for the ice to thicken on the Mill Pond; for the first heavy snow. Waiting for the kittens to be born (it was Luther, not Flora, who told her when they were coming); for the sound of the sawmill that meant it was spring. Waiting to get over mumps and whooping cough and especially measles. Waiting for the first arbutus to bloom, half hidden in Dunbar's pasture; for the first berries to ripen (she had quick fingers for picking); for the seeds she had planted to spring up in her garden. Waiting for the day that school would begin. Waiting for Joel.

5

They had played together as children. Never very much, for Joel preferred to play at his house, and he never asked her there. She liked him because he was different from most of the boys she knew, boys who swore and used bad grammar—*ain't, hain't, northin'*—and hung around the bathing houses at the shore, peeking through the knotholes when the girls were undressing. She liked him because he was always good to Harry, Flora's son, born not long after the accident, a fat red-cheeked boy whom the other boys mocked because he talked with a stammer. In spite of the difference in their ages, Joel always included Harry in their games, treating him as an equal, drawing pictures to please him. Joel could draw remarkably well, making quick lines that seemed at first to have no connection merge into an exciting pattern. Trees. Birds. Animals. Even faces you could recognize, though one feature or another was always exaggerated.

But playing with Joel meant waiting, just as she was waiting now. Just as she waited every Friday when he came in Ed's truck to take her back to Millboro for the weekend. Ed Levesque was Doris's husband. He worked as caretaker and gardener for some of the summer people, and right now Joel was helping him out.

Laura looked at her watch again. It was almost five o'clock, and Joel had said he would be there for sure by four. Here she had washed the boards at noon. Here she had hurried the children off—something she never liked to do—in order to be ready. She felt a touch of exasperation. But this was no time to get exasperated, she told herself, for she had made a definite plan, and she did not want anything to distract her from it. This plan had to do with waiting. She had waited long enough for Joel to make up his mind about them. Before they got home she would find out exactly what he wanted.

She heard a horn touched lightly. Then she saw the truck coming with Joel at the wheel. It always stirred her to see him

—his face with its olive skin and well-proportioned features; his dark thick hair, carelessly parted, with a cowlick where the part began; his deep-set, guarded gray eyes; his mouth that, unlike his eyes, betrayed him, changing with his moods. A year older than she, he was about her size and height, but he had an aloofness—a haughtiness, Flora called it—that made him appear taller than he was.

The truck drew up and stopped before her.

"Waiting long?" he asked.

"Quite a while," she said, careful to keep her voice even.

He grinned. "That's what you get for being so smart."

She flushed a little, set her satchel in the seat, and got in, still holding her bag. She didn't like to hear people say she was smart, though they said it often. Especially she didn't like to hear Joel say it, even when he was teasing her like this. "How's everything?" she asked.

"All right, I guess."

"You been busy?"

"So-so."

Normally she plied him with questions, for he never came right out with anything, but only revealed things piecemeal— where he had been, what he had been doing, whom he had seen, what each one of them had said. The questions over, she would tell him what had gone on at school, though he seldom asked. But today such things seemed trivialities.

"Don't you have any plans, Joel?" she asked abruptly.

He looked surprised. "Why, to get myself a regular job," he said. Right after high school he had worked three years in the woods, marking trees for cutting, but after a series of accidents, one of which had injured his back, he had given it up. He had taken this work with Ed only temporarily.

"You know what Luther said."

"A-yuh." When Harry left school, despite his mother's protests, to learn the plumber's trade in Lubec, Luther had offered

Joel a job in the store. He had turned it down immediately. He was looking for an outdoor job, a job where he could be his own boss, make his own hours; above all, work at his own speed. Just the thought of a schedule riled him.

"I wish you'd tell me what you've got against the store, Joel."

"You wouldn't understand."

"You could try me, Joel."

He shook his head curtly, and she knew there was no use pressing him further.

There were a great many things about Joel she did not understand. Actually, that was the core of his fascination for her. Everyone else she knew was all of a piece; Joel was full of baffling contradictions. He was one of the boys, and yet he wasn't. He professed to scorn their games, yet he hung around the field willing enough to umpire or keep score. He never missed one of the dances, yet for the first hour at least he stood off by himself in the back of the hall, looking bored. Sometimes the evening was half over before he came out on the floor. Though he was a poor dancer, he never lacked for partners, for, the girls all agreed, Joel had class. He was clever, too, and singing along with the music, he made up his own words, mocking words generally. *Margie, you are my aggravation* . . .

In school he never volunteered, but when someone happened to say something he disagreed with, he would start up a real debate. Though he was bright, he never applied himself to his lessons. When the others were doing theirs, he would sit with a pencil in his hand drawing caricatures that he would cover immediately if anyone looked over his shoulder and then destroy. Grades meant nothing to him. When rank cards were ready, he never even bothered to go to the desk for his.

Would he have been different if his mother hadn't been the kind of person she was? Laura often wondered. Joel's mother was "from away," as the people of Millboro put it. His father, who had gone to sea when the coastwise schooners were running, had met and married her in Boston, where she had worked in a shoe factory. It was apparent that she was older than her husband, and people figured that she was sick of the factory and looking for a way out.

If this was true, she did not find it, for she had scorned Millboro from the start. The place was dead, she told her neighbors, the women dowdy. She mocked at the local dialect, and scoffed at the wooden sidewalks, complaining loudly when she caught her high heels in their cracks. To her neighbors she complained about the lack of conveniences. In Boston, she let it be known, her flat had a gas stove and, more than that, plumbing. She didn't go to church, nor did she join any of the local organizations.

But the thing people disapproved of most was the way she brought up her children. She fed them whenever they were hungry and never said a word to them about cleaning their plates. She bought them anything they wanted, usually from mail-order catalogues that she kept piled on a shelf above the sink. When she ordered, it was always C.O.D.—something frowned upon by the best people in Millboro—and when her husband came home, he sometimes found six or seven parcels waiting for him to redeem.

They disapproved of the way she let Joel's sister, Emmie, eight years younger than he, go around in "boughten" dresses that needed to be shortened and hair ribbons that had never been pressed. They disapproved of the way she taught her children not Flinch and Jack Straws, but games with real playing cards. People who went by sometimes as late as ten o'clock at night saw her and Joel playing double solitaire at the kitchen table. They had a good deal to say, in lowered voices, about her partiality to Joel and the way she let him follow her everywhere. Yet when she had disappeared six years before, it was Emmie she took with her.

Would he have been different if his father had kept within

the law? When he had stopped going to sea, Joel's father had become a lobsterman, but after a time people began to notice that he wasn't setting out his traps any longer. (A lobsterman without traps meant only one thing during Prohibition along the coast of Maine.) Until then everybody had liked him, thought him a quiet, respectable man, and felt sorry that he had been taken in by such a wife. But when they found out what was going on under their very noses, a good many, especially women, changed their attitudes considerably. Every now and then the W.C.T.U. threatened action, but nothing ever came of it.

"Don't you make long-range plans, Joel?"

He shook his head. His mother had never planned ahead. She had believed in taking one day at a time, and so did he. If he had any plans, they were to stay right there in Millboro. He hated cities. It was the one thing on which he and his mother had really disagreed.

They rode on in silence. Occasionally they passed a farm where a man was clearing out his cornfield, and the earth gave off its smell, heady and half forgotten. There was the smell, too, of sap, thinly sweet; the pungent smell of pitch; the acrid smell of late bonfires. Where the road neared the sea, there was the brackish smell from the clam flats, especially strong in spring, when they had been freed of their covering of ice and snow. Spring was late this year, and the maples, like the alders, were just beginning to show their buds. But her thoughts were not on spring.

"Well, I'm making plans," she finally said.

All her life she had been making plans. To say she had been dreaming dreams would have been more accurate, for never before had she been in a position to make them come true. Now she was twenty-one years old. In a little more than three years of teaching at District 3, she had saved nine hundred dollars.

When she was fifteen she had brought up the subject of normal school to Flora, but Flora wouldn't even consider it. "I promised Mama that if anything ever happened to her, I'd look after you and Doris," she said. "How could I do that with you gallivanting off somewhere? You won't even have to go to Normal if you teach around here."

At first she had thought she would never get over it. She had stayed in her room hours, days at a time, and for weeks, in spite of Luther's distress, had broken out crying even at the table. Then Joel's mother left, and though he had tried hard to cover it up, she saw he was miserable too. Things changed for both of them. He needed someone. She needed someone to need her. No one really ever had. So they felt a kind of bond. He began walking home with her from school, sometimes from socials. He took her sliding and skating, often with Harry along, though secretly she would have preferred that just the two of them go together. At the graduation ball, he danced the last dance with her, and when the orchestra played *Whispering*, he tightened his hold on her hand until her class ring cut into her finger. He sang, too, not saucy, made-up words then, but the real ones. *Whispering that you'll never leave me.* That night he had kissed her for the first time. It wasn't much of a kiss, just a quick brush against her forehead. But since then a new dream —a vibrant, consuming dream—had taken over. Mrs. Joel Closson . . . Joseph . . . Jesse . . . Josephine . . . Julie. And another dream had blended right in with it—a dream of escape from Flora. *Sit up straight, Laura . . . look, you've got the light coming over your wrong shoulder. . . . You've forgotten to put on your apron. . . . If only you'd think before you do things, Laura.*

She smoothed back her hair, adjusted her bag, then looked at Joel from the corner of her eye to see if he had heard and decided that he had. But he said nothing, just drove on, his hand, faintly shaded with dark hair, jerking the wheel. Her glance moved and lingered on it. It was an interesting hand, sensitive and finely proportioned, with long fingers and narrow well-kept nails—the kind of hand not often seen in Millboro.

Five minutes went by. He was putting all his attention on the road, taking exaggerated care to keep out of the muddy ruts. A wind blew in from the sea, and the bell buoy on the Point sounded, hollow and deliberate. A long procession of crows passed silently overhead.

If only he would talk with her, she was thinking. If only he would tell her what he wanted. If he didn't want her, bitter though it would be, she must know and accept it. She couldn't spend her whole life waiting to find out.

"What are these big plans?" he asked suddenly.

He had asked. He had wanted to know. There had been a taunting note in his voice, but he had asked.

"Going away," she said. "Maybe to Normal."

She waited, this time eagerly, hoping he would protest, say he loved her, needed her, wanted her, vow that they must never be apart. But again he said nothing.

A slow, hot flush spread over her. She felt scorned, humiliated. Then, upon impulse, she looked in his face and saw the panic in it.

It was enough for her.

2

Millboro had a population of about six hundred. Like most Maine coastal villages, it had seen better days. In its center was the elm-shaded green where the Soldiers' Monument stood, fronted by a rusty cannon. Directly opposite, on the road that enclosed the green, was the Post Office, white, squat, and blunt-fronted, about half large enough for those who crowded it twice daily with the coming of the mail. Its outer wall served as a bulletin board for the village, announcing Grange suppers, Fish and Game laws, lost dogs. Inside, behind a partition of boxes, Mrs. Hattie Blaisdell, the postmistress—tiny, agile—worked, stamping the letters that came in and went out with the skill and rapidity of a woodpecker. Those who had prestige in the village had a box with a key. Others had to wait their turn at the Delivery window when the mail was open.

To the right of the Post Office was the Grange Hall, white, too, but seeming, by contrast, to be more commodious than it was. Its second floor housed the Selectmen's office and its upper entry the Ladies' Social Library. (Hours: Saturday, 2–4) In its cellar was the village lockup, a huge iron cage divided in the middle, where perhaps two or three times a year some tramp or alien drunk reposed. Any serious offender—such as a man who had killed a moose or set his neighbor's barn on fire—was taken to the county jail.

Next to the Grange Hall, but set a little back from it, was the grade school with its high belfry, shedding its ugly pumpkin-colored paint. In front, centered by a flagpole, was a yard of hard-packed gravel, and in back, set primly apart, were two outhouses that had never known paint.

To the left of the Post Office was Peasley's Grocery, weathered and sagging, where Mr. Peasley, with grimy hands and dark-rimmed nails, measured and packaged his meager stock. The fastidious never traded at Peasley's, even though prices were often cut there, for everything in the store tasted faintly of kerosene. It might have come from the barrel itself, set too close to the flour and crackers, or it might have come only from the smoky lamps that burned there on dark afternoons. Had it not been for the income from the pool table in the back room, the place could never have stayed open at all. A crowd of boys always hung around Peasley's, watching the game, or stood on the steps, shouting remarks to the girls who passed.

Directly across the green stood Luther's grocery—yellow, with a brown mansard roof, twice as big as Peasley's and twice as flourishing. SAWYER'S—ALMOST EVERYTHING, the sign above it read. The sign did not exaggerate. On the first floor, carefully organized, were staples; dry and canned goods; meat, fresh and pickled; fruit; cheeses; strings of dried fish; kegs of salt pork; tongues and sounds; patent medicines; penny candy. Everything shone. The windows with their displays, the counters, the showcases, the cabinets, the scoops, the scales, the oilstove surrounded by four or five chairs (loafing was not encouraged at Sawyer's); the old roll-top desk that nobody but Luther could manage. In the annex, itself as clean as Flora's kitchen, were grain and barreled goods; upstairs, hardware and a few furnishings.

Just beyond was the high school, a one-story building, brown-shingled, with worn steps and long rows of narrow windows where the shades always hung unevenly. It had a central hall with a large hot-air register in its floor on which the girls stood at recess on cold mornings, their skirts circling, the metal of their garters burning into their thighs; a main room where boys and girls, carefully segregated, studied, regarded benignly by a plaster bust of Shakespeare set too high for dusting; two classrooms, bare except for a teacher's desk on a platform, faced by two lines of scarred settees; and two entries smelling faintly of the inside water closets beyond.

On a knoll between the grade school and the main highway leading to Cherryfield stood the church, white and dignified, with a tall, graceful spire. Inside, the floors were carpeted in red, rich and dark, well-worn in the vestibule, especially under the bell rope and in the back pews. The pews themselves were cushioned in the same color. A line of small red panes edged

14

the plain glass windows, making, on sunny mornings, a rosy reflection of little squares on the white woodwork. The top of the pulpit, behind which the Reverend Bigelow stood, was red too. So was the fringe on the bookmark in the big Bible that he fingered while he fumbled through his prayers. Downstairs was the vestry, with long, high windows through which the boys who refused to attend Christian Endeavor—Joel among them —peeked while the service was in progress. Flanking the church was a shaded graveyard.

About half a mile from the green, as a gull flies, was the bay. At its head, on the mouth of a brook leading into it, stood the mill Laura's father had once owned, almost dwarfed by its pile of sawdust. Its slip led down to a coffee-colored pond, where willow seedlings floated like giant insects above a rotting, rough-edged dam. Around the pond was a line of alders and above it a bridge with a high, narrow railing where the boys walked, arms outstretched, swaying precariously, Joel the least skillful, the most reckless of them all. At one time this mill had sawed lumber for a shipyard on the cove. Now it ran for only a few weeks in the spring, turning out staves and shingles.

A road led from the mill to the wharf that, in the past, had been the heart of the village. When Laura's grandparents were living, the harbor had been crowded with vessels, waiting their turn to unload provisions and take on lumber or ice from the nearby ponds. Her father and mother had taken their honeymoon trip on one of them, the *Sarah Marie*. In her own childhood a few schooners had come in—four or five a month, maybe—mostly for shingles, but now everything was shipped by truck and put on the freight cars at the Junction, eight miles away. Yet the harbor was not entirely deserted, for a few fishing boats, neat and businesslike, were anchored below the tide line, and half a dozen fishhouses, festooned with nets and lobster traps, dotted the shore. Standing on posts close to the wharf itself, narrow and weathered, was a sardine factory with a large smokestack and a high sharp whistle that blew to call the packers whenever a boatload of fish came in. Beside it were the ruins of the old shipyard.

Leading off from the green were three branch roads, dusty in summer, drifted in winter, muddy in spring, near which fifty or so houses stood. Roughly a third of these were old colonial houses, with big chimneys, broad roofs, and wide windows. Once the finest houses in the village, they were now shabby and no longer fashionable. Their furnishings were those that had always been in them, the old bureaus too often "modernized" by paint, the old tables half hidden under tasseled scarves. One was the old Leighton place where Doris and Ed lived—purchased, they were careful to specify, when the estate was settled. A few of them had been made into double dwellings, two serving for business as well. In one, Miss Marie Hodgkins, ginger-haired and ginger-tongued, operated the village switchboard. In another, Mrs. Nelly Eaton, with a knack for style and a partiality for purple, ran a millinery shop. People came from all the surrounding towns for the benefit of her skill.

Another third of these houses were of more modern design, mostly Victorian. Built during the last era of shipping, they had elaborate scrollwork, wide piazzas, turrets, and bulging bay windows. Some had bathrooms, a few had central heat. Their furnishings ran to brass beds, oak sideboards, Morris chairs, and Mission rockers. The largest of them, brown with a cream trim, belonged to Luther and Flora.

The remainder of the houses, most of them some distance from the green, were of no period whatever. They were similar in design, being of one and a half stories, small, narrow, and gabled. Some were shingled, others were covered with cheap siding. All had thin chimneys and meager windows. Their furnishings came from mail-order houses—iron beds, varnished chiffoniers, wicker rockers. They had no lawns, only back yards, invariably cluttered, and in each yard an outhouse stood. It was in one of these houses that Joel lived with his father. The only thing that differentiated it from its neighbors was a profuse and vivid garden growing from a rowboat set beside it.

Except for twenty or so scattered farms and a dozen summer estates, called cottages, along the shore, this was all there was to the village of Millboro.

3

It was after church on Sunday that Laura had her first opportunity to tell Flora. She dreaded telling her, for Flora would disapprove. Flora didn't like Joel. He took too much after his mother, she thought. It irked her to have Harry seek out his company. If pressed, she would have been forced to admit that as far as looks and brains went, he was head and shoulders above the other boys his age in Millboro—but that wasn't saying a great deal, she would have been sure to add. Then there was the matter of his father. . . . Yet she must tell her, Laura knew. She must tell her that they would be married in September.

She must tell Flora before she told anyone else because Flora was the oldest. That was the way things had always been done in the family—"in turn," her mother had called it. What it amounted to was an assumption that as the family increased in size, it diminished in quality and especially in privilege.

Flora had always been first in everything. The new clothes had always gone to Flora. Doris had worn them second, Laura, third-hand. When there was only enough money for one to take music lessons, it was Flora who took them, and when their mother had made a trip to Boston and only one child could go with her, it was Flora who went. Doris was to go the next time, but all of them knew there would be no next time, for Boston was a long way off. So it had been as long as their mother had lived, and when the will was read, it was Flora who was to have first choice of the things in the house.

Being first had become a habit with Flora. At one time or another she had been president of all the organizations in the village—the Ladies' Aid, the Eastern Star, the Ladies' Literary Club, the Relief Corps, the Sidewalk Society, and the W.C.T.U. Her competence was generally (if sometimes grudgingly) recognized. No one could run a church supper as smoothly as she could. No one could make so much profit from a bazaar. No one could put a drive so quickly over the top. Except in her marriage, Flora had always presided. But Luther knew how to manage her—he was the only one who did.

Flora and Luther made an impressive couple. Both were large. Flora had big shoulders, a big bust, a big waist (well-corseted, even at breakfast), big arms and legs. "A damn fine woman," men in Millboro said, though most of them were careful to keep out of her way.

Luther was taller and broader, with wavy reddish hair—sorrel, he said it was, like an old mare—curly in his ears and eyebrows. He had skin that would have sunburned easily had he stayed outside, a large mouth and jowls that on anyone else would have been disfiguring. But to look at Luther was to look only at his eyes; bright blue, warm and kind and honest. Flora idolized him. He was the only one whose opinions she rated with those of her mother.

His own mother had died when he was a baby, and her place had been taken by an elderly cousin, thin, pale, and sickly, who had made it clear that he was a burden to her. This had shaped

18

his taste in women toward the vigorous and the stout. Remembering his aunt's reluctance, he was constantly grateful to Flora for taking him on. Indeed, he could never get over being astonished by it. What made it more astonishing was that of her own free will she had stood up against her mother to do it.

The sight of her, trim and neat at breakfast, always gave him a good start for the day. Even though they had been married for fifteen years, his face still lit up when she came into the store. "Smart woman, Flora," he would pause to say while a customer waited. In small matters he gave in to her, but on real issues he took a stand. He never let her know how much money he had or how he invested it. He had done all he could to stand between her and Harry (still red-faced, still stammering a little). Flora had been determined to have Harry graduate and then go into the store. When she found out that he wanted to leave school and that Luther had backed him up, she locked herself in her room, until, realizing that she was beaten, she had come out as composed as though the idea had been her own. Nobody ever heard Luther give his ultimatums, but everyone noticed how kind he was once they were given.

Laura and Flora were alone in the kitchen when Laura began the conversation. It was a large kitchen and the most modern in Millboro. The walls, the cupboards, the built-in porcelain sink were paneled and varnished the color of light molasses. Cottage curtains hung crisply at each window. The table where they ate, except when company came and on Sundays, was covered with a clean red and white linen cloth, set for the next meal, and covered again with white mosquito netting. Above the sink, bonneted with fresh paper bags, stood three kerosene lamps, ready for service should the electric current go off, as it often did. They were alone except for Beauty, the cream-fed cat, who lay in a basket under the stove, as black and shining as the stove itself.

Laura had hoped that Luther might be there when she broke

the news, for she could always count on Luther for understanding, even when he sided with Flora. But right after church he had gone back to the store to take inventory before his summer stock came in. Flora disapproved of his ever going to the store on Sundays, but this was another of the things on which he held his ground.

Flora was standing by the sink, an apron over her Sunday silk, running the water into the dishpan. Laura took a wiper from the rod behind the stove and stood beside her. She was glad she had something to hold in her hand, for she had learned at school the support that just a pencil could give.

"There is something I ought to tell you, Flora," she began. So many of her words and thoughts about Flora had the word "ought" in them. After all, Flora had raised her, given her a roof over her head—the broadest roof in town—fed her, sewed for her unceasingly, and allowed her to do nothing in return but take care of her own room and wipe the dishes on Sunday. Since she had been teaching, she had tried to pay her back, but Flora would have none of it. No one could ever get even with Flora. That was the way she wanted it.

"Well," Flora said, shaking in the Boraxine. "Go ahead."

"It's about Joel." Laura hesitated. She wanted to see Flora's reaction, but she dared not look at her face. Laura thought a lot of both her sisters ("love" was a word seldom used among adults in Millboro), but something troubled her concerning them, something hard to put into words. Away from them she felt a person in her own right, strong and ready for anything. In school her classmates, even her teachers, had deferred to her. At District 3 the school board consulted her constantly and listened to all she said. So did the family with whom she boarded. But with Flora and Doris it was different. With them she felt nobody much. All the strength somehow went out of her. As a child she had felt it was because they breathed up all the air. She had that feeling now.

20

"What about him?" Flora's voice thinned a little as she reached for the tumblers. Where Joel was concerned, she was always on the defensive.

"Maybe you've noticed that things are getting serious."

Flora's hand stopped moving for an instant. She had noticed nothing of the kind. Joel had been coming to the house for years. But it was always Harry he asked for. After Harry left, he had driven Laura back and forth on weekends, but that she had seen as a favor to Luther. He seldom took Laura anywhere, and when he brought her home he showed none of the marks of a suitor. Even if she had suspected anything, she would have given Laura credit for remembering she was a Leighton—and a Blodgett as well. A Leighton had founded Millboro. For sixty-two consecutive years a Leighton had been among the Selectmen. Blodgetts had sat in the State Legislature.

The Clossons, on the other hand, were relatively new in Millboro. They had come from Portsmouth way, and most of the men had gone to sea, never as officers or owners of their vessels, but as fishermen, cargo handlers on steamers, deck hands on tugs. Joel's grandfather had come to Millboro on a schooner whose company had gone bankrupt and left its vessel there. While he was waiting for another berth, he had married a girl from one of the outlying farms and settled down near the Junction. That was all anyone knew. Of Joel's mother's family no one knew anything at all. A woman from Boston, who had worked in a factory and took too much time buying her groceries at Peasley's when the poolroom was full. Worse than all this, there was the matter of Joel's father. . . .

It wasn't. It simply could not be. The shame. The talk. There was a ringing in her ears. "You can't mean it, Laura," she said hoarsely.

Laura flushed. "I know what you're thinking," she said. "Well, I don't approve of his father either, if those rumors are true." At first she had blocked her ears to the things people said, yet at the same time she was careful to keep away from the shore at night when she might have heard the sound of his boat going out. But gradually she had had to admit—though only to herself—there might be some truth in the stories.

Recovering herself a little, Flora shook in more Boraxine and swished it vigorously into a lather. It isn't true, she told herself again. It simply could not be.

"And I know Joel wouldn't approve," Laura added quickly. Everyone knew that Joel had no use for his father. Even as a small boy he had made his dislike clear. "Yer Pa's back, Jo," some child would say, seeing his vessel docking. But Joel never went down to the wharf as Emmie did, and he lost no time in swapping all the presents his father had brought him.

Flora wasn't listening. "You can't mean it, Laura," she said again. "You just can not."

"Well, I do. And if you're blaming Joel for what his father may or may not do—"

Actually, the rift had brought Laura some satisfaction, for it showed everyone clearly that Joel was not involved in what might be going on. But it brought a shadow, too, for, having so few memories of her own father, she idealized the relationship between father and child.

"I'm not blaming him," Flora interrupted, seizing one of her best plates and scraping it violently. Had everyone else known? Had there been talk already behind her back? "He's a good boy enough as far as I know. He doesn't smoke or drink, and that's something in these parts. But I just can't believe . . ." Her voice faded, "Why you had to pick him . . ."

"Who did you expect me to pick, Flora?"

For three generations now, hundreds of Maine boys, seeing the end of sailing, had left their towns and villages. At first they had gone West, to Ohio and beyond; later to cities where there were mills and factories. Those who stayed behind took such work as they could get. They fished; they cut pulpwood;

22

they were carpenters and small farmers. A few—those who had something to start them off—had their own businesses. From the point of view of marriage, eligible men were very scarce indeed. Girls who themselves had stayed behind had to make the best of it.

Flora knew this, but she hadn't planned on Laura's marrying a boy from Millboro. She had kept telling herself that someone more suitable would turn up—a county agent, a minister in one of the surrounding towns, or, more likely, a teacher. It struck her forcibly for the first time that she had been wrong to keep Laura from going away. The realization made her speak more positively. "That's neither here nor there. The fact remains that Joel has no real job."

"He's sure of one now, Flora." She could not bring herself to tell her that Joel had agreed to take the job working for Luther in the store. Flora wasn't going to like the idea of his being the one who took the place she had intended for Harry. That had been settled, like the wedding date, the night before on the steps of the piazza.

"Well, even if he gets one," Flora went on, breathing heavily, "he's not the kind to get ahead. Joel's got no drive."

For as long as she could remember, she had taken Flora's criticisms. As a child she had taken them meekly, in silence or in secret tears. But as she had grown older she had grown rebellious, too. Yet she was an orphan, she always remembered, and, like beggars, orphans couldn't be choosers. So she had never really talked back. But this was different. Flora wasn't criticizing her now. She was criticizing Joel. "That's not true," she started to say, and stopped suddenly, for she knew it was true in a way. But that was because Joel had no purpose, she told herself now as she had told herself many times before. But with her to help him, to show him how to plan, that would all be changed. "That's a very mean thing to say," she said instead, surprised by her courage.

23

"Mean or not, it's a fact," Flora retorted. "You'd be throwing your life away."

Laura set the glass she had been wiping unsteadily upon the shelf. "Well, I'm going to marry him," she said, her voice thinning. "In September. And feeling the way you do, I guess we'd better have the wedding at the notary's in Cherryfield."

Flora's hands sank into the pan. Her face was very pale. "After all we've done for you, all the years, all the care— If I had known or even suspected. . . . After my promise to Mama. . . ."

Laura felt a desperation. "I guess you're forgetting how Mama thought that Luther wasn't good enough for you," she said.

She had felt the words coming and tried to stop them. But they had not stopped. Now she was appalled by the sound of them. This was a story she was not supposed even to know. She could not remember when she had heard it. Perhaps she had pieced it together from fragments picked up here and there—a few words spoken when she was supposed to be sleeping, a phrase or two from behind a half-closed door. It was a story that, to her knowledge, no one had ever mentioned in Flora's hearing. Not even Doris. But then, Doris hadn't argued when she had decided to marry Ed. Doris had merely said what she was going to do and gone out, slamming the door behind her, leaving Flora shouting things about Catholics and foreigners. But remembering didn't console her. She lowered her eyes.

For an instant Flora stood rigid. Then, her hands dripping, she stumbled to the roller towel and buried her face in it.

Flora was crying. She hadn't even cried when Harry left, though she had been haggard for weeks afterward. The only time Laura could remember her crying was at her parents' funeral when, there in the cemetery under the big maple, she had seized one of the handles of her mother's casket and sobbed until Luther almost had to carry her away.

Now she had brought it all back. Laura felt submerged in

guilt and shame. Her strength wavered, then steadied again. If she backed down, if she gave in now, she would be caught in Flora's house forever. More than that, she would have lost Joel. He had his faults. She knew that. But he was all she had, really. She clenched the wiper tight in her hands and fixed her eyes on Beauty.

Gradually Flora's sobs subsided. Without looking at Laura, she took a clean dish towel from the drawer, soaked it under the faucet, and held it up to her face. When she laid it down, she was completely herself again. "If you're bound to marry him," she said, "there's no point in my talking any longer. But there's one thing I do expect, and I think I've got a right to expect it. I expect you to be married from this house."

4

Luther was sitting on the steps of the store, wearing his blue serge suit that he kept on all day Sunday as a concession to Flora. He was waiting for her, Laura knew, and she hurried to sit beside him. There was, as always, a smell of the store about him, a smell pleasant and reassuring, a blend of grain and molasses and leather and Lennox soap.

Luther was not a native of Millboro. Born on a farm on the outskirts of Lubec, he had left school at fourteen, working for his father during the spring and summer and in the fall picking up potatoes with the migrants in Aroostook. His ambition had always been to strike out, not for the mills and factories of Massachusetts, but for the West, the real West of the magazines. He wanted pinto ponies instead of farm horses, long-horns instead of Jersey cows. He wanted prairies instead of ocean, meadow larks instead of gulls. He wanted to sit by a campfire at night and from the distance hear coyotes bark at the full of the moon. But things hadn't worked out that way. When he was eighteen the barn had burned and his savings had gone to his father, who had to start all over again. Then he had come to work for his uncle in the store he now owned.

Everyone in Millboro except Flora's mother had liked Luther from the start. He was always pleasant and accommodating, ready to open the store at all hours, even on Sundays, as interested to sell a yeast cake as a bag of flour and as willing to deliver it. Since he had owned the store, you could exchange or return anything without being made to feel it was an imposition. He never sent out a bill when a man was down; yet, when a creditor could pay, he saw that he did. There wasn't a more respected man in the county.

They sat for a time in silence. This had been a habit of theirs over the years. It had begun on the back steps of the kitchen when Flora and Doris had been quarreling inside. The quarrels were less frequent now, for Doris seldom came over except for holidays and for brief unannounced visits at outlandish hours. (Snooping, Flora called it.) But for Luther and Laura the habit of sitting silent had continued.

The village was quiet. At the shore a man worked on his boat and way out near the Point two small gnome-like figures with bags on their backs gathered seaweed for fertilizer, laboriously lifting one foot and then the other as they crossed the sucking flats. Except for a few loafers on Peasley's steps, stilled by the sunshine, no one else was in sight. The only sound came from the church, where the Junior choir was trying out the new hymnals, half-humming, feeling their way.

I come to the garden alone. . . .

It was Laura who spoke first. "Have you seen Joel?"
"A-yuh. He's just left. He's out lookin' for Ed."

26

"Did he—?"

"A-yuh. Things is all fixed."

"He told you everything?" she paused. "About our being married?"

"A-yuh." He knew he ought to say more, but he couldn't seem to. So he just put his hand over hers for a moment. The news hadn't really surprised him, for he had noticed lately the way things were going. He had intended to point it out to Flora, but put it off, knowing how upset she still was about Harry. Now she would have another bitter pill to swallow. And he couldn't help her much.

He liked Joel. He was grateful to him for the way he had let Harry tag after him. Grateful, too, that unlike the other boys he had never made fun of Harry's stammer. Joel was a good boy, but not, he felt sure, the one for Laura. Just why, he couldn't say. The boy was hard to know. There was something about him—nothing you could point your finger at—that made you think he had been scarred somehow. Maybe if they would just hold things back a little. . . .

He was sorry now that he hadn't put his foot down when she wanted to go to Normal. He had wanted to, started to once or twice, and then backed off, feeling it wasn't his right, not being related by blood. Maybe it still wasn't too late. He could at least try.

He took his hand away from hers and cleared his throat. "Laurie."

"Yes, Luther."

"Sure you don't want to put this thing off a bit? You used to talk 'bout goin' way to school." He paused and watched her face anxiously. "If you want to go now, I can swing it easy."

She shook her head. Once she had wanted to go more than anything else in the world. She had thought about it almost constantly. At school, impatient with the inadequacies of her teachers, she had promised herself that before long she would be sitting in a classroom with a real professor. In the library on Saturday afternoons, handling the ragged old books, she had dreamed of new ones, shelf after shelf of them, available at any hour. At home, alone in her room, she had dreamed of a roommate to talk to, perhaps even to visit. At socials and dances, when the noise was too loud and the contras rowdy, she had thought longingly of feather fans and tasseled programs. Every time she watched the stage leaving, she had imagined her luggage strapped on with the freight and herself on the seat, waving good-by to Millboro.

But that was all over. The time had passed. She was too old to be a freshman. She would feel too conspicuous, too out of place. Besides, she could not leave Joel now, now that she had known the new ardor of his kisses. And she had promised.

She shook her head. "Thanks just the same," she said warmly. "You've told Flo?"

"Yes, Luther," she said, coloring. There was another silence. In it she might have heard the sharp staccato of hammering as some Sabbath-breaker began to shingle his house or shed. Or a mock fight starting up at Peasley's. Or the Junior choir, confident now, beginning the third verse. But all she did hear was the echo of Flora's sobbing when she had said the words she had never meant to say, the words that had burst right out of her.

"Luther, I've upset her. She doesn't approve."

"It's 'cause she thinks an awful lot of you, Laurie."

Tears filled her eyes.

Luther reached over and covered her hand with his. It was a big hand, rough and reddened from the brine of the salt pork and pickle barrel.

The tears spilled onto her cheeks. "I didn't tell her about Joel working in the store."

"I'll tell her." What would he say when he told her? he wondered. He wouldn't tell her about the lack of enthusiasm Joel

28

had shown when he brought the matter up. Or about the look on his face when the agreement was made, a look he himself wasn't smart enough to read. Or about the generous wages he had offered.

Laura drew her hand away, took out her handkerchief and wiped her eyes. There was something more. Something she must tell him. Something she must admit. "Joel may take a little breaking in, Luther. You see, he—" She stopped and looked at him appealingly.

He smiled warmly into her face. "Don't you worry 'bout a thing, Laurie. Joel will do all right. You just leave him to me."

Relieved, she put her handkerchief back in the pocket of her sweater. "You've always been awfully good to me, Luther."

"I look at it 'tother way round," he said.

5

Laura crossed the green and approached the old family home— white and green-shuttered, with a long ell that led to the barn, now used as a woodshed. She had no special feeling about it. The few memories she had of her father had been of him at the mill. The touch of his hand, always cold; his face—not at all like the somber face in the album—peeking at her as they played Hide and Seek among the piles of lumber; his clothing, smelling of pitch. But better than she remembered him, she remembered the raucous whine of the saw and the bounce of her feet over the thick layers of sawdust. Her mother's image she could not disassociate from Flora's.

Looking the house over, she saw that it needed paint badly,

especially on the sashes. The yard, once a lawn, was bare of grass, and planks lay end to end across the mud and up to the ell piazza, where a rocker left out over the winter swayed dismally. The steps sagged, and a rusty clam hoe lay near the door. Flora was right in saying that Doris and Ed had let the place go. She was sorry she had allowed them to have it in the first place, she often added. And for next to nothing, too.

There had always been hostility between Flora and Doris. For the first fifteen years of her life, Doris complained, her mother had thrown Flora up in her face. Flora's neatness. Flora's energy. Flora's rank card. Her record of four hundred and sixty-nine consecutive Sundays in Sunday school. Then, her mother gone, Flora had aggressively taken her place. But not for long, for on her seventeenth birthday Doris had eloped with Ed.

"You'll be an outcast," Flora had warned her when she suspected what was going on. There were very few French Canadians in Millboro. Most of them were farther down the coast. "And how will you live?"

"The way I want to," Doris answered, saucy as she always had been.

All her life Doris had tried in every way she could to be different from Flora. Nature had helped her. Flora was oversized; she was small and shapely. Flora's face was staid and ruddy; hers was pert and freckled. Flora had a small, firm mouth; Doris a large one. She had stretched it as a child, she claimed, so it would be different from Flora's. Both had dark hair, but where Flora wore hers sedately in a figure eight, Doris had had the first bob in the village. But Flora had one advantage—a pair of fine, dark eyes. Doris had small gray ones over which she wore heavy glasses, which she despised.

Flora's friends worked hard for the good of the village. They organized bake sales; they packed missionary barrels; they sold tickets for all benefits; they supervised the care of the

30

graveyard and planted salvia around the monument on the green. Doris's friends, numerous in spite of Flora's predictions, were less serious-minded. Her house was generally crowded. At almost any hour of the day or night someone was sure to be there, making coffee, or playing the Victrola, or just taking a nap on the sofa. The telephone rang constantly. *That you, Dottie? That you, Ed?*

Ed had come to Millboro to haul pulpwood. When he wasn't on the road, he had built himself a boat (half launch, half scow) and once it was done he cruised the shore, slowing down at the floats of the cottages and starting up conversations with the summer people, who fell hard for him and his stories about vandals and arsonists and rumrunners looking for hide-outs. The result was that nearly all of them hired him to take care of their places. Before long he was able to give up trucking and work when he pleased. He was one of the fellows who loafed on Peasley's steps. It was from there that he had first seen Doris. He had tripped her as she went by, and she had slapped his face. That was the beginning of their courtship.

Ed didn't look at all like a Frenchman. He was a good deal taller than Doris, light-complexioned and, like her, freckled. ("See. Catchin'," he often said, touching his nose or cheek to hers.) The only thing that set him off from the natives of Millboro were the quick movements of his hands, his sideburns, and his flashy dress.

Ed was a tease. People put up with his jokes (a pinch on your buttocks, for instance, while you were asking for your mail) because he was always good-humored and ready to lend a hand. "Oh, that Ed Levesque," they would say with a kind of affectionate exasperation. He was a born mimic, and his take-offs of the summer people, given at local affairs, brought down the house.

He and Doris dressed alike when it was possible, with matching sweaters and raincoats and mackinaws. Each called the other Buddy. With their dog Butch (a monstrous English bull), they were always on the go. At least one night a week they drove, considerably above the speed limit, into Machias to bowl. On Saturday nights they played Bingo or went square-dancing, getting home at two or three. On Sundays, in full view of people going to church, Ed taught Doris (wearing a pair of his trousers) to box in a ring he had set up in the orchard. This was Flora's greatest mortification.

Ed and Doris had no children. They never would have, Flora predicted, until they settled down. But settling down was something they had never even considered. They were full of impractical plans: sailing in an open boat to Florida; opening a sporting store in Cherryfield; running a hunting lodge in Alaska. Eventually they discovered that such ventures cost money and then one plan was dropped and another begun.

Laura dreaded telling Doris nearly as much as she had dreaded telling Flora, for Doris always made her feel inexperienced and, worse than that, prim. "Lord, kid, but you're green," she was always saying. Or "What you don't know would fill an awful big book." Or, to Ed, "Now, Ed, careful what you say in front of Laura." Doris wouldn't disapprove— she would like the idea of Laura's marriage being no more acceptable than hers. But she might try to take the edge off somehow. You never knew about Doris. She could be generous to a fault, almost; but she could be mean, too, though the meanness never lasted long, except to Flora.

Laura opened the door, called Doris's name, and went inside. For a wonder, Doris was alone. She was in the kitchen, washing her hair. It was a bare room. The wallpaper was dark and spotted near the stove and table. On the shelf by the sink was a pile of unwashed dishes. Two chairs with damaged cane seats were drawn up before what had once been a fine gate-leg table, now ringed from hot dishes, and near the window was a Boston rocker with a grimy cushion, covered with Butch's white hair. His smell permeated the place.

32

"Hi, there," Doris said. "Sit down."

Laura took a magazine from the seat of the rocker. "Where's Ed?" she asked.

"Down to the shore, calking the boat."

Then that was where Joel was too. "Butch with him?"

"Oh, sure." Wherever you saw Ed, you saw Butch's ugly, crumpled face. "Any news?" Though secretive about her own affairs, Doris was avid for news of others and managed always to be well supplied with it.

"Why, yes, there is." She had not intended to begin so abruptly, but she had business to transact.

Doris reached for a towel and wound it around her dripping head. "What's up?" she said.

Laura flushed a little, as she always did when she was about to talk of Joel. "Joel and I are going to be married in September."

Doris drew out one of the chairs and sat down by the table. "Fancy that," she said. "Little Laura." Her face was expressionless, but then, it always was without her glasses. "Have you told Flora?"

"Yes, I told her this morning."

"She surprised?"

"I think so," Laura said cautiously. She was always careful in reporting what one sister said to another, especially when she was quoting Flora. Doris had a way of twisting words when she repeated them.

Doris looked scornful. "Whatever happened to her premonitions?" Luther and Harry showed, or at least pretended, a respect for Flora's premonitions. Laura had resigned herself to them, though for years they had curtailed her activities, preventing her from having a bicycle, from learning to swim, from skating on the bay. But Doris ridiculed them openly. "Just what did she say?"

Laura knew better than to mention Flora's objections to Joel's family, for the Levesques had far less status than the

Clossons along the coast. Ed used to say with a laugh that he had never even known his father's real name. "Mick" Levesque was what people called him. "She says Joel's got no drive," Laura said.

"Just like her," Doris sniffed, ready as usual to defend any one or anything that Flora condemned. "Well, Ed's not complaining."

Here was another tender spot. Doris wasn't going to like the idea of Joel's leaving Ed and going to work for Luther in the store. She would take it as a slight. Laura told her quickly, conscious that she was stiffening, then added placatingly, "I've counted on you, Doris, to help us find a house."

Doris sold real estate for a company in Cherryfield; that is, she sold it when there was any to sell. People didn't move around much in Millboro. "Joel got any money?" she asked, relaxing a little. After all, a sale was a sale, and it had been almost a year since she had made one.

"Yes, we have," Laura said, hedging. "Almost nine hundred dollars."

The pronoun did not deceive Doris, but for the time being she let it pass. "That won't buy a house, kid," she said. "Not any more. Not today."

"Not any house?"

"Not any you would want to live in."

"Oh, we're not particular," Laura said quickly. "Just a house anywhere. Just for a time." Until Joel gets ahead, she meant. Hadn't Luther begun in a job like Joel's? Besides, there was Joel's drawing. She would see that he kept at it and enter a great many contests. The magazines were full of them. He was sure to win one sooner or later. That would open the door for him and then, working right at home, he could do cartoons. "You must have a house somewhere," she added.

Doris reached for the sugar bowl where she kept her bobby pins and took them out with an expression of great concentration. Laura watched her anxiously. Doris had always plagued her, held her off, but, when it came right down to it, she seldom failed her.

"I do have one," Doris finally said, her voice distorted by the bobby pins she held between her teeth.

Laura brightened. "Where?"

"You wouldn't want it."

"How do you know? Where is it, Doris?"

"Way off. Away from everything. It's been empty for years."

"But where?"

"On the barrens."

The barrens were twelve miles to the northeast on a high plateau—a fenceless wasteland stretching for thousands of acres, almost treeless, where once a great forest had stood. Fires had swept over it, one after another, impoverishing the soil, until now it was an area of weeds and ledges and gravel dunes with a few cart-wide, almost indistinguishable roads that wandered over it. Among the scrub and bushes wild blueberries grew. When Laura's grandmother had been a girl, anyone could pick there. Then, when her mother was young, the land had been posted against trespassers. Pickers were hired and the berries shipped off in boxes and crates to Boston. When she herself was small, picking gave way to raking for the factories in Cherryfield, Jonesboro, Harrington, and Columbia Falls. Almost nobody lived on the barrens, though a few tarpaper shacks had been put up for the migrant rakers who arrived every August.

At first Laura rejected the idea of living there as quickly as Doris had. But they must find something soon. They must settle things before Flora began planning for them. Before she said, "We have a big house here. . . ."

"Can we see it today?"

"How'd you manage without a car?"

"Luther would let Joel take the truck. Just at first," she added quickly.

Doris shrugged and put on her glasses. "I'll see if I can find the key," she said, getting up and going into the pantry.

"I suppose the house has a well," Laura called after her, fearful of her reply.

"Oh, sure," Doris said. "And the shed's not bad."

It really sounded possible. "How much land?"

"Twenty acres."

Laura felt her excitement mounting. Except for the money she had saved, she had never had anything that wasn't really Flora's. It had been Flora's home and Flora's food. It had been Flora who, until a few years ago, had bought all her clothing. Now here was something that could belong not just to her, but to her and Joel. Not just a house, but twenty acres.

Doris came back with her key. "Thanks, Doris," Laura said, reaching for it. "Thanks a lot."

"Don't mention it," Doris told her. Then, unable to hold back any longer, she added, "Well, congratulate Joel for me. Not many fellers are lucky enough to find a girl and have a house thrown in."

6

Late in the afternoon Laura and Joel set out in Ed's truck, taking a gravel road that led inland. Even in the past two days, spring had come closer. Green was beginning to show up on the slopes and in the ditches. The maple buds were pink, and yellow tassels had appeared on the willows. Once a flock of wild geese flew over in formation, high and honking.

36

They rode on in silence. Joel's face was closed and sober—not at all the face she had seen the night before when they had sat together on the piazza steps. He had been ardent then, desperate almost, begging her not to go, not to leave him behind. Promising that if she would stay and marry him, he would take any job she wanted him to. Vowing that he would work hard, harder than he had ever worked before. She had never seen him like that. It had surprised and shaken her, but thrilled her too. She had promised. They had kissed and clung together, talking in whispers until the town clock had struck ten. (She always had to go in at ten.) Saying good night, she had seen his face in the moonlight, so different from now.

"There'd be no electric lights," he said abruptly.

"I know."

"No telephone."

"I wouldn't mind."

"There'd be no water in the sink."

"The well's good. Doris said so."

"No furnace."

She laughed. "There aren't half a dozen furnaces in Millboro."

"You'd be alone all day."

Wasn't that exactly what she wanted? A place where she could be herself, not bossed, not smothered, not patronized. A place where no one could reach her. Not Flora. Not Doris. A place where she could be alone with Joel.

"What would you do?"

She laughed again. "Well, first I'd clear up the place. That is, of course, if we take it," she added quickly. "Then I'd paper and paint."

"Ever do it?"

"No. But I can learn."

He gave a quick look at his own slender hands, incompetent with every thing except a pencil. "What after that?"

She laughed. "Why, Joel, there'd be cooking and washing

37

and ironing and sewing and canning. And if I had any time left, there would be reading and walking."

"Sounds like you've bought the place already," he said.

She touched his arm. "We won't even look at it, Joel, if you don't want to."

Sensing her disappointment, he spoke more affably.

"Sure we'll look at it," he said.

Again he fell into silence. He was not sure he liked the barrens. They were too open, too exposed. Driving over them, he felt himself also exposed, and it made him uneasy. He wished Harry was with them.

She looked about, careful to miss nothing, for she had never been out this way in April. As they drove on, the country became flatter. Trees grew farther apart, shrank in foliage, then almost disappeared. A wind sprang up suddenly. What had seemed to be a monstrous, unending shadow ahead became, as they approached, a blackened land, bordered only by the sky and, far in the distance, a faint line of hills. It was the burn. You burned in the early fall or spring for blueberries. Like pruning, it made them grow more profusely. At the end of the second season you harvested. After a few years, depending upon the crop, you burned, waited, then harvested again. You harvested by raking.

"Is raking hard, Joel?"

"Darn hard," he told her. "I tried it once—for almost a day."

"What makes it so hard?"

"The heat," he told her. " 'Tisn't just from the sun. It's from the black ash left from the burn. Comes right up and hits you in the face."

It was hard to conceive of heat with such a wind blowing. She raised her hand to hold her hat on. The sun was setting, leaving the sky dull. Above them, a flock of crows made a dark canopy.

The burn was all about them now—a great black smudge

stretching as far as she could see, broken by the road and the ledges, some flat and smooth like the ledges around the school-house, some great boulders. She remembered what she had read in her Latin class about land devastated by conquerors. Gaul must have looked like this after Caesar had passed over it, the grain fields of Italy when Hannibal had gone.

"How long does it stay this way?" she asked soberly.

"Oh, a month or six weeks, I guess."

She sat very still as they passed through it, seeing the gaunt, singed bushes that had survived. A few trees, half charred. The desolate, gravel dunes.

Then, abruptly, it ended. On one side of the road was a thinly wooded area; on the other, blueberry vines from last year's burn already showing signs of bearing.

Then they didn't burn the whole place at once, she thought, relieved.

They went on. There was no sound except the rattle of the truck and the skid of the wheels over the wet, loose gravel. There was nothing to see except the somber sky, the crows with their black, beating wings, the winding roads. Then, once more, the desolate, scarred landscape. Two miles. Three. The wind was stronger now, and with the sun down, the air was chilly.

"Like it?" Joel asked, half teasingly.

"Maybe," she answered.

He looked at the speedometer again.

"Getting close?"

"A-yuh," he said.

Then he pointed. The black floor ended. Just beyond it was a hedge of scrawny hackmatacks, and beyond that was the house—small and narrow, with a high, pitched gable and clap-boards that had never known paint. But there was a kind of dignity about it, standing there, withdrawn, in its little oasis of green.

"Must be it," he said.

"It's not bad, is it, Joel?" she asked, looking it over carefully from doorstoop to gable.

"Can't tell yet."

They drove into the rutted driveway, got out, crossed the little dooryard that would have seemed meager in Millboro, but which looked really luxurious here, went up the steps, put the key in the lock, turned it, opened the door, and stepped inside.

The hall was dark and filled with the smell of a house long closed. Her eyes adjusting, Laura saw a door and opened it. It led into a sitting room—small, clean enough, well-lighted, and furnished with a rusty stove, rather elegant in design.

"Why, it's not bad at all, is it, Joel?" she said again. She thought of the family furniture that belonged to her, now stored in Doris's attic. The sofa here, the table there . . .

They went into the hall again and opened the second door, into what, judging by its faded wallpaper, was a bedroom. It was narrower than the sitting room and had only one small window.

"No opening to the chimley," Joel said.

"We could use an oilstove," Laura told him. "Besides, it's right next to the kitchen."

The kitchen was a bare small room, with high, built-in cup-boards, a table, a rusty stove, and a sink. Above the sink was a little round window, like a porthole. To Laura there seemed to be something special about that window, something that gave the house an air. Through it, by bending a little, she could see the hills.

"Look, Joel!" she cried.

Joel came closer, looked out, and saw, not the hills, but a stain of sawdust where the woodpile had been and a rusted axhead beside it. When he was a child his mother had never allowed him to handle sharp things, afraid he would damage his fingers. If something needed repair, she would simply let it go until his father came home. "He might as well make himself useful," she would say. In the woods, marking trees, he had used only a hatchet, and never with skill.

"And look, Joel, the shed."

The shed was, like the house, unpainted, but obviously in poorer repair, its wide front doors sagging a little on their hinges. Above them hung a large rusted bell with a thin, knotted chain attached to its tongue, the kind of bell farmwomen used to call in their men.

She took his arm and drew him closer to the window.

"I can see it," he said.

But his eyes were not on the shed. They went instead to the well-curb, rotted around the pump; then to the bulkhead, warped at the bottom.

"What do you think, Joel?" Laura asked, turning.

He looked down at his hands again and said nothing.

She studied him earnestly. "Are you sure you don't want to change your mind about our getting married, Joel?" she asked. "It's not too late, you know."

If he changed his mind, she would go away. She would leave him just as his mother had. He couldn't bear that. He drew her roughly to him, pressing her hair against his trembling mouth. "Course I don't want to change my mind," he said.

7

Once the place was theirs, they went out every Saturday and Sunday to explore. Already the new vines, pink-tipped, were

beginning to appear, smothering the black. Ferns were springing up within the charred skeletons of the bushes.

With the change in the barrens, there was a change in Joel.
All his doubts about the place left him. After a week in the
store, its openness was just what he needed. He liked to take
the narrow roads, with no idea where they led; to stand, with
Laura, alone in a great expanse, seeing no one—only rabbits,
hawks, partridges, crows, a gull or two that had strayed inland,
and occasionally a deer. He liked to climb with her to the top
of one of the big boulders, then to lie there, counting the
crows, chanting a rhyme every Maine child knew:

> One crow sorrow,
> Two crow joy,
> Three crow letter,
> Four crow boy.
> Five crow silver,
> Six crow gold,
> Seven crow secret
> Never to be told.

Or just talking.

He talked more now than Laura had ever known him to talk
before. He told her about his work in the woods, about trees—
which ones went for pulpwood, which ones made good lumber
for building. He talked about forest fires and how they started
—from lightning, from campfires, from portable sawmills,
some, now and then, from a man burning a bee tree. He talked
about surface fires, running through the flash fuel that littered
the forest floor; about duff fires, burning the leaf litter or the
peat that was underground, smoldering sometimes for days
with almost no smoke or flame; about crown fires that swept
through the foliage, common among dense stands of evergreen;
about spot fires, carried ahead by sparks sometimes as much as
a mile.

He talked about the soil. It had been burned over too often,

42

he told her, except in places like theirs. (He said "theirs" now, not "hers," as he once had said, she noted joyfully.) Once, when a pheasant flew by, he talked about hunting. He had a gun, he said, but he hardly ever used it. "Except when I'm sore," he told her. "When I'm sore, I go off as far as I can and fire one shot right after another." When she brought the subject up, he talked a little—not much—about the store. Things were going all right, he guessed, he said without enthusiasm. He was doing the best he could. But there was one thing he did not talk about—the thing she wanted more than anything else to hear. He did not talk about his family.

She remembered every detail of the morning she had first heard about his mother's leaving. Luther had brought the news when he came back for breakfast after sweeping out the store.

"I hear Jim Closson's wife's gone," he had said, drawing out his chair.

Flora was cutting bread for toast. "Gone?" she echoed. "Gone where?"

"Couldn't say that," he answered. "All I heard was that she's left him. Took the girl with her."

"Who told you?" she demanded.

"Tim Conary." Tim Conary drove a public car. "She hired him to drive her to the Junction. Told him she was leavin' for good."

Flora laid the bread on the toaster and held it over the flame. "I knew t'would happen sooner or later," she had said complacently. "I've known it for years."

Laura went to school reluctantly, dreading to meet Joel there. But Joel had been absent. He was absent for at least a week. He had come back, not mortified, as everyone had expected, but so aloof that no one, not even the cruelest boys, had dared say a word to him about what had happened.

She had recognized his misery and, young as she was, had sensed that there was some mystery about it. What had he been

43

doing that week? Where had he been? No one had seen him. These questions had plagued her for years. It wasn't like Joel to hide. He was too proud for that. But of one thing she was certain. There had been a change in Joel's attitude toward his father then. What had once been only antagonism had become bitter enmity. Something terrible and violent had happened. Would he ever tell her what it was? she wondered. She had thought that as soon as they were engaged he would want to bring up the past and get it off his mind. But he never had. As far as any mention of family was concerned, he might never have had one.

Late in May, when, except for a few charred bushes, the barrens were entirely green again, they put in a garden. It took a long time, for making a garden on the barrens wasn't like making one anywhere else, since new soil had to be brought in and fertilized. In it they planted vegetables enough to last them all winter and, in a special corner, set off with string, pink and white asters for the wedding bouquet.

As soon as school was over, Joel drove Laura out every morning and she began cleaning the house. Distraught as she was at the idea of a house on the barrens, Flora wanted to help, but it seemed important to Laura that she should do it alone. It was her house, she told herself. Flora must get no foothold there.

She made slow progress. Every time she went outside for water, she paused to look at the miracle of new green about her, or stood in the wind, for the wind nearly always blew there, feeling its vigor against her face. Now and then she stopped and sat on the steps, watching the crows flying, some-times high—calm, rhythmic—as though they were rowing; sometimes low—agitated, swooping—teaming up to have things out with some perky blue jay.

Luther had taught her the rhyme about them. It was one of

the days he had taken her with him when he went to deliver groceries. He often took her along. In summer they sat together on the high seat of the wagon under the big umbrella with the words SLOAN'S LINIMENT on it; in winter wrapped in a fur lap robe on the low seat of the pung. Luther would never acknowledge seeing just one crow. "See that t'other feller flyin' right up close. See!" he would say, pointing to the empty sky. "Look. Look hard. You've got mighty poor eyesight, seems to me."

Sometimes she lingered at the sink, peering out of the little porthole window. It was not like any window she had ever seen before. Things looked different from it—brighter, more exciting, especially the sunset, making a vivid backdrop for the hills. As long as she had that window, life could never be humdrum, she told herself.

Joel came a little after five, and they picnicked leisurely, sitting on one of the ledges. Then they walked along the wandering roads where the tall red grasses grew between the ruts. Sometimes they broke into a sudden run and then stopped, breathless, laughing with happiness.

Free, free, she thought. Free from Flora. Free to be alone with Joel.

Free, free, he thought. Free from a house he hated. Free, forever free from memories.

Free. Free . . .

They could hardly believe it.

One evening, just at sunset, in the northeast corner of their land, sheltered by a few pine trees, they came upon a tiny graveyard surrounded by a crumbling stone wall and half hidden by a patch of darkened, matted blackberry vines.

Laura pointed. "Look, Joel."

He followed her as she hurried up the two flat rocks that served as steps and bent over the lichen-covered stones.

45

"Osgood," she read. "Did you ever know a family around here by that name?"

"No," he said shortly. "How would I?" Joel was touchy on the subject of genealogy. Whenever he went to the Post Office, he was very conscious of the box marked L in gold, and whenever he had sat with the other boys on the steps of the village graveyard watching the Christian Endeavor meeting, his eyes had wandered uncomfortably to the substantial monuments that bore the Leighton name. He was only a Closson, he always remembered.

"Osgood," Laura repeated thoughtfully. "David. Hannah. They must have been the people who built the house." She bent lower over the stones. 1856. Because of the lichens and the dusk, that was all she could make out. "What do you suppose they did for a living?"

"Farmed, p'raps."

"Of course." She remembered the bell. "But on this land?" she asked, looking about.

"They might have raised cattle," he told her, pointing to a strand of rusted barbed wire lacing the wall. "They must have had a hoss, at least."

It would have been a long trip into town with horse and buggy, she thought soberly. Her eyes moved to the sunken graves. David. Hannah. "What do you suppose they died of, Joel?"

"Consumption, maybe. A lot of people had it then."

Had they come out there young together, the way she and Joel had? Had they, too, been full of hope? "How old were they when they died?" she asked suddenly. "Let's look at the dates and see if we can make out."

He took her arm. "Too dark," he said. "We'd better be going."

They started, and almost at once she stopped suddenly, looking back. "Joel, just as soon as you can get to it, I want you to fix that wall," she said.

All day people had been pushing him at the store, asking for three or four things all in the same breath—*two pounds of brown sugar, one pound of prunes, one package of cream of tartar, Arm and Hammer if you have it.* . . . Tapping their coins on the counter when they thought he was slow. Breathing down his neck when he was trying to add. Now Laura wanted things in a hurry too. He dropped her arm. "Well, come on, I can't do it tonight," he told her brusquely.

8

As the days passed, one question plagued Laura. Had Joel told his father? So far as she knew, he had told no one but Ed, and he had to tell Ed because he worked for him. Ed and Doris together had lost no time in passing it on. For one thing, it was news; for another, it was distressing to Flora. Flora herself had told no one, but she met questions with dignity, and the prospect of having a wedding to manage had somewhat softened the sting. But what about Joel's father? Laura didn't like the idea of his just hearing it somewhere. Besides, since he went so few places, he might not hear it until everyone else had. That did not seem right.

Joel's father was a stranger to her, really, a man not much taller than Joel, but heavier, with a paunch that hung over his belt a little; dark hair allowed to grow long on one side, then carefully combed over his bald spot; and a shaggy, untrimmed mustache. He walked, like men who have spent most of their life at sea, with a gentle roll.

The first time she had seen him was when Luther once took her to the wharf to watch a vessel unload. The only thing that

47

had stayed in her mind about him was that, unlike the other sailors, he had no visible tattoo. He had been away most of her childhood. When he was at home, he was always busy—fitting wood, cleaning up the yard and shed. She had never talked with him. When she was a child, she had avoided him because Joel did; when she was grown, because of the embarrassment that anything connected with Joel's family, even his house, brought. Nowadays she rarely saw him. When she did, it was always with a pipe in his mouth, working in his garden or walking in his rolling gait alone along the shore.

It was time, she thought, to bring the matter up.

"Joel," she said one evening while they sat together on one of the ledges, "have you told your father yet?"

His mouth hardened. "Told him what?" he demanded. For the last six years he had lived in his father's house only because he had nowhere else to live, all the time taking care to keep out of his way. That wasn't hard to do, for his father left before he got in at night and was asleep when he got up in the morning. As long as he was in school, he had used some of the money his father left on the kitchen mantelpiece beside the lamp. But he had used no more than he had to. He had bought no class ring, pretending to scorn the idea of a fellow wearing one, and, short as it was in the sleeves, he had worn his old blue suit for graduation. He had kept track of the money he had spent and as soon as he had got a job, put every cent of it back on the mantel. It wasn't his fault that his father hadn't touched it—that the bills still lay there, clearly visible through the glass base of the lamp above them.

He had bought his own food, too, and cooked it, keeping his supplies carefully on one side of the cupboard. Granted, he hadn't done his washing, but he tried not to notice the clean sheets on his bed or the neatly ironed shirts hung on hangers in his closet.

"Why, told him about us, Joel."

48

"What about us?" he asked coldly.

Laura tried not to show her hurt and her exasperation, knowing she was on tender ground. "About our getting married, Joel."

He picked up a twig that lay beside him and regarded it, scowling. "It's none of his damn business," he said.

The wedding was to be on the second Saturday in September. About the middle of August, Joel began to get uneasy. He loved Laura and he wanted to marry her, but now that he had her word she would stay, he would have put things off as long as he could. All summer he had spent his free time doing work in their garden—work he enjoyed. That work was almost over. Now there were other things to face. The sawdust stain, the sagging door . . . When he went down cellar or into the shed, he was careful never to take a light with him for fear of what he might see that needed doing.

Moreover, he dreaded the wedding. "Why can't we just go to a notary?" he asked. "What have we got to have a wedding for?"

"Because I owe it to Flora," Laura told him.

"You don't owe anything to Flora," he insisted. The dislike between Flora and Joel was mutual. It had begun when he was a child and he had come to play with Laura and Harry. At home he played what he wanted to and gave no thought to time. At her house, Flora chose their games for them. "Get out the dominoes, Laura," she would say. Or "Open the drawer and take out the parchesi. Joel can stay an hour if you're good." His dislike had grown with him. He knew how Flora felt about the marriage without ever having been told. "She's bossed you around every day of your life," he went on. "The only reason she wants you to have a wedding is so she can run it."

"Oh, Joel, that's not true." Even if it was true, she was determined that until the wedding was over Flora should have things her own way. She had disappointed Flora in marrying Joel. In her distress and her guilt she had spoken words she would have given much to retract. She had put Flora—the president of the W.C.T.U.—in the position of having to invite Joel's father into her house and, in a way, into the family. Yet, since that Sunday morning in the kitchen, Flora had said nothing to show her disapproval. If she was not really cordial to Joel, at least she treated him civilly. The wedding must be just as Flora wanted it. "Flora cares a lot what people think," she added, realizing uncomfortably and for the first time just how vulnerable she had already made her.

"What people think means nothing to me," he told her.

"But for my sake, Joel."

There was so much to do. There was the wallpaper to pick out. Joel was no help here, for he didn't like making decisions any more than he liked making plans. So that had been up to Laura. With some misgivings she had finally settled on a landscape for the hall; green medallions for the parlor; ferns for one bedroom, pink and blue morning glories for the other; a spray of pine on a white background for the kitchen.

Then there were the plans for the wedding itself. First, there were the dresses—white, of course, for Laura; blue for Doris, who was to be matron of honor, and rose for Flora, who was to play the march and lead the line at the reception.

Things got off to a bad start. Flora wanted yokes. Doris despised yokes. Flora wanted full sleeves. Doris wouldn't be caught dead wearing them. Flora wanted long skirts. ("Why wouldn't she?" Doris asked, glancing down at her own trim ankles.) Laura said little. She was almost free, wasn't she? She could afford to give in.

Since Flora was making the dresses, she eventually had her way, and the trouble about fittings began. Half a dozen fittings weren't enough for Flora. This was not because she lacked skill, but because she demanded perfection. Every night when Laura got back from the house on the barrens, hot, sweaty, exhausted, Flora would hurry her through her bath, then, with a dozen or so pins in her mouth, she would begin to adjust the neckline or, sitting heavily on the floor, re-measure the hem. "I don't know how you expect this to look like anything," she would say, sighing. "I just have to catch you when I can."

It was even harder to catch Doris. All day she was out on the road, looking up real estate with the idea of buying ("On what?" Flora said tartly when she heard) and then selling when the market went up. Every evening she and Ed and Butch were off to see the local ball teams play. She had no taste for satin anyhow, she told them, and would sooner come in a pair of Ed's old khaki pants. "I wouldn't put it past her," Flora said.

When Doris did come for a fitting, she brought Butch with her. Everything about him upset Flora—his ugly, crevassed face; his deep, hoarse bark; his sudden snores; his rheumy pink eyes; his smell, overpowering in the heat; most of all, his slobbering. Now, with the dress material spread around, Flora wouldn't let him in the house, and he stayed outside the screen door making piteous, repulsive noises. In retaliation Doris affected a sudden allergy to cats and broke into frequent jolting sneezes, causing Flora to drop her scissors, once prick herself badly, leaving a clearly distinguishable spot of blood on the hem she was turning.

But gradually things straightened out. The cake was ordered in Bangor. The other refreshments were planned—chicken salad, hot rolls, cheese sticks, white cake, chocolate cake, sponge cake, and, of course, three kinds of ice cream. People kept offering flowers from their gardens, dishes, silverware, napkins. . . .

The night before the wedding, everything was well in hand.

The house was cleaned, the clothes were pressed, the food was ready, the flowers were in water in the shed. After supper, Luther, Ed, and Joel brought over the chairs from the church vestry and set them up, leaving a space just big enough for the bridal party. It was the only time that day Laura had had a glimpse of Joel.

"Is your father coming tomorrow?" she asked him. She had not mentioned his father to him since that day on the barrens. Someday, she decided, she would bring the subject up again, find out what the matter was, and maybe help to smooth things over. But her only real concern now was the wedding. Would he come? It would be easier for Flora if he didn't. And for everyone else, really.

Joel did not look up at her question. "How would I know?" he said irritably, and went on counting chairs.

It was a good day for the wedding, sunny and clear, with just a touch of fall. When breakfast was over and Luther went off to the store, Flora began the last-minute preparations. She did not allow Laura to come into the kitchen, yet she took no stock in the idea that a bride be neither seen nor heard before the ceremony. "You can answer the door," she said, "and the telephone if it rings."

People kept coming. Mrs. Hattie Blaisdell, wearing her usual black apron, brought over the mail. "I thought it might help out a mite," she said. Mrs. Marie Hodgkins left her switchboard briefly to bring a crocheted doily she had made between calls. Miss Enid Baker, who would miss the ceremony, not feeling she could close the library until four, dropped by to explain and leave a bookmark she herself had embroidered. Mrs. Amos Bigelow, more eloquent than her husband, brought a poem she had written, together with a comb of honey from their bees. Miss Nellie Eaton brought three jars of jelly wrapped in tissue paper and decorated with artificial purple pansies selected from her trimming stock.

People kept telephoning.

"Yes, this is Laura. Not too busy to talk with you."

"Four o'clock. That's right."

"Yes, promptly at four."

If Joel were late. . . .

She had reminded him half a dozen times, and she had meant to remind him the night before, but their conversation about his father had thrown her off the track. She had not seen him again. After the chairs were arranged, he had gone out to pick the asters for her bouquet. Before he got back, Flora had sent her upstairs. "You look tired to death," she had told her. "You go right straight to bed." She hadn't wanted to go to bed. She had wanted to say good night to Joel, to remind him to come early, to part his hair and shine his shoes carefully, but she remembered how things must be, and went.

At eleven, Ed arrived with Doris (still in curlers) to freeze the ice cream in the shed. A little later Julia Wass, who had been Laura's best friend in high school, came to help her weave the flowers and cedar in and out of the chicken wire that Luther had strung up above the fireplace and along the banisters in the hall. So many had sent flowers that Laura abandoned all idea of color scheme. Calendulas crowded purple petunias, and yellow snapdragons crept in among pink sweet peas. At noon Luther came home, having closed the store for the day. For lunch there was soup, made from the bones of the chicken, and eaten standing.

By one o'clock Flora was lying exhausted on her bed. Luther was on call in the kitchen, holding Beauty while he waited. Doris and Ed were in the garage, secretly tying strings of tin cans to Luther's Buick, which Joel and Laura were to use for a honeymoon in Bangor.

Laura was in her bedroom, lying down, waiting to dress. At times like this a girl was supposed to have misgivings, to have regrets about leaving the house in which she has grown up. She had none. She could hardly wait to get to their own house on the barrens. She didn't really want a wedding trip, for there was so much to do, and she was anxious to start. But she didn't want to disappoint Luther. The wedding trip had been his present to them. He had been so good about everything, so patient breaking Joel in, overlooking his blunders, sparing his back. So good about putting the truck at their disposal. So interested in all their plans. Yet she couldn't quite relax. There were still things on her mind.

She heard a car stop in the back yard, then Harry's halting voice in the kitchen. She knew he would come, yet she felt touched somehow that he had. She hadn't always been as kind as she ought to have been to Harry, for it had seemed sometimes that he was in the way when she wanted to be alone with Joel. She was sorry for it now.

Flora's door opened. "That you, Harry?"

"Yes, Ma. It's me."

"How come you're so late?"

If Joel should be late today, with the eyes of the whole town on him. . . .

By three o'clock Laura was ready and standing to keep from getting wrinkled. Doris had left to dress herself in Harry's room. Flora, ready for an hour, was checking up on things in the kitchen.

There was a knock on Laura's door and Luther stepped inside. "Whew," he said. "By gorry."

But she was blind to his admiration. "Has Joel come?" she asked anxiously.

"A-yuh." He did not say that he had just come, that Flora had been about to send Ed for him.

"Did he bring the flowers for the bouquet?" She was not worried about the ring, for, unwilling to trust either Joel or Ed, she herself had given it to Luther the week before.

"A-yuh. Flora's fixin' 'em now."

"How does he look?"

"Jest fine."

"His hair?" she asked, her mind on the cowlick.

"Slick as a whistle."

This was a real relief. "Does he seem nervous?"

"Maybe. A mite." Actually, he had seemed very pale and very nervous. His hands had shaken, holding the cup of coffee Luther had given him. "But then, every man's nervous on his weddin' day."

"Has his father come?"

"Haven't seen him."

She relaxed. Her last worry disappeared, leaving only a trace of guilt.

Luther took both her hands and held her off, turning her slowly so that he should miss nothing. Her dark eyes. Her high color. The crisp little shoulder veil. The long row of tiny buttons down her back. The point of her long, tight sleeves. "By gorry," he said again.

"You look pretty nice yourself," she told him, smiling.

He did. He wore his best blue suit and the necktie she had given him at Christmas—the same startling blue as his eyes.

But as she watched, his face sobered. "Laurie, I want you to promise me somethin'."

"Anything, Luther." Next to Joel, he was the one in all the world she loved best. She was going to miss him terribly.

"I want you to promise me that if they's any trouble, you'll let me know. That you'll never keep it from me."

There would be trouble, of course—sickness, accidents—there was always trouble as you grew older. How could he help knowing? It would be there for everyone to see. But if a promise was what he wanted. . . . "Of course, Luther."

He released her hands. "That's what I wanted to hear," he said.

At half-past three, the guests began coming. Women grateful for a chance to wear their white gloves, yellowing from disuse; men reconciled, once they had arrived, to leaving their gardens or fishing boats or woodpiles; a few young men (there were not many of them left in Millboro) with new haircuts that left a line of white above their sunburned necks; young women, overexcited and overdressed; little boys, bribed by talk of the table the Sawyers set; little girls, crackling with starch and lively with anticipation. They gathered on the steps and on the piazza, the men leaning against the rail; most of the women, conscious of their corsets, standing; the children everywhere. There was talk about pulpwood, the weather, the blueberry yield, the Grange supper ahead. About local baseball, radio, the new teachers, how the mackerel were running, what a relief it was to have the summer people gone . . .

At a quarter to four, Harry led them all inside. The little girls seized the front seats, the little boys gravitated toward the kitchen. At exactly four, Flora sat down at the piano.

Oh, promise me . . .

Standing by the front door with Ed, Joel felt a surge of revolt. He hated promises. People caught you by promises you weren't ready to give and held you to them. He had promised too much already.

He felt a revolt against Laura. She expected too much of him. She expected him to make plans and decisions. His mother had never expected that. "Take one day at a time," she always told him. "Just play things by ear." He felt a revolt, too, against Laura's family. Against Flora, for putting him through a thing like this. Against the job they had fixed up for him—an inside job where all day long he had to make small talk. Where he had to be pleasant, even to the summer people . . .

His mouth tightened. Sweat broke out all over him. He

grabbed the handkerchief he had placed just so in his pocket an hour before, crumpled it, and wiped his brow. If only he could bolt. . . .

He felt a hand on his arm. "What's eatin' you, boy?" Ed asked.

He yanked away. Then his eyes rose to the top of the stairs where Laura stood, waiting—lovely, confident, smiling. "Nothing's eating me," he said hoarsely. "Nothing at all."

9

By the time Laura and Joel returned from their trip, the blueberry foliage had begun to turn to delicate shadings of red. By the middle of October it had become a floor of copper flame. Mile after mile it stretched, set off by the grayness of the ledges and the blue of the sky. The sky was full of birds now— shrikes and pine grosbeaks, migrating from the north; robins, swallows, finches in great flocks, heading southward; crows congregating for the winter. The insects were gone. The air was clear, almost intoxicating. It seemed to Laura that she had never seen such beauty before.

Nights were even more beautiful than days. Some nights moonlight fell, silver on the gravel dunes and ledges, white on the ruts of the cart-wide, wandering roads. Some nights were dark and full of mystery. Outside it was pleasantly cold—just cold enough to keep you moving when you went to the shed. Inside there was the fire snapping, smelling faintly of pitch, the kettle humming. There was work to do together—cracks to fill in, windows to putty. And later there was love.

The moves of love, beyond kisses, were all new to her. They

were new to Joel too. He was not one of those boys who took the fast girls of the village into the fishhouses or on the piazzas of the cottages along the shore. Their honeymoon had been almost a failure. For three nights they had lain still and silent in the hotel bed together. For three days they had walked for hours along the river, like strangers, pointing out this or that— pleasure boats, tugs, barges, a ferry called the *Bon-Ton*, the Boston boat arriving, a schooner loading—seeing, yet only half-seeing. They had walked up and down the city streets, looked in shop windows, made comments, eaten together, yet seldom met each other's eyes. Instead of bringing them closer together, marriage was driving them apart, it seemed.

She was the one who had made the start. She had not wanted it that way. She had wanted him to come to her, to teach her, to take her, she supposed, though she hadn't quite known what "taking" was. But when he didn't come, she must go to him, she knew. So finally she had stretched out her hand.

But her disappointment was soon over, for once the start was made, things happened that she had never even suspected. Things that shook her out of her childhood. Things that could happen again and again and lose nothing.

Though she was by herself a good deal, she was never lonely. There was always work to do. During the summer she had spent most of her time on the garden. Now, before she could paint or paper, she must put up the vegetables. Flora had never taught her to do things, and she made many blunders. Much of her time went into just keeping the old cook stove going, for they burned slabs from the mill, saving the hard wood until winter. It wasn't easy to get a slab fire started. Then it burned out before you expected it to and you had to start another.

Once the canning was done, she tackled the kitchen. First there was the old paper—four layers of it—to peel or generally soak. Then there was the paint to scrape, a real job where it had been blistered by the heat. Once the new paint was on, there were the walls to size. Then there was the paper to cut and match. And always, when Joel was home, there were the meals.

It all took longer than she had expected, for sometimes when the sun was warm she could not resist going outside to stretch out on one of the low, flat ledges or walk with long brisk strides across the barrens, ankle deep in its bright red carpet, deepening daily to a color she could not name. She spent hours, it seemed, studying it. Not ruby. Not plum. Not garnet. Perhaps magenta . . . No, not quite magenta.

And there were always interruptions. Doris and Ed came often, full of mysterious talk about their new scheme, which was all but ready to be revealed. Butch came with them and stayed outside snapping at bees or scratching in the garden. Flora and Luther drove out two or three times a week when the weather was pleasant, and Luther always brought something with him—a pan, a ladle, a breadbox—something he claimed he wanted to get out of the way. They never stayed long. Luther saw to that. "Come on, Flo," he would say at the end of half an hour. "An old man needs his sleep, you know." Flora seldom protested, for she was always hoping for a call from Harry when the night rates went on, and she wanted to be there when it came. Besides if the phone kept ringing, Beauty got all wrought up, she claimed.

When Luther was in hearing, Flora seldom made suggestions, but one night, when he and Joel had gone to look over the blueberry vines, she brought up a subject that had been in Laura's own mind. "I've been hoping to see you at church," she said. "Folks keep asking questions. But I don't s'pose there's any chance of Joel's coming."

"Oh, I don't know, Flora." She wasn't like Flora. She had never given religion much serious thought, finding, outside the church, something vaguely embarrassing about it. She wasn't

59

like Doris either, who brushed the whole thing off as humbug. She believed, she supposed, in what the Bible taught. She prayed, but not every night as Flora had insisted she do when she was small. But going to church had been important to her. It had meant security, something to center on—the same place, the same time, the same familiar hymns each week. It meant solidarity. No matter how provoked she got at Flora, there was real satisfaction in sitting beside her and Luther in the family pew.

But would Joel go? The only church service he had ever attended was the Christmas concert, and then he had sat in the very back pew. Should she ask him? Sunday was his one full day free from the store. Besides, things were going so well now. He did the chores regularly. He sawed the wood and kept the woodbox filled. He carried the water. He shored up the cellar stairs, replaced some boards in the bulkhead and several panes of glass in the window of the shed. Sometimes she had to ask him for help inside, and he gave it willingly, though she did not ask often, for she had learned that it was simpler to do things herself, especially things that took quick and skillful fingers. But to ask him to go to church . . .

"Perhaps later, Flora," she said without much confidence.

There had been other visitors—schoolmates, old neighbors. Jams and jellies were delivered. Shoppers going to Ellsworth took the back road in order to stop by. Everyone tried to be enthusiastic. "As long as you don't mind being by yourselves," people said. Or, "As long as you don't get sick of each other's company."

As if they ever could!

10

By the end of October the kitchen was finally done. The floor was painted. The cupboards were dry and ready for dishes again. There was a new metal-top table from Luther's store, bought and paid for, though Luther had tried to give it to them. There were four straight chairs, painted to match the pine needles of the wallpaper. There was a low, varnished rocker from Flora's attic, newly cushioned in yellow and set by the window where white dimity half-curtains hung. On the mantel above the stove, now respectably polished, stood three lamps and a tall walnut clock that had been Laura's mother's. Above the table was Luther's calendar, showing a sunrise over a mesa.

Now Laura was ready to begin on the bedroom. Here she ran into real trouble, for she hadn't stopped to consider what the walls of an old house were like when she picked out a design of climbing morning glories. But finally it was done and passable. The furniture was painted white. The rag rug from Sears and Roebuck was laid and the curtains were hung. A picture of her mother, which Flora had framed and brought out, was placed dutifully on the bureau.

Dropping by to see how things were going, Luther had insisted she needed a trip to town. "Flo will be tickled to see you," he told her. Already Flora had begun to complain because they never came in. Their excuses—that Joel was tired at night, that there was always work ahead—failed to impress her. Their not going to church was still a sore issue. Not that she brought it up again—that is, in so many words. "People were asking about you Sunday," she would observe, or, "That was a fine service you missed." Laura knew, of course, what Flora was thinking, but there was a change in Laura now. She could know what Flora thought and it didn't upset her the way it used to. It wasn't the time to make an issue of church, she had decided.

Flora was upstairs when Laura opened the kitchen door. "Who's there?" she called.

"Me."

"Oh, Laura."

"Shall I come up?"

"I'll be down in a minute."

Standing there, Laura looked about the familiar kitchen with its radiators, its electric lights, its enormous cookstove with a gauge in the door of the oven, its sink of white porcelain, and found it a poor room indeed, compared with her own. Then she bent to pat Beauty, who lay quivering in a dream.

There were heavy steps on the stairs and Flora came in, buttoning her cuffs. "In all these weeks you've never been in when you weren't on the run, and now you come at a time like this," she scolded.

"Are you going somewhere? Luther didn't know, I guess."

"The Sidewalk Society. A special meeting."

"Oh." A meeting of any kind, even a special one, seemed remote and unimportant to her.

Flora reached for the clothes brush that hung on a hook by the window and whisked it vigorously over her shoulders. "They're talking about taking out the boardwalks and putting in gravel ones. It was Mama that got the board ones in, you remember."

Laura hadn't remembered, but she thought it best not to say so. "I'll just run over and see Doris," she said.

"You'll never find her," Flora warned. Then, as Laura turned to leave, she called after her, "You'll be back here for supper, anyway."

"No, thank you, Flora."

"But—"

"Not tonight. Some other time."

Was that really *me* who said that? she asked herself, closing the door quickly behind her.

Before she reached the back steps of the old house she heard the gramophone, full blast, playing *"The Isle of Golden Dreams,"* and saw Ed, unshaven, in a red flannel shirt and khaki trousers, sitting at the table surrounded by papers and the remains of dinner—a pile of potato skins, the ragged remnants of a dried fish, and half of a very moist pumpkin pie.

"Well," he said, looking up, "if it ain't Teacher."

"Busy?"

"Never too busy ter talk ter a dame," he said gallantly, tipping back in his chair. He was making out his bills. When he had worked for the pulpwood company, he had done his figuring on Luther's machine, but for the summer people he used a lead pencil instead. Summer people liked "characters" and, finding it profitable, Ed was glad to oblige. Along with each bill, itemized on rough tablet papar, he sent a letter, its contents varying only with the season. "Dear Frend," each letter began. Then, "Fokes will sure be glad to see you," or, "The town sure seems dead with you fokes gone." The writing was large and childish, not at all like Ed's usual flourishing hand.

Butch was spread out in a rocker, half his great bulk hanging over the edge, so Laura went to the table and drew out a straight chair.

"Is Doris around?"

"Sweepin' out the barn," he said.

"The *barn*," Laura echoed. It was surprising to find Doris sweeping at all. And that barn, crammed with everything that had been discarded for generations, to say nothing of the old family surrey, a mowing machine her father had taken as payment for a year's supply of firewood, a dumpcart from somewhere, old wheels by the dozen . . . "Why in the world would she be sweeping out the barn?"

"Part o' the new scheme," Ed said, putting on a mysterious expression.

In the past she had been envious sometimes of Doris and Ed and of the excitement they found in living. Now that envy was gone. Everything except her life with Joel had faded. But she tried to sound interested. "Tell me what it is," she urged.

"Oh, I dunno." Ed was visibly enjoying the suspense he believed he had created. "Things ain't quite ready yet."

"Just give me a hint then." She liked Ed and she would not willingly disappoint him. She appreciated, too, how understanding he had been when Joel left him to work in the store.

The door opened and Doris came in, her face smudged, her hair trailing cobwebs, the red of her skirt dulled by dust. "Shall we tell her?" Ed asked. They exchanged one of their sly, secret looks that so infuriated Flora.

"Sure. Go ahead. Why not?"

They both started talking together. They had cleared up the barn. Piled all the stuff out in back. They were opening a gym there.

Ed pawed over the papers on the table and eventually pulled out a printed notice, obviously intended for the Post Office. He handed it proudly to Laura.

KEEP FIT WITH ED AND DORIS

Want to multiply your muscles?
Reduce your wasteline?
Enlarge your bust? Get rid of your belly?

Latest Equipment
Trapeses. Paralel Bars. Punching
Bags, Dumb Bells, Flying Rings

ADVICE FOR NOTHING, TREATMENT REASONABLE

64

Once, younger though she was, Laura would have reasoned with them, asked who would come, why people who had rowed or hoed all day should be concerned about their muscles, reminded them of the sagging floor and rotting beams. Reminded them, too, that they would have to answer to Flora. But today she only listened while they talked on with mounting enthusiasm—half-listened, really—wished them good luck, and made an excuse for leaving.

As she went, the feeling of detachment grew. It was as if she had been away for a long time, as if the two or three people she met, people she had known all her life, were mere acquaintances. When she stopped to talk with them, she had a hard time thinking what to say.

Nowhere was the feeling so strong as when she approached the high school. For four years that school had been the center of her life. Every day she hurried through her breakfast and dinner, impatient to get there. When school was out, she had lingered, to Flora's annoyance, long after she might have left. With the slightest excuse she was ready to go back evenings. Every minute of the time she spent there had been charged with excitement—the excitement of bells and of lessons, of rank cards, of basketball games and socials, of school annuals, of friendships that, so she thought, would last forever. She had left it sadly, believing that nothing could take its place. Even when she had taught at District 3, her feeling had not changed much. She had still gone back for games and debates and reunions. Now she looked at it almost without interest, the way you look at a dress or a coat you have loved and worn, but have outgrown and hung away.

Nearing Joel's house, she saw his father carrying water to the rowboat garden. He appeared not to have seen her, but she was sure he had.

In her happiness, she had almost forgotten Joel's father. Seeing him now, she felt the old guilt that she had not wanted him to come to the wedding, and a new guilt besides. Hadn't she promised herself that, once the wedding was over, she would try to heal the breach between him and Joel? Here she hadn't given it another thought, and now she must either pass without speaking or meet his eyes. There was no choice really. "Hello, Mr. Closson," she called.

"Why, hello," he answered, feigning a start.

"Your flowers are lovely," she said, thankful that there was something to talk about. He had pulled out all the dead annuals so that only the chrysanthemums were left and a little English ivy, trailing over the gunwales.

"Here, I'll pick yer some." He set down his pail and began to break the brittle stems.

"Just a few, now."

He kept on picking, reaching for the best.

"Oh, no more," she said, protesting.

"The frost'll git 'em. Might 'swell."

Bending over the flowers, he didn't look at all like a man who would take his motorboat out after most people were sleeping and get back just as the sun came up—part of a chain, so people said, that operated from Canada. Like a man who could go to prison if the revenue officers caught up with him. He just looked like a mild-mannered, aging man who was desperately lonely. Having known too much of it herself, loneliness of any kind had always touched her. Now, in her guilt, it touched her more.

He handed her the flowers, his eyes down, his fingers fumbling their stems.

Once again words broke out of her, words she had never intended to speak. Words that had never even crossed her mind. "We want you to come to supper tomorrow night," she said.

For the first time his eyes met hers, and she saw the incredulity in them.

66

"Why, thank yer," he said. "But I dunno. Lotsa work here on the place."

"Work can wait," she told him, feeling an odd exhilaration. "We'll look for you around five."

11

As soon as she had started off, the exhilaration left her and she began to worry a little. What would Joel say? Ought she to have done it without talking it over with him? She remembered again the night before the wedding when she had asked him if his father was coming, remembered not only his exact words—"How would I know?"—but the frown on his face as he had spoken them. In retrospect, they seemed more ominous than they had at the time. She wished she had not come into town at all. At the store she did not go inside as she had planned, but went instead to the truck and waited there.

"Where'd you get the flowers?" Joel asked, coming out promptly at five.

"From your father. I spoke to him going by."

He put the groceries in the back, got in, started the engine, and stepped on the accelerator.

"We got flowers in our own garden," he said coldly.

They rode on in silence. His eyes were on the road, hers on the flowers in her lap. If only I had not stopped to admire them, she thought, then one thing wouldn't have led to another.

Her eyes moved to the roadside. The ferns had turned tawny, but the scrub still held its color. Woodbine crept crimson along the stones in the ditches and festooned itself around the trunks of infrequent, undernourished elms. The red in the sumacs was working upward. Luther had laughed at the sumacs. "Look like giraffes, don't they?" he had said once when she was a child and they were out delivering. "See them long legs and long necks with their little heads atop 'em?" She thought of this every year, and it never failed to amuse her. But it did not amuse her now. She had done something, maybe, that she shouldn't have done. But she had done it, and at least it would give them a chance to clear the air. Besides, Joel might not be mad about it. Things had been going so well lately.

"Joel," she began.

"What?"

From the tone of his voice she knew that this was not the time to bring the subject up.

"Nothing." I will tell him tonight, she thought, when supper is over.

But all that evening he was quiet and withdrawn. He glanced at the paper, filled the portable oilstove, and brought in the last of the squashes. Then, before she had finished picking over the beans, he started for bed. When she came, he was lying for the very first time with his back to her, as if asleep.

They lay stiff and silent, just as they had lain the first nights of their marriage. What could it have been, she kept asking herself, that had come between him and his father? Not just the rumrunning, she was sure. There was nothing righteous about Joel. It was something else. She ought to know what it was, she told herself. She was his wife. He ought to tell her.

The clock in the kitchen struck ten.

"Joel."

He did not answer.

She waited a few minutes, then spoke again. "Are you awake, Joel?"

Silence.

"Please, Joel."

Still there was neither sound nor motion.

She stretched out her hand as she had done that night in the hotel in Bangor. This time she might have been touching stone.

At breakfast he was civil but withdrawn. She gave him fritters and molasses, which he especially liked. She herself had just a cup of coffee. If only I didn't have to tell him, she thought. But she had to. There was no way out. And in a few minutes he would be leaving.

"More fritters?"

"Guess not," he said without looking up.

She refilled his coffee cup. "You'll be here for supper?"

He looked up, surprised. "Where else would I be?"

She did not answer, but only turned her spoon in her cup.

His face grew suspicious. "What are you driving at?" he demanded.

"I'm not driving at anything."

"Well, what's on your mind then?"

It was impossible to put it off any longer. She took the spoon from her cup and placed it carefully in the saucer. "I invited your father to come out," she said.

He stared at her. "You invited my father?"

She nodded.

"For supper?"

"Yes."

"Here?" He looked incredulous, almost stupid.

For an instant she felt that she had the advantage. "Well, Joel, where else?"

He got to his feet and stared down at her angrily. "Just what did you say when you asked him?"

"Why, Joel, I—"

He seized her wrist and began to press it. "Answer me," he said.

Shocked, she looked down at his hand. She had never realized he had that much strength in his fingers.

He pressed harder. "Answer me!" he said again.

"Just that we—"

"*We!*" he shouted. "You mean you brought me in on this?"

"You're hurting me, Joel."

He dropped her wrist. So she had gone prying into the past. Cozying up to his father. Digging up memories. First she would find out one thing, then go after another until she knew all of it. All that had gone on that terrible night. Worse than that, she had spoken for him, put words in his mouth, words he would never have said. "Just what right do you have to go meddling in my affairs?" he shouted.

She couldn't answer. She just sat there, staring down at her wrist. Wasn't a man's business his wife's too? Weren't a husband and wife supposed to be one?

"And behind my back at that." He lowered his voice, but it was still bitter. Here he had changed his entire way of life for her. He had taken a job he hadn't wanted. He had given her an accounting of every cent he made. Every night of his life and every Saturday afternoon he worked around the place. And this was the thanks she gave him.

"But Joel—" He must understand. She must make him. "Listen."

He grabbed his mackinaw. This was what he got for tying himself down. For breaking his neck on her account. He opened the door and started out.

"Wait, Joel." She jumped up to follow him, jolting the table and upsetting her coffee. "Wait." She wanted to tell him how it had happened. How she hadn't planned it at all. How as likely as not his father wouldn't come anyway . . .

But he had left, banging the door behind him. Looking out, she saw him stop in the shed, pick up his gun, and drive away.

70

She sat down at the table and stared at the spreading coffee stain. All her life she had hated quarrels and taken great pains to avoid them. She had never had a real quarrel with Joel, even when they were children. Joel got moody, but never really mad. Now, when they were just two months married . . . Why wouldn't he listen? . . . let her explain . . . To go off like that . . . It would have been different if he had told her how strongly he felt about his father. Warned her.

You knew, her mind whispered. You *knew*.

For a long time she sat there, confused. Miserable. Then suddenly a thought struck her. He had given in about working in the store, about the house, about having a wedding. . . . He would give in now. He would turn around and come back . . . not to say he was wrong—Joel would never say that—but to give her a chance to explain. Most important of all, to say he wouldn't be mad any longer. He would come back. Perhaps even now he was on his way.

She got up, grabbed her sweater from a chair, and hurried outside. He would come back and find her coming to meet him. Perhaps if he hadn't gone far she could meet him halfway. The thought pleased her.

It was a gray day. Big clouds hung darkly over the barrens, muting the colors of the foliage. The air was cold and a strong wind blew. She shivered as she walked. She should go back and get a coat, she knew, but she could not bring herself to delay the reconciliation. She pulled her sweater tight about her and kept on. He would come back.

A quarter of a mile from home she heard a crow calling, and though she knew it was nonsense, she still could not look up for fear there might be only one in sight. He would come back, she kept telling herself as she stumbled along the frozen gravel. He might take his time about it, but he would come.

She heard a car and, laughing aloud in her relief, she hurried faster. Her hair slipped down; her ankles turned. But it did not matter. He had come.

It was only Tom Pinkham, earlier than usual, with the mail.

She stood still without waving until he had passed. She had been so sure. Then she sat down dejectedly on a rock by the roadside. Tears started, and she wiped them away on the sleeve of her sweater. She listened again, but all that she heard was the wind moving in the dried weeds and bushes, and the caw, caw of a string of ragged crows flapping over.

Joel's father came exactly at five, parking not in the drive, but down the road a little way. Through the window Laura saw him coming, walking with his gentle roll. He was wearing a neat dark suit, a white shirt with a stiff collar, and he carried his hat, turning the brim with his fingers.

Laura waited at the door for him. Until noon she had been telling herself that though Joel had not come back to make up, he would come at dinnertime, just as he did every Saturday. He could come then and still save face. She had cooked a special dinner for him—biscuits, beets, finnan haddie—trying all the time to block her mind to questions. *How do you know he will be back at all? How can you be sure?*

At one o'clock she had put the food away, gone into the bedroom, and cried for what seemed hours. I cannot go through with this, she thought. Had there been some way to reach Joel's father, she would have told him not to come. But there had been no way, and here he was. She was composed, she thought. At least the traces of her tears were blotted out. "Come in, Mr. Closson," she said.

He wiped his feet carefully and stepped inside. "Real breezy out," he told her.

"Yes, I guess it is." She had started this thing, and she had to see it through. Joel's father had come at her invitation, and she must keep him from knowing what had happened.

"Joel home?" he asked at once before she could even take his hat.

"Not yet."

His glance fell on the table set for two.

"There's been a mix-up," she said lamely. "Joel—" His eyes met hers squarely.

Her own eyes fell.

"I couldn't of stayed, nohow." His voice was dry, though his face showed nothing. "All I come out fer was ter bring yer this." He drew a loosely wrapped package from his inside pocket and handed it to her. "Better late than never, I guess."

She opened it shakily. It held six silver soup spoons. "They belonged ter Joel's mother," he told her. Then, before she could collect herself enough to thank him, he had opened the door and was hurrying off.

It was half-past eight when Joel turned into the driveway. He had left the store at noon with a few cookies in his pocket and headed for the woods. Every time he had heard a rustle in a thicket he had let go with his gun. Yet he never went to find out if he had hit anything. He just fired off another shot or two and kept on walking, his feet cold and wet in the light shoes he was wearing.

Mad as he was at Laura, he was madder still at his father. He had thought he was quit of his father for good, and now he was barging in, giving Laura flowers, working on her sympathy. What had he told her? What were they talking about now? Ganging up on him, he supposed. Getting him in a corner. With no sound at all from a thicket, he had fired off all his remaining shot.

About four, tired out, he had come back to town. He would look up some of his old friends, he decided, especially some that Laura didn't like. But who could he look up? Roland Graw was working on the Boston boat. Jim Hodgdon had just found a job in Ellsworth. Tom Gillis had married a Harrington girl and taken over her father's business. He ought to have gone away too, he told himself. Then he would never have got himself into a mess like this. What he really ought to have done was to have left six years ago, when it all happened.

Thinking back made him sweat, then shake with chills. To get warm he went into Peasley's. He had never hung around Peasley's, for he hated the smell of tobacco smoke (he had had enough of that in his father's house) and he was no good whatever at pool. But he couldn't go home, at least until his father had left. Besides, Laura disapproved of Peasley's.

He bought two candy bars and ate them, keeping close to the stove so that he could dry his feet. No one had said anything except "Hello," but he saw a wink or two that made him burn. *Henpecked. Henpecked already.* So, just to show that he could spend his money as he pleased, he shot five games of pool, losing every one. At eight, hungry and still bitterly angry, he started home.

When she heard him come, Laura was sitting in the rocker, waiting. After his father left, she had become completely calm again. She had thought things out. She was ready for him. She would say nothing at all about the way he had acted. Nothing at all about his leaving her all day. She didn't expect him to talk about his mother, for she respected his silence there. But he would have to tell her about this trouble with his father. Then, when it was all out in the open, she would be able to decide where the fault lay. If it was with his father, she would side, of course, with Joel. If it was with Joel, she would reason with him, and together they would work out some kind of understanding.

She heard the truck stop, then his steps at the door. The door opened and she saw him standing there, his eyes accusing, his mouth dejected, his shoes stained from dampness, streaked with mud and clay, bits of leaves still clinging to them.

A great rush of love engulfed her. Right or wrong made no difference. She ran to him, threw her arms around his unbend-

74

ing neck, and began frantically to kiss the shoulder of his mackinaw. "Oh, Joel," she cried. "I'll never ask him here again." When he did not respond, she clung to him harder. "I'll never mention his name to you again, Joel, I promise, promise, promise."

12

Indian summer came suddenly after the first heavy frost. The wind died, leaving the bushes stripped and the birds' nests bare. The sky was cloudless. There were few birds now except for the crows and the pheasants that came for the last of the seeds. The air was clear and so still that the sound of a hunter's gun could be heard for miles. Daily the color of the blueberry vines deepened, making a vivid contrast with the sky. It was a breathless time, too good to believe.

All was harmony inside too. Laura's humility had moved Joel deeply. Words that he had spoken during the quarrel kept coming back and shaming him. He was anxious to atone. In addition to his own chores, he tried to help her with hers, stopping on his way in to take the clothes from the line or even helping her in the kitchen. Once he made the bed, but so badly that they both broke out into laughter. When Flora came, he went out of his way to be pleasant to her, and when Ed wanted him to go to Ellsworth, he said he had something more important on his mind.

To please Laura, he tried a dozen drawings and even submitted two of them to a contest in *Collier's*. He made love more often and less hurriedly, giving her time, not falling asleep, as he had begun to do when it was over, but singing to her, singing their song, *Whispering while you cuddle near me.* . . .

On the second Sunday of November he suggested suddenly that they go to church. They were sitting at breakfast. The sun was spilling in, spreading its beams, and through the little port-hole window Laura could see the hills, sharper than they had ever seemed before. At Joel's words she turned her eyes from them and looked, startled, into his face. A few weeks before she herself had brought the subject up and got nowhere. Now, of his own free will . . .

"Your suit is all pressed," she said quickly before he could change his mind. Then she got up at once, trying not to show how pleased she was, and started to clear the table.

They were going to be late. But she would not ask him to hurry. She did not even look at the clock while he shaved and dressed, taking twice as long as either Luther or Ed would have taken. She did not even mention the sound of the last bell that reached them through the clear air while they were still more than half a mile from the village.

They got there just as the scripture lesson was beginning. As they stood in the vestibule by the coat rack, waiting, Laura scrutinized Joel anxiously. Yes, his cowlick was damp and down. His tie was neat, his shoes still shone from their wedding polish. Reassured, she peeked inside.

It was the usual congregation—thirty or forty men and women, most all of them elderly, the hard-of-hearing near the front, the others scattered in their family pews. At the base of the pulpit was a bouquet of dahlias in a Mason jar, and behind it Reverend Amos Bigelow stood, reading haltingly, his finger following the text.

> The earth is the Lord's and the fullness thereof,
> The world and they that dwell therein,
> For he has founded it upon the rock. . . .

With Joel there beside her for the whole congregation to see, Laura felt a buoyancy she had never felt before. Reverend

Bigelow's stumbling words took on a new resonance and a new beauty. Her eyes lifted to where the dust motes quarreled gently in the sunshine and squares of dark rosy light flickered on the wall, making almost the nameless color of their land. It seemed to bind them all together—the Lord, the land, herself and Joel.

She turned to look at him.

He smiled. It was an open smile, full of love and gratitude— one such as he had never given her before.

She felt warmed, lifted, exultant. I shall remember this day as long as I live, she told herself.

The organ creaked, then burst into melody. It broke what had seemed almost a spell. She straightened and, signaling for Joel to lead the way, started up the aisle and slipped into the Leighton pew.

Sitting, she gave Flora a flushed, triumphant glance.

See, it said. *See.*

13

Callers became less frequent, for now that the weather had changed, a trip to the barrens meant a long, chilly drive. But Luther came often, taking the back road when he had business in Ellsworth, and Doris and Ed dropped in now and then to report progress on their venture, held up temporarily because of a new and better scheme that was already hatching. One Saturday morning Julia Wass, now teaching at District 3, came out with the mail and talked about things that were happening at school. Poor Julia, Laura had thought, only half listening. When she thought of school now, she thought only of its nuisances—the head colds, the tale-telling, the mixed-up rubbers.

The whole family had spent Thanksgiving congenially at Flora's. Joel's behavior had been all anyone could have asked for. At the table he drew out Flora's chair, to the bewilderment of Ed, who, unaccustomed to such finesse, thought he intended to pull it out from under her, said so, and set them all laughing. He praised the dinner. He even helped clear away. Afterwards he joined the others in games and puzzles. Even Beauty and Butch (actually invited) caught the spirit and passed the entire day in complete peace. It had been, as Luther observed, indeed a day to remember.

Persuaded by Luther, Flora had finally consented to the whole family's coming to the barrens for Christmas. Laura had everything planned. The house must be finished and shining, the sitting-room furniture in place, the ruffled curtains ironed and hung. In spite of the cookstove, the dinner must be creditable, though of course it could not be as good as Flora's. Joel would preside at the table, polite, hospitable, the head of the household. Christmas would be her vindication.

She thought of nothing else, neither the weather nor the calendar. Indeed, most of the time she did not even know what day it was. At noon she ate her dinner standing, using up the odds and ends or occasionally baking a potato to go with a piece of stripped fish. She hardly took time to glance outside. What she saw when she did was an unending, swirling plateau of white, broken only by the bushes that huddled against the wind and the tracks Joel made, filled in by mid-morning.

The wind would get on my nerves, if I had any, she thought. It never stopped blowing. It blew down the chimney, making the stove smoke. It rattled the windows; it came in under the doors. Sometimes when she went to get water it all but blew her off the steps.

But that was a small worry. Early in December the sitting room was finished. In it they put the things from the old house —the green velour sofa; the drop-leaf table; the brown leather

Morris chair Luther had given them, a leftover from the time he had carried furniture in the store. The little oak desk that had been in Laura's room for as long as she could remember. Above the mantel they hung the picture of the Coliseum that her pupils had given her when she left District 3, and on the floor they laid a braided rug—a castoff from Doris that, after three scrubbings, still smelled faintly of Butch.

When everything else was done, Laura hung the curtains and tacked up the tiebacks, measuring them critically with her eye. Then, she sat down and looked about. There were flaws, of course—several places where the medallions on the wallpaper didn't quite match; a few spillovers on the sashes; a spot right in the doorway where she had tested the paint too early after she had used the last drop and thrown away the can. . . . But no one except Flora would notice them.

She got up and walked from room to room, pausing in every doorway to look critically about.

Then she tried a new approach. She put on her overshoes, seized an old afghan that she kept out of sight in the bedroom closet, wrapped it around her, and went outdoors. There, one hand cupped over her eyes, the other clutching the afghan, she looked inside. It was only then, shivering, the wind against her, the snow above her overshoes, that she realized completely how beautiful it was.

Our house, she thought, her heart swelling. Our home.

Joel had worked hard getting ready for winter. He had filled the holes in the foundation. He had hauled a truckload of sawdust from the mill for banking. He had piled the hardwood in the shed. He had mended the roof and fixed the flashing around the chimney. All these things he had done without a hitch. Then, on the night of the sixteenth, while he was just carrying a pail of water from the well, he slipped and strained his back badly.

Laura helped him into the upstairs bedroom where the mattress was firmer. Then she got the hot-water bottle for his feet and started the little portable oilstove going. He refused to have the doctor.

"How could you get him anyhow?" he demanded, then held his breath while a pain passed.

"I could walk in." She could do anything for Joel.

He turned his face away. "Don't talk so crazy," he said.

She said no more. He was in no shape, she saw, to be left alone. Luther would come out when Joel didn't show up in the morning.

When he was settled, she wrapped herself in a blanket and sat in the chair beside him. The room was cold and drafty. Every hour or so she went downstairs to put more wood in the cookstove and fill the hot-water bottle. Around midnight the oilstove faded, flickered, and went out. She would have to go to the shed for more oil.

She lighted the lantern, put on Joel's big boots, threw his mackinaw over her shoulders, and, picking up the can from the back entry, started outside. It was still snowing and the large flakes sputtered against the lantern.

She didn't like to go out to the shed at night. It wasn't that she was nervous; it was just that, once the sun was down, she never felt relaxed there. Now, through the darkness, she saw it looming ahead. She walked slowly, picking her way. The night was very quiet. The only sounds she could hear were the creak of her lantern and the grating of the door when she yanked it open against the hard-packed snow.

Inside, she set the lantern down and stood rigid for an instant, startled by the grotesque shadows of herself and the oil can upon the wall. Other things looked different from the way they looked by day. Joel's gun, pointing at her. The woodpile crouching. The saw, hanging threateningly on a rusty nail overhead. The ax, slashed into the ragged block.

Shivering, she unscrewed the top from the can and placed it

under the spigot on the spot where the drip of the kerosene had darkend the floor. Then she tried to turn the handle. It did not even loosen. She lifted the lantern. Its gleam fell on a piece of pipe. She picked this up and fitted it over the handle. Turning it, she caught the smell of kerosene.

She put her hands under her armpits to warm them, listening for the change in tone as the kerosene poured into the can. When she decided it was almost full, she closed the spigot and, picking up the can and lantern, started back, a great gust of wind slamming the door noisily behind her. It had taken her longer than she had expected.

When she stepped inside the house, Joel, barefoot and wearing only his pajamas, was standing in the middle of the kitchen.

"Why, Joel, you . . ." she began. Then she saw that he didn't look like himself at all.

"Where in God's hell have you been?" he shouted.

She stopped still and stared at him. She had seen him arrogant, stubborn, furiously angry, as when she had interfered between him and his father, and scared, as when she had told him she was planning to leave Millboro. But she had never seen him like this. Never seen him out of control. For an instant she lost her own composure—the dark, the cold, the isolation, Joel out of his head, it seemed. Then the sound of his chattering teeth brought her back to her senses. She set down the can and lantern, took the mackinaw from her shoulders, and slipped it over his. "Just out in the shed," she told him. "You ought not to be up like this."

He stood rigid. "Why did you have to go—" He clutched his back again. "Why did you have to go and do a thing like that?"

"Why, for oil. We've got to have heat." She moved to take his arm. "Come back to bed, Joel, this very minute. The house is freezing."

He pushed her away. The mackinaw slipped to the floor.

"How was I to know?" he demanded. "Going off like that. Why didn't you tell me?"

"But you were sleeping." She picked up the mackinaw, put it back on him again, and, still wearing boots, tried to lead him toward the hall. "Come now. Back to bed."

He was shaking all over, but he still resisted. "I heard a door slam," he said.

"'Twas just the door of the shed. Come on now." She guided him firmly toward the stairs. "You're not even awake, Joel. You've had a bad dream."

When she got him upstairs he sank, still trembling, against the pillow. She went back into the kitchen, took off her boots, and blew out the lantern. Then, shaken and shivering herself, she filled the oilstove, wrapped herself up again in the blanket, and sat down in the chair beside his bed. Why should anyone be so upset by just the slamming of a door?

Joel was in bed for a week. At least a dozen times a day Laura stopped her work to take him something—trays at mealtime, broth, gruel, custards in between; a second hot-water bottle before the first had cooled. She was distressed, yet at the same time she was stimulated. It was so wonderful to have him home, so wonderful to have a chance to serve him.

When he was up again and back at the store, she insisted that he take things easy. Yet from six in the morning until bedtime she herself kept busy. She did all the chores, carrying the oil and wood and water. She cleaned the upstairs bedroom. (Flora would be sure to go there on some excuse or other.) She papered the water closet, though it was so cold there that the paste kept thickening. She put the cellarway in order. She made mincemeat and plum pudding.

Where does the time go? she kept thinking. Often she had to stop what she was doing and figure what day it was.

Not until the twenty-third did she start out to get the tree. The snow was deep, far deeper than she had realized, and beyond the shed she sank halfway to her knees with every step. Plodding along, she watched the patterns the birds had made and the grotesque shapes of the drifts about the ledges. Now and then she came on the track of a deer, and once, that of a bear crossing a swale. Though her exertion made her a little short of breath, she kept humming a song they had always sung at Christmas concerts:

> The bells are ringing,
> Sweetly ringing. . . .

It wasn't easy to find a suitable tree on the barrens, even a small one, for those that grew there were scrubby and one-sided from the continuous wind, but at last she did find one that would do. It was larger than she had wanted, but Joel could cut it off. She started back, dragging it, turning it now and then to equalize the weight on the branches. It was heavier than she had expected, and she was walking against the wind.

When she reached the little graveyard, she decided to rest for a minute. She sat down on the stone step, which the wind had cleared of snow, and began to think about the people who lay there. They were dead, and she and Joel had the house they must have loved, the room they must have slept in. The little porthole window . . .

Impulsively she took off her mittens and, using the ax, began to scrape the dry, shell-like lichen from the stone.

DAVID OSGOOD
1854–1880

She paused to substract. Twenty-six. Not much older than Joel . . . Soberly her eyes moved to the stone beside it.

HANNAH OSGOOD
1856–1900

Twenty years she had lived on without him. . . . Had she lived there alone, looking out on the burns, seeing no green anywhere? Alone, in winter, hearing the wind at night? She thought of what it would be like and shivered.

Lying flat at her feet, stripped now of the weeds that had covered it, was a small stone she had not seen before. She bent to read it.

HOPE
10 mo.

Just that. No date. The name . . .

Suddenly she began to feel the cold. Another shiver struck her. I'd better be getting on, she thought. She picked up the ax, seized the tree by its base, and headed home.

In the open again, the drifts seemed deeper, the wind stronger than before. Every now and then she paused and turned against it. The tree, picking up snow as she went, grew heavier and heavier. Her feet grew heavier too.

She tried to hum again, but her teeth were chattering. Once she dropped the tree, deciding to leave it for Joel to bring in. Then she remembered his back and picked it up again. Her teeth chattered now so that she could not control them.

If she came down with the grippe for Christmas . . . If all her plans should come to nothing. . . .

Then, relieved, she saw Joel driving into the yard. She could get there. She had to. But the tree seemed to be dragging her backward, backward. . . .

She yanked at it fiercely and, as she did, she felt a sharp pain in her pelvis, then a warm, quick flow.

"Joel," she cried. "Joel."

PART TWO

1930

1

Laura Closson stood by the cookstove, lighting the fire. The edgings were damp this morning, so she poured on a little kerosene. Not much, of course, for in times like these everything had to be watched and measured. As soon as the fire blazed up, she closed the damper and went to the window. It was April, and the barrens were brown and bedraggled. The birches, few and fragile, were thin, bent from the weight of ice and the force of the wind. In the ditches by the roadside last year's cattails grew, blanched, overblown, and ragged.

Another slow spring, she thought. In five years she had changed very little. She was thinner. She wore her hair short and shaped to her head. Her motions were quicker than before.

They had been good years, by and large. They had brought Jesse, now three and a half. ("Smart as a whip," people said of him. "Bright as a button, Jesse.") They had brought improvements on the house, outside and in. It was painted now, gray against the smoke of the burns. Joel had done the upper part and she the lower. There was a new green velour chair in the sitting room; a new set of maple furniture in the bedroom; a sewing machine, kept in the hall; a pump in the kitchen; and a new cookstove set on a zinc platform. As she turned to close its draft, she looked it over with satisfaction.

Yes, the years had brought her many good things. They had brought an increasing love for the barrens themselves—of the sunrises so red and violent that she could never get used to them and woke up time and time again with a start, sure the whole place for miles around was burning. Of the sunsets that she could watch through the little porthole window while she was doing the dishes at night—colors sometimes quiet and harmonious, sometimes so dramatic that she lifted Jesse up to watch them. Of the northern lights, cold and mysterious, that sent her thankfully to bed. A love of the animals—the deer that came out early and late and twitched their tails before they listened; the foxes, arrogant and handsome; the rabbits, changing color with the seasons, like the land they lived on.

A love of sounds in the quiet. The shrill of the locusts; the clamor of the katydids; the dry rattle of grasshoppers' wings among the tall red grasses; the soft, haunting hoot of an owl at night; the faint chorus of frogs in gravel pits and far-off marshes; the single strident cry of the kingbird; the bold, abrupt note of the brown thrasher; the slow, rough whistle of the meadowlark that nested in the little graveyard. She even liked the rusty call of the crows. She used to say, laughing, that she'd got so she could tell one old crow's caw from another's.

The years had brought her a closer relationship with Luther. He drove out often and at almost any hour of the day. "Got time to waste on an old duffer like me?" he would ask before he turned off the engine. (As though her time meant anything!) He always brought some little surprise—a can of a new sandwich spread he was carrying, or perhaps a box of Nabiscos and a bottle of Moxie. "How's everything?" he always asked.

He didn't ask it in the way Ed asked, "How's tricks?" He asked it quietly, and he listened and looked while she answered. He helped her finish whatever she was doing, and then they sat down at the kitchen table together.

In his own home, Luther had never talked much, especially about himself. Here, in the quiet of the kitchen, he told Jesse stories of his boyhood. How he had fancied himself a cowboy and rounded up his four old cows with a yippe-hi-hey, drying up their milk and scaring the daylights out of them. How he had practiced with a rope, never coming anywhere near his target until one day, not knowing anyone was within a mile of him, he'd heard a yell like blue murder, and saw that he had caught the sheriff right around the collar, as neat as could be. How one afternoon when his father had gone to town he'd got down the shotgun and tried it out, sitting on the fence by the pigpen. The darned gun had kicked him right back in against the old sow. While he was telling these stories his laugh would ring out, big like the rest of him, filling the kitchen, with hers and Jesse's joining in.

The years had brought excitement, too. Before Jesse had come, they had gone to basketball games at Sullivan and Jonesboro with Doris and Ed; to Grange suppers; occasionally to Saturday-night dances. (Once they had gone to a dance marathon where Doris and Ed had kept going six hours and eighteen minutes, dropping out then only because someone had knocked off Doris's glasses and broken the nosepiece.) Best of all had been the trips to Ellsworth, just the two of them, doing errands for Luther. When the errands were done, they had walked about, taking in the sights. The hotel, its broad piazza lined with rockers; the river, spilling evenly over the big dam; the Courthouse, staid and forbidding on the hill, with the jail beside it. (They always walked by the jail very slowly, careful not to stare, yet never missing a thing.)

Their longest trip had been to Bangor. It had been Luther's

present to them on their first anniversary. Of course it hadn't been like the first trip, for she had been pregnant again, and her legs had begun to swell so that she couldn't stand for long at a time. But they had watched the river as they had done before —the tugs; the coal barges; the ships weighed low with lumber and pulpwood; the pleasure boats, cruising or tied up at the slips; the Boston steamers (once the *Belfast*, once the *Camden*) turning slowly, grandly, before they could dock. They had gone to Brewer and back on the busy little ferry, watching the drifting logs, the churning pulpwood, the old sailors lining the stringpiece. They had gone to Freese's for baby things, then to the Palace of Sweets, where, just as on their first trip, they had a butterscotch sundae and bought two boxes of Pine Tree Toffee, one for Flora and Luther, one for Doris and Ed. They had planned to eat again at a restaurant, but at the last minute changed their minds and decided to go to a drugstore instead. The hotel seemed noisier than before, so they hadn't slept much, and the second day they started home at noon. The drive back had been the nicest part of the trip, for Joel had been in one of his best moods, singing crazy songs all the way. Luther would have given them a trip every year had they been willing to take it, but of course after the first year there was Jesse.

Added to all these things was the money she herself had earned—$516. The first summer after they were married she had picked their own berries and sold them through Ed to the people he worked for. ("Twenty-five dollars a basket," he used to say airily.) The next year she had begun making jam, getting orders sometimes for as many as a dozen jars from each customer. At first she had made it only from their own blueberries. Then one day Luther had sent her half a crate of oranges (he had been overstocked, he said) and, following a receipt of Flora's, she had made a bitter marmalade that had caused quite a sensation. Luther sold it in the store. Later, one

90

of the traveling men took it on, and she had as much business as she could handle. Except for buying the green velour chair for the sitting room, she had invested all she had earned in a building and loan company whose offices she had seen in Bangor. It would go for Jesse's education.

Of course there had been disappointments, even disasters. The miscarriage (no baby, she had once believed, could be quite like the first). Then the hard pregnancy with Jesse and his chronic croup. There had been a summer of drought, when the only water they had was what Joel had brought in from town, which meant they had lost the garden. There had been windstorms that blew off shingles and let the rain inside. One of them had knocked down half the chimney. There had been blizzards, when for days they had been cut off completely, even from the shed. There had been burns that had gotten all but out of hand.

But no disappointment had been quite so great for her as Joel's disinterest in getting ahead. He did his job—she granted him that—though probably not quite so well as Luther said. Yet he took none of the opportunities that Luther offered. He wasn't interested in learning how to buy and keep accounts, though Luther was always ready to teach him, hoping, as she had, that since Harry didn't want to stay in Millboro, Joel would someday take over the store. She was disappointed, too, that he had given up his drawing. He seldom drew now unless he happened to find pencil and paper within reach. Then he drew idly, as if he had no real idea in mind, rarely finishing a sketch.

She went to the cellarway, took out a plate of smelts she had cleaned the night before, rolled them in corn meal, and set them frying. Then she looked at the clock on the mantel. It was quarter to six.

"Joel," she called.

There was no answer.

She lifted the cover of the cookstove and put in another stick of wood.

"Joel," she said again.

Still no answer.

Perhaps if she pumped. . . . She began noisily to move the handle. She hated to keep at him. It made him irritable when she did. Yet how would he get to work on time if she didn't? Once when he had told her to leave him alone she had, and he had overslept. Then he had acted as though it was all her fault.

She stopped pumping and turned to open a jar of applesauce. After all, her own worries had been small, she told herself, compared to those other people were having. Over the radio she had heard about hard times in the cities, unemployment, soup kitchens. Remote as these things had seemed, they were beginning to have their effect even in Millboro. Summer people who had lost heavily in the stock-market crash were not opening their cottages. That meant less business for Luther, part-time for Ed. The sardine factory was still closed, and, according to Tom Pinkham, the blueberry factory in Cherryfield would be hiring only half its usual crew.

I ought to be thankful for all I have, she thought. Her love for Joel was as strong as ever. She was still stirred by his presence, still confident of his love for her. If she for a minute doubted it, she had only to remember how distraught he had been during her pregnancy; how, even now, when she left home just on an errand, he either came for her or watched the road for her return. After five years of marriage she did not expect him to be demonstrative. Yet sometimes it did seem as though he went out of his way to exasperate her.

"Joel," she said again. "It's after six."

Still silence.

She put the dishes, the silverware, and the oleo on the table. Then she went to the door of the bedroom. Joel lay quiet, his eyes closed, but she knew he was awake from the feel the room gave her. Besides, she could see a faint look of guilt on his face.

"Joel."

"Mmmmm."

"It's late."

"I hear you," he said. "You don't have to yell."

2

After Joel had left, Laura piled up the dishes and went into the front room to listen for Jesse. Since the days had grown longer he awoke at dawn, talked to himself a little, then went back to sleep and slept sometimes until eight o'clock. That let her get the house picked up before she got his breakfast.

Hearing nothing from him, she went into the downstairs bedroom. She did not raise the shade, for the sun was bright this morning, and she was still careful about the paper. Already the morning glories had begun to fade a little—the blue more than the pink, it seemed—especially above the bureau. She picked up Joel's pajamas, which he had thrown on a chair, his stockings, left where he had dropped them the night before, his tie, hung on the doorknob. Then she made the bed.

This done, she went into the sitting room, pausing in the doorway to look at the curtains. They were wearing out, and no wonder, for though she took them down while the burns were in progress, all summer long grime kept seeping in from the ash. That meant frequent washings with strong bleach. Curtains cost money, and this wasn't the time to spend a cent. The room was in order, for they seldom sat there. Except for the new chair, the pictures of Jesse on the walls, and a small braided rug she herself had made, the room showed no changes.

She went into the kitchen, put another stick of wood in the stove, moved the coffee pot forward, folded Joel's napkin, and slipped it into his ring. Then she sat down in the rocker and stirred her coffee thoughtfully. Women were supposed to follow. But what if men didn't lead? Women were supposed to wait. But what if they waited and waited and nothing happened?

She took a sip of coffee and then stared out the window. How would they get anything done unless she reminded and coaxed and, yes, even nagged? Take painting the house, for instance. After she finally persuaded him that the two of them could do it, she had to pick out the paint, buy the brushes, even borrow the ladder from Ed. Yet—and here was the crazy part —as soon as it was done Joel was as proud of it as she was and brought out every traveling man on the road to show it off, relishing the compliments they gave him.

The clock struck seven. She got up and went into the hall. Listening again, she could hear a sluggish fly buzzing. Jesse's watching that fly, she thought. He loved small things, buttons and thimbles and spools to play with, birds and insects to watch. Crouching or lying flat on his stomach, he would follow a beetle with his eyes as it crawled up a blade of grass. She had known him to spend an entire afternoon just watching an ant-hill.

Back in the kitchen, she did up the dishes, swept, and made a custard pie. At eight she heard the mail truck coming. Now that her ears were trained to quiet, she could hear it long before it was in sight. Mail was never an event for her. There was the paper, of course, and now and then an advertisement and a magazine. Though it was sometimes noon before she went out to the box, she always waved as the truck went by. When she waved this morning, Tom Pinkham waved a letter back at her.

She got very few letters. Right after she had moved to the

barrens she had often heard from Julia Wass and some of her old pupils at District 3, but it took time to keep up a correspondence, and time had been at a premium.

Who was the letter from? It wasn't an advertisement, or Tom wouldn't have waved it the way he had. It couldn't be a bill. They didn't owe anyone a cent. It wasn't likely to be an invitation, for no one was entertaining these days. She had never known Joel to write a letter to anyone, so it wouldn't be his. Unless, perhaps . . .

She had always thought that someday he would hear from his mother. He must have thought so too, for right after that first week had passed—that week he had disappeared from everyone's sight—she had watched him go past their house to the Post Office just in time for the early mail. He had gone regularly every day until after graduation. Then he had suddenly stopped.

Or perhaps the letter was from his sister Emmie. She could barely remember Emmie. The only image picture she had was of a small pale girl, with big blue eyes and an untrimmed Dutch bob. Emmie would be nineteen now, old enough to take things into her own hands. Perhaps . . .

When she opened the box, she saw that the letter was from Flora and felt let down. Still standing in the road, she tore it open. *Dear Sister, Have Joel bring you in tomorrow morning. Important that I talk to you.*

What was the trouble now? Some complaint about Doris and Ed, most likely. About the way they were neglecting the house, or the way they were still spending money now that Ed's income had been cut. Or maybe it was another out-and-out quarrel, like the time Doris claimed Beauty had killed a sparrow and ought to be made to wear a bell, and Flora had retaliated by twitting them about Butch not having had a license for three years.

She looked down at the letter again. *Have Joel . . .* Annoyed as she was, she was curious too. When Flora had anything to say, she always sent a message by Joel. Why? . . .

She put the letter in the pocket of her apron and went back inside to check on Jesse.

Joel drove them in the next morning. He looked considerably older now than Laura. He was very thin and his eyes seemed more deep-set and guarded. He was silent and glum. He was always glum when they headed for Flora's, for the peace between them had been a temporary one. Whatever side Flora took, Joel increasingly took the other. Until Flora headed the Republican women, he had never taken the trouble to vote. Then, at a time he knew she was sure to be in the Selectmen's office, he registered as a Democrat. He resented the fact that though she rarely held Jesse and never offered to help with his care, she was forever studying his face for resemblances. "Look at his brow," she would say. "All Leighton." Or, "Look at his chin. That's Grandpa Blodgett all over again."

Jesse, still half-asleep, was leaning against Laura. Small for his age, he had Laura's dark eyes, deep-set like Joel's, but open and spirited; hair that was dark and heavy; fair skin so transparent that his veins showed bright blue at his wrists and temples; a straight nose and a small sensitive mouth. When the three were together, he kept as close to his mother as he could. Though he admired his father, especially for the way he could draw (when he would), he was a little scared of him, too. He never knew just what to expect from him, not being sure whether a slap was a pat or a punishment. He'd think they were getting alone fine; then all at once his father would snap out something at him. *Shut up, Jesse*; or, *Talk to yourself for a change*. The best thing, he thought, was to keep out of his way.

Halfway in, Laura looked at her watch. "It's ten minutes past seven," she said.

Joel said nothing. If he stepped on it, they could make it on

96

time. But he didn't feel like stepping on it. He had awakened in a bad mood. He did that more and more lately, for now that people were buying less, there was less to deliver, and that meant staying inside all but an hour or two a day. The small talk, which he despised, had grown depressing.

Things sure look bad around the country.

Sure do.

Reckon we're luckier than most.

Reckon we are.

Besides, heading for Flora's always made him drag his feet.

"Are we going to see Uncle Luther?" Jesse asked. The quickest way Laura had of getting him to do things he disliked (taking his sulphur and molasses, going to bed at seven o'clock) was to say that Uncle Luther liked boys who did such things without a fuss.

"For a minute."

"Then are we going to see Uncle Ed and Aunt Doris?" Uncle Ed always had some new tricks to show him, some new jokes or riddles to tell. Besides, he and his Uncle Ed had secrets from his mother, like standing up in the rowboat (Jesse loved boats) or going swimming without any clothes on. Aunt Doris let him play the gramophone all by himself, eat anything he wanted, and feed Butch at the table. She and Ed had taken him to every county fair for miles around even before he could walk. Right now they were teaching him to box. He did not want to box, but he thought if he learned he could surprise and maybe please his father.

"If you are good at Aunt Flora's."

He sobered. He didn't like staying at Aunt Flora's. He much preferred the store.

"Listen, Jesse." His mother put her hand under his chin and looked directly into his eyes. "You're to do just what I say and never once ask how soon we are leaving. Do you understand that?"

He stiffened a bit, but nodded.

"That's the boy," she said.

3

Flora was sitting at the kitchen table when they opened the door, working the puzzle in the morning paper. She had already done up the dishes, made a pie, swept the floor, and polished the cookstove.

"Late, aren't you?" she asked with a glance at the clock. She had grown heavier with the years. Flesh cushioned her arms and legs and padded her shoulders, but her hair was as dark and vigorous as ever.

Laura could feel herself flushing. "Oh, I don't think so. Not much, anyway. We stopped in awhile at the store." Actually, they had stayed only long enough to say "Hello," but Luther would never betray them.

"Didn't Jesse need a coat?"

"I wasn't cold," Jesse said. Young as he was, he understood that his mother was being criticized, and he was ready to defend her.

"Here's Beauty," Laura said, bending to look under the stove where Beauty, overweight as well as aging, lay breathing heavily in a basket padded against possible drafts. She lay regal, and, like her mistress, indifferent to children. "Take her out in the shed."

Jesse picked up the basket reluctantly and moved slowly toward the door.

Flora looked at her pie in the oven, adjusted the damper, and turned to Laura, who was hanging her things on a peg in the entry. "Come into the sitting room," she said.

"Why don't we stay right here?" Laura suggested, drawing one of the straight chairs from the table. She always felt stronger in the kitchen, remembering that she had won her first battle there.

Flora moved over to the rocker, sat down, and with a fleshy hand smoothed out her apron.

"What's on your mind, Flora?" Laura asked. "Tell me while Jesse is outside. He's getting to be all ears."

"Well," Flora began, "I'll come right to the point. I think you ought to join the W.C.T.U."

Only this, Laura thought, after all the mystery. She felt annoyed. "I can't join things now, Flora," she said. "Living way off as we do, having no transportation and nowhere to leave Jesse." Actually these were among the greatest advantages the barrens offered her, and she was thankful for them each day. "I've told you so a lot of times."

"But this is different," Flora spoke urgently, and the color began to rise in her face.

"How different?"

Flora paused and smoothed out her apron. "Well, there's a lot of talk going around."

"What about?"

"About Jim Closson."

Hadn't there always been? There was talk, too, about Mr. Peasley selling vanilla and canned heat to the boys on Saturday night. They'd given up trying to get them, even in small amounts, at Luther's. "Fresh out of stock," he always said.

"Women always talk," Laura said quickly.

Flora stopped rocking and leaned forward in her chair. "It isn't just the women. Didn't you hear about what went on at Winter Harbor?"

"No. What did?"

99

"A rum boat came in there just last Tuesday night. The word got around and pretty near all the men in town went out and threw the stuff overboard."

Then picked it up when it floated ashore, Laura thought. Her mouth hardened a little. She said nothing.

"Well, the men here are beginning to talk."

Still Laura did not answer. She was disturbed, but she tried not to show it. She did not doubt Flora's word. Whatever her other faults might be, Flora did not lie.

"Lots of men can't make a living," Flora went on. "That puts them on the town. Then the rest of us have to pay the bills. And there's Jim Closson, making money hand over fist."

Laura reddened. She had tried to keep Joel's father out of her mind. It wasn't hard to do, since she almost never saw him except at a distance—which, she had a feeling, he, too, was careful to maintain. On the two or three times she had run into him, she had been careful to speak pleasantly.

Nice day, Mr. Closson.

Sure is.

A little chilly.

Chilly. A-yuh.

But when she did think of him, her thoughts had often turned in this very direction. What did he need that money for? How did he spend it? Not in ways that were apparent, surely. He drove the same old car, wore the same old mackinaw.

"There may be trouble," Flora went on, lowering her voice. "Anyway, it's time for you to show where you stand. You owe it to the family."

"The family" meant the Leightons and the Blodgetts. All of them had been Prohibitionists. It was a Blodgett in the legislature who had introduced the first dry law. No one in "the family" had been known to touch liquor—not even Doris and Ed, though they were deterred not because of moral scruples, but rather because, having naturally high spirits, they felt no need of stimulation. But was she a Leighton and a Blodgett, or was she a Closson now? And if she was a Closson, then what? Where would Joel stand, feeling toward his father the way he did? She couldn't talk to him about it. There was her promise.

"Maybe they wouldn't have me anyway," she said, trying to speak lightly.

"Oh, they would," Flora assured her. "As a matter of fact, it came up in the meeting on Thursday. Your name was the first one mentioned for the membership crusade." The clock struck the half hour, and she got up laboriously to look at her pie again.

So it had come up in the meeting.

Laura could see the meeting as clearly as though she had been there. The women gathering in the vestry with none of the decorum that they showed on Sunday; hanging their coats in the entry, putting their hats on the shelf above, their rubbers below; moving inside noisily, crowding for the front seats, saving places for special friends by putting hymnals on them. She could see their banner on its pole set up before them, hear the chords that Flora struck on the piano, hear the singing:

> Wine is a Mocker
> And strong drink is Raging. . . .

She could hear the pledge, spoken with new fervor because at last they had won support from some of the men, men worked up not because someone broke the law but because he was making money doing it. She could hear the fervor of the new crusade. "What about Laura Closson?" someone would ask, and the rest of them would nod slyly, all anxious for her to take a public slap at Joel's father.

She stiffened. She liked Joel's father. She had been touched by his gentleness and dignity. She could have no part in a thing like this. Yet she hated to upset Flora. She had upset her enough by her marriage. If she could only put her off, she thought, as likely as not the whole thing would blow over. If it didn't, there was always Luther to turn to.

"Wait a little while, Flo," she began. Then, when Flora leaned forward ready to speak again, she interrupted her. "Remember how you always said I didn't think before I spoke, Flo? Well, I'm trying to think now. Can't you give me time?"

Flora was caught and she knew it. "Well, I suppose," she said grudgingly.

4

The last week in April, Laura began her spring cleaning. No house ever got so dirty as theirs, she thought, with the smoke from the burns and the wind that never stopped blowing. At the end of two days she hadn't quite finished the kitchen. This year she had promised herself that when the house was done she would tackle the attic of the shed. But she wasn't making her usual progress. Her zest was gone somehow. Part of it was because of her concern about Joel; part because of the news she heard from town. Half the summer cottages would not be opened. Hotels along the coast were cutting down on their staffs. (Fewer guests meant fewer lobsters.) For every package of nasturtium seeds that Luther sold, he sold six of carrots and squash.

And there was this new worry. Not a worry, really, for if any more was said she had only to go to Luther. Not a worry, but a nibbling . . .

Jesse slowed her up too, keeping right at her elbow. "Read to me, Mama. Read." When he wasn't outside, it seemed he always had a book in his hand.

"I can't read to you now, Jesse. I'm busy. Can't you see?"

"But I've got nothing to do."

"Go watch the crows." Usually he liked to watch the crows, for they were always up to something—carrying on a conversation, picking a quarrel. But today he didn't feel like it.

"There aren't any crows around, Mama."

She took her hands from the suds and thought a minute. "Then go out to the little graveyard and see if you can find a jack-in-the-pulpit like the one we saw there last year."

He started off reluctantly. She had barely had time to clean a shelf before he was back again.

" 'Tisn't there," he said. Then his voice grew teasing. "Read, Mama, please."

"But I have work to do, Jesse."

"Read first," he said.

She sighed and poured out her pail of suds. Then she dried her hands on her apron and sat down in the rocker.

"All right. What shall I read?"

He gave her one of her own books he had found in the shed. "Read here," he said.

She read for twenty minutes. When she paused for breath, he still studied the page. "What's that letter, Mama?"

"B."

He looked at it soberly; then slowly, deliberately, he moved his finger. "Here's another B," he finally said, and pointed.

"Why, Jesse, good for you." Her worries faded in the face of her pride. "Look, Jesse. N. Can you find another?"

His eyes moved down the page, then again his finger pointed.

"Good work," she said. She would get him more books. Tomorrow was Saturday. She would go to the library then. If she helped him a little, he might skip the whole first grade. Then he would be only seventeen when he graduated and went to college. She had $516 already. In twelve more years . . .

He was going to get ahead, Jesse.

The next morning Doris and Ed came out to get Jesse and take him fishing. Laura never worried about his going. Ed's boat was a monstrosity, but you could say one thing for it—it was perfectly safe. After they left, she hurried through her work and had her dress changed by the time Joel got home at noon.

"Could you drive me to the library this afternoon?" she asked as soon as he had sat down at the table.

He took her willingly everywhere she asked him to—to church (though he never went inside now), on visits or errands in town; sometimes to Cherryfield or Ellsworth just for the ride. But he didn't like to have her spring things on him. When she did, he felt compelled to hold her back. It was an old tactic of his, one he was using more and more. By it he could assert himself and still not risk a quarrel in which, not being as quick as she, he might lose face. "Can't you wait until next Saturday?" he asked, reaching for a biscuit.

"Not very well," she told him. Once the excitement had begun, she had hardly been able to wait at all. Jesse would graduate at seventeen. He would win the Valedictory as she had. He would go the very next September (this was important) to the state university, or maybe to Bowdoin. It wasn't too early to start planning. "I'd like to start as soon as dinner," she said.

He could have gone then. In a way it would have been more convenient. But he was determined not to give ground. "Can't make it before two," he told her.

When Laura climbed the stairs of the Grange Hall and entered the library, Miss Baker was standing facing the shelves with an armful of books. Miss Baker had been the librarian for as long as Laura could remember. A spinster who kept house for her elderly father on a farm three miles outside the village, she walked back and forth every Saturday, in all kinds of weather, swept, dusted, kept the fires in winter, gave out and took in books methodically—all for a dollar a week, raised at the annual food sale put on by the members of the committee. The heat and the books (budgeted at $25 a year) were supplied by the town.

She looked no different now from the way she had looked all those years ago when, sitting on the stairs, Laura had waited for her to open the library door. She was tall and thin, with legs that seemed stretched from all her walking, arms stretched too from years of reaching for the highest shelves.

"Why, Laurie Leighton," she said, turning at Laura's greeting. "I'm tickled to see you. It's been a long time."

"Too long, Miss Baker." She had forgotten what it did to you to stand in that crowded entry—drafty, badly lighted, boxed in by books with faded bindings. How it quickened your blood. Her eyes moved to the hard, straight chair by the window where she had spent so many hours. She could lose herself in a book there as she could never do at home. No one told her to sit up straight or to move into a better light. She had read *Black Beauty* there, *The Secret Garden, Little Women, Great Expectations. Great Expectations* had been her favorite of all, for as she read she saw herself as the orphaned Pip, Luther as Joe, and Flora as Mrs. Joe. She remembered guiltily how, with flaming cheeks, she had read of Mrs. Joe's death over and over.

She took a deep breath. "This place has a smell of its own," she said. "What is it?"

Miss Baker laughed. "Dust and kerosene, I guess, with a whiff of fish and tobacco thrown in." She picked up a book she had laid on the window sill. "From Ed Bowden's pipe," she said, making a face. "I've put it here to air." She picked up another lying beside it. "Sniff this."

Laura sniffed. "What is it?" she said. "I can't make out."

"Sloan's Liniment. It's Nathan Wiswell. He reads to take his mind off his rheumatism. Every Western story we've got just reeks of it." Miss Baker sniffed again, made up the same face, then opened the window wider. "Sit down and visit."

"I'm afraid I can't," Laura said regretfully. "Joel's waiting. He's anxious to get back and spade up the garden."

"Oh, dear. Well, what can I get for you?"

"It's not for me," Laura admitted, half-ashamed. How long had it been? How many books had she taken out since her marriage? Not more than a dozen—and most of them had gone back unread.

But later . . . when Jesse was older. . . .

"A book for Jesse," she said. "He's beginning to pick out his letters already."

"Why, you don't say," Miss Baker exclaimed. "How old is he? Around four?"

"Not for seven more months," Laura said proudly.

"Why, goodness me," Miss Baker obligingly gave an astonished look. "And not quite four! Think of that." She set down the books she held, then bent to the lowest shelf. She had her own system of cataloguing. Children began on the bottom shelf and worked their way up.

"Let me see." She ran her long fingers thoughtfully over the bindings. "How about this?" She handed Laura a picture book in large print. The pictures were of birds and insects.

Laura's face lit up. "Just the thing," she said. "The very thing."

"I've got a library card for Jesse," Laura said as soon as Joel started up the engine. She remembered her own first card and the event it had been. As long as she had lived at Flora's she had kept it in the sideboard drawer lined with purple plush, where Flora kept her mother's silver.

"Took you long enough," he said.

"Jesse's picking out his letters now." She had delayed telling Joel because it was so good to have a secret . . . something exciting to hold back, then to reveal. "He'll be reading in a year, I think. So he can go right into second grade. He's really smart, Joel."

Joel knew he ought to be proud of Jesse, and he was. Just because he didn't make a fuss over him like everyone else didn't mean he wasn't proud. But two things galled him. Every time he tried to teach the boy anything, like the name of a tree, for instance, he knew it already; and every time Laura talked about how he was going to be a success, he felt a reproach that he himself was not.

"Smart like the Leightons and the Blodgetts," he said.

5

Laura sat by the kitchen window waiting for Joel to come home for supper. It had been a fine day. In the afternoon while Jesse was napping she had walked over the barrens where the new tender vines were beginning to put out tiny pink buds. She had picked arbutus in the graveyard and seen a scarlet tanager on top of one of the little pines. Spring, she thought. It's spring at last. Yet, in spite of her pride in Jesse, somehow she could not feel the exuberance spring normally brought.

She set the alewives back in the oven and went into the sitting room to look out, for she could see farther down the road from there. No sign of Joel. He was always on time at night. Luther himself took care of any late customers and closed up the store.

It must be a flat tire, she decided. She hoped someone would come along to help him fix it, for his hands had grown no more practical with the years. She would stand by, watching him struggle, sweating and exasperated, with screwdriver or awl. "Let me do it," she would finally say, and he would give it over to her, willing, but injured, too. She ought to be the helpless one, she told herself over and over, and she tried to be. But how far was she supposed to go? Was she supposed to let things fall to pieces before her eyes? How would anything ever get done if she did?

She watched until a line of crows flew by, stiff-necked and cawing. Then she went back into the kitchen. Supper wouldn't amount to much. She was glad Jesse had eaten when things were hot. She took a drink of water from the dipper, then went and stood again by the sitting-room window. The questions came back. One plagued her especially. How could someone rely on something, as Joel did on her competence, and still resent it? It seemed unreasonable, ungrateful, unjust.

At the sight of his car, she went back to the kitchen, took the alewives from the oven, and moved the kettle forward. By the time she had drained the greens, she heard him on the steps. "Hello," she called.

He did not kiss her when he came in. Kissing at such a time was something men at Millboro stopped with marriage. Instead, he went directly to the sink and began washing. At the end of a day he did not look his best, for he shaved at night, never having quite enough time in the morning. Now he looked more than untidy. He looked tired to death.

"What kept you?" she asked.

He splashed water on his face, then spoke from between his fingers. "Luther wanted me to drive him to Cherryfield."

"What for?"

"To see a man there."

"What man?"

"Oh, somebody he knows."

She filled his plate and set it on the table. "Why did he want you to drive him?" she asked, watching his face.

He grabbed a towel and mumbled into it.

"It's funny he didn't drive himself." Luther was a better driver than Joel. With Joel at the wheel, he was always uneasy.

Joel made no answer, just threw the towel on the shelf and pulled out his chair without meeting her eyes.

She poured his tea, puzzled and troubled. She knew Luther was worried about business, but did he have some new worry that she knew nothing about? She seldom saw him alone now. On Sundays he went right from church to the store. Driving by, she could see him bent over his books, one big red hand shielding his eyes, the other holding a pencil. If there was something else. . . . She felt relieved that she hadn't bothered him about the W.C.T.U., especially since the whole thing seemed to have been forgotten.

She sat down at the table. Joel shook out his napkin. He ate barely a few mouthfuls, then pushed back his plate. She decided to risk one more question. Joel might answer and he might not. But if he did answer he would tell her the truth. He was like Flora in that.

"What did he want to see this man about?"

His eyes met hers briefly. "I figger that's Luther's affair," he said.

6

Soon the blueberry vines were hung with delicate cream-colored blossoms, shaped like blunted bells. Bees, sometimes in great clouds, hung over them. Listening on a still day, you could hear their gentle, steady humming. Jesse was intrigued by them. If he had been allowed to, he would have sat by the hour on the ledges, letting them light all over him.

"He's going to get stung," Laura said.

"Teach him a lesson," Joel answered.

By the end of the month, ground laurel bloomed, deep pink among the bearing vines. Wild roses and vetch crept in from the ditches, and in the stretch of tall grass between the ruts of the roads a few daisies and devil's-paintbrushes grew.

By the first of July, heat came suddenly. It was hot enough in the village—as hot as anyone could remember—but far hotter on the high, almost treeless barrens. There was still some wind, but when it came it brought only heat. The berries began to ripen early, bringing the gulls in great flocks. Usually the operators tried to scare them off by setting up whirligigs that turned in the wind. They also tried to keep away the deer by spreading blood meal, but this year, with berries worth so little, it hadn't seemed worth the trouble. Ironically, now that the demand was small, the crop was going to be one of the biggest ever.

Every morning Laura and Jesse picked, filling their pails in no time, and in the evening, when it should have been cool again but never was, Laura put up the berries she had not saved for themselves and the family. Then she went to sit on the back steps with Jesse, watching the fireflies, hundreds of them, flashing low over the barrens—here, there, there, here—some bright, steady for an instant; some faint, as though the light brought pain with it; some lingering; a few soaring, a few nestling—each for himself, finding his own way.

When Jesse spoke then, it was always in a whisper.

"I like them, Mama."

"I like them too."

As soon as the black flies drove them in, they sat together in the kitchen, watching again through the little porthole window until time to go to bed.

People didn't use their cars now unless they had to, so Laura had given up expecting company. But one afternoon in the middle of the month, she looked out to see Doris and Ed drive into the yard. Butch was with them. Heavier now, half blind and completely deaf, he lay across Ed's lap, his head hanging down, apparently dozing. The truck, a 1923 model, showed its age more than Butch showed his. But neither Ed nor Doris had changed at all. They were still as jaunty as they had ever been, still as full of plans and enthusiasms. "I never worry about nothin' 'til it hits me," Ed had always said. And now that it had hit him, he wasn't worried either. The less work he had, the more time he had for his boat and his ball games.

"Come in," Laura said. "Come in and stay." She was especially glad to see them, as she hungered for company. Joel was less talkative than ever. He came home late—something he had never done before—seemed very tired, ate quickly, and worked in the garden until time to go to bed. He made love absently and less often. He was restless at night. She felt sure he was worried about something, yet when she tried to question him, he only brushed her off abruptly.

"Can't stop," Doris told her. "Not more'n a minute."

"That's right," Ed said. "On our way ter Ellsworth."

Laura looked at the tires, worn thin by one excursion after another. "How come you take the back road?" she asked. The back road was considerably longer than the one through the Junction. If you had car trouble, you were likely to be stuck for hours before anyone passed.

"Wanted ter see yer," Ed said. "Ain't yer my best girl after Doris?" Considerably hindered by Butch's bulk, he reached over and hugged her hard.

It was impossible to be provoked at Ed. "Then get out and come in," she said.

"We can't stop, honest," Doris said, bending to wipe Butch's eyes with her handkerchief. "We just thought we might get a look at Jesse."

"What's your rush?"

"Got to get to the bank before it closes."

"Sounds prosperous," Laura said.

They poked each other vigorously, then burst into gales of laughter.

"Come on in," Laura urged. It was so good to hear laughter that she did not think to ask the reason for it. Not that it always took a reason to send them off. "Come on."

"Jest long enough ter see Jesse," Ed said when he had sobered. "Got some business ter transact. He sleepin'?"

"Should be. You can go and see."

"All right if he wakes up accidentally?" he asked, winking. "Sure."

Ed heaved Butch from his lap, shut off the engine, jumped down and went inside.

"Don't stay more'n a minute, now," Doris called after him. She took off her heavy glasses, fogged from laughter, and wiped them on her petticoat. Then she began to tell the news. The barber who set up his chair every Monday at Peasley's had stopped coming. Fern Gott had lost his job in Bangor and come home to live with the folks. On and on. One discouraging thing after another. "I guess Jim Closson's the only one who's making money," she finished. "He must be really raking it in."

Laura felt her color rising. Just when she had thought the whole thing had faded, here it was again to plague her.

"Winter Harbor scared the others off, folks say, so now Jim's got all the business on the stretch," Doris went on, watching her closely. "He'll be rich for sure. If he can keep it up," she added ominously.

Laura's mouth dried. Her knees weakened. To cover her confusion, she bent to pat Butch's great head with its pink flesh showing through the sparse, dry hair until, relieved, she heard Ed's quick feet on the stairs.

112

"Was he awake?" she called.

"Sure was," Ed called back. He came striding out, got into the truck, and Butch resumed his position. "Some fella yer got. Told me what he wanted fer his birthday."

"Now, Ed," Laura said, recovering, "don't you give him one thing. Besides, his birthday is six months off."

"Gives us time ter hunt up what he wants," Ed said, chuckling. "Yer'd never guess."

Laura seized his arm. "Listen, Ed, I shall be mad if you give him anything at all this year. So will Joel."

"Course we'll give him something," Doris said. "Why not?" She leaned over and wiped Butch's eyes again, then put her handkerchief back in her purse. "We've got to get a move on, Buddy."

Ed started the motor and waved a lanky arm. "Ta-ta," he said. "Ta-ta."

Laura stood looking after them and then went soberly back inside.

That night she did not sleep well. She heard the clock strike ten and eleven. Then, lying quiet so not to wake Joel, she heard the sound of voices.

In the five years they had lived on the barrens, there had never been prowlers about. Now and then tramps had come, but she had locked the doors as Joel told her, and they had gone away. Occasionally a motorist had stopped by, trying the back road, which was poorly marked, and wanting to know which turn to make for Ellsworth. But prowlers, never.

Startled, she got up and went to the window. Though heavy clouds covered the moon, she could make out the road, for she knew its every line. No cars were on it, yet she continued to hear the sounds. Who could be out there at this hour? What could be going on?

She saw a match blaze, flash, almost go out, then steady itself. Someone had lighted a lantern. She watched it as it appeared and disappeared around the hummocks. Then she saw it set down on one of the ledges.

Again she heard the voices. Gypsies, she thought. Gypsies stole anything they could lay their hands on, anything lying around loose. They even stripped gardens. Joel sometimes left the key in the car at night. If they lost that car. . . .

"Joel," she whispered.

He grunted and turned over.

"Joel." She went back to the bed and shook his shoulder.

"Hmmm."

"Get up. There's somebody outside."

He got up sluggishly and followed her to the window.

The moon was out now, and in the distance it showed four figures—bending, crouching—and the glint of a pail.

"Someone's stealing berries," he said.

"Stealing berries," she repeated. It seemed impossible. "Why, it's never happened in other years." She kept watching, curious, yet fearful of recognizing a voice she knew.

"This isn't other years," he said dryly. "Come back to bed."

7

It was a relief when the rakers came. Normally these were regulars who lived within a radius of fifty miles and worked the barrens year after year—handy men; high-school boys; farmers waiting for their corn to ripen; a teacher or two who needed summer work; sturdy housewives, conscious of the long winter ahead; just drifters. They arrived in a long procession—in cars, some respectable enough, some ancient jalopies, their radiators sending up clouds of steam, their thin tires stirring the dust; hitchhiking; on bicycles; even on foot. But this year the procession was longer than usual, for every man in the area who was idle came looking for work.

Half of those who came were turned away. (There were berries, yes, but who would buy them?) They left, dejected, lingering to fill their hands, their hats, whatever they had with them, determined to get something at least for their trouble. Meanwhile the trucks were bringing in the half-bushel baskets and boxes, the winnowers were being set up, the land divided into aisles by string.

Jesse and Laura sat together in the shade of their hackmatacks and saw the workers bending in the hot sun, each with his own rhythm, running their rakes under the low vines until they were full and heavy, then emptying them into their baskets. They saw them carrying their baskets to the winnower, where the machine blew out the leaves and dust and the slow-moving belt carried away the green clusters. As the sun grew hotter, they saw them pause to wipe their faces, or drink from the bottles of water they carried, or discard clothing on nearby bushes. At noon they saw them seek out some shade and eat their lunches, then lie flat, some on their backs with hats over their eyes, some on their stomachs, their heads resting upon their folded arms. They saw the trucks, loaded high, lunge—rocking, swaying—along the narrow roads to the highway.

Jesse was reluctant to take his nap.

"They'll still be here when you wake up," Laura answered him. "They'll be here for days and days."

A little before six o'clock, a dilapidated car drove up and stopped by the roadside almost in front of the house. It had a frame but no top, and Laura could plainly see the people who were in it—a man, obviously an Indian; his wife, very thin, holding a baby; two small boys; two broad-faced girls in their teens; a grandmother with just enough flesh to make wrinkles. They stopped the car and simply sat there. Harmless as they looked, Laura felt uneasy.

"Jesse," she called. "Where are you?" He had been wandering away a good deal lately. Twice because of it she had sent him supperless to bed.

"Here."

She went to the back door and saw him at one of his favorite games, making a village from the chips from the chopping block.

"Don't go away."

"I wasn't."

Back at the front window she watched the Indians for half an hour, sitting there almost motionless. She ought to go and talk with them, to find out what they wanted. But Joel wouldn't like it. He had warned her repeatedly against strangers who might come by. He wouldn't be home until nine or ten o'clock, for the red feed was in, coloring the bay, and he had gone after mackerel with Ed.

As she watched, she saw a word or two pass among them. What were they talking about? Jobs? She could distinctly remember the last raking. There had been no Indians then. Or had they only lost their way? If they had, she ought to help them. Even Joel would say that.

She waited a few minutes, indecisive. Then she went outside. Approaching the car, she could see things she had not been able to see from the window—a dirty blanket, a bottle of water, a hardened rind of cheese. "The foreman has gone," she began. "He won't be back until morning." She could not bring herself to tell them that the hiring was over.

They all stared at her, but no one answered.

Then she realized that they were Canadian Indians—Micmacs, people called them, and they didn't speak English. She had heard something about Micmacs, for they were beginning to drift down to work on the barrens. They were fast workers, people said—some of them could rake a bushel in ten minutes in a good harvest, and they could keep going for hours at a stretch in the hottest sun. But still they were "foreigners." No one knew just where they came from or how they lived; this put them in the same category as gypsies and tramps. Whenever they came in town, people locked their doors and sometimes pulled their shades. (Once, through confusion or curiosity, a man and a woman had come into church, causing the Reverend Bigelow to lose his place completely. Though they stayed the service out, no one spoke to them at the door.) When, occasionally, one or two of them got a little rowdy around Peasley's on a Saturday night, they were rushed into the lockup, something that almost never happened to a local boy, whatever his offense.

She stood helplessly for a minute, then she started inside. All the time she was making the thick pea soup for supper she kept her eye on them. Were they lost? Exhausted? Bewildered? Certainly they were hungry.

Perhaps if she fed them, they would move on. Joel ought not to object. They hadn't come to the door. Actually, they were neither gypsies nor tramps. Anyway, they made her nervous, just waiting there.

She picked up the kettle and some bowls, then remembered spoons. She had only six spoons of any size, for she was getting her set gradually with coupons from rolled oats. The soup was too thick for drinking. Suddenly she thought of the spoons Joel's father had brought. She had never shown them to Joel, for to do that would have been to break the promise she had made him. She had merely put them away for Jesse. It could do no harm to use one of them now. Nothing could happen to it, for she would be right there all the time they ate, keeping a sharp eye on them.

They watched her come, but their faces still showed nothing. When she got there, the man reached a broad brown hand for the kettle. The old woman put out a tiny claw for the spoons.

Just then she heard Jesse calling. "Mama." He had come in for supper, found her gone, looked out and seen her. "Mama." He sounded scared.

She turned and moved a few steps toward the house. "I'm coming."

As she spoke, she heard the motor start. Then, as she stood there watching, helpless, the car drove off, taking her kettle, her soup, her bowls, and her spoons.

In other harvests, rakers had stayed in great numbers on the barrens all during August and sometimes into September. But this year, after the first two weeks had passed, only scattered groups remained.

Evenings Laura took Jesse on excursions, rewards for his patience while she canned or worked in the garden. Often they passed the tarpaper shacks and stopped to speak to the workers who still stayed on. It was in the door of one of these shacks that they first saw Mr. Pettigrew—an old man badly stooped and brown as November, who looked frail until you were near enough to see his sinews. He and Jesse took to each other immediately.

"Set awhile," he urged, indicating the ground beside him. He came from over Larrabee way, he told them. He had been raking the barrens for more than sixty years. Jesse listened fascinated while he talked about the old days when whole families had come by wagon, bringing pots, pans, mattresses, and all the clothing they could muster, for there was no water for washing on the barrens. They set up tents and cooked outside them, baking their bread in tin gadgets and their beans in a hole lined with rocks. It took two days to get them real tasty, he said. There was real sociability then, bonfires at night, singing.

Children up to ten or so took care of the little ones. Everyone else raked. They used round wooden boxes, not baskets then. They had no winnowing machines, but held their boxes as high as they could, poured, and counted on the Almighty to send the wind. Instead of trucks, wagons took the berries to the factory. A single trip took all day. "Good times them was," Mr. Pettigrew said with satisfaction. "Families workin' together, makin' maybe two-three hunnerd dollars. Enough ter git the winter through." Then his eyes lingered with nostalgia over the barrens. "Kind er gits in yer blood," he said.

When Laura and Jesse went back over the wandering road in the twilight, the whole area, depleted as it was, had a cast of blue.

8

On a morning not long after the raking was done and a touch of red was beginning to appear on the vines, Joel came home suddenly just before nine o'clock. He looked pale and worried.

"It's Luther," he said. "He's bad."

Laura looked up from the sink where she was washing dishes. "Bad?" she echoed. "Bad" meant sick, dangerously sick, in Millboro.

"Yes, bad."

Luther bad. It seemed impossible.

"But what—"

"It's his heart."

"His heart—" she echoed. Then, "How bad is he?"

119

His eyes did not meet hers. "Real bad," he said.

She stood without moving, still holding the wiper. If anything happened to Luther. . . .

"He wants to see you."

"I'll get Jesse," she said.

She dressed him, still half-asleep, hushing his questions. "Not a word out of you, now. Not a word. You hear me?" Then she closed the draft of the stove and put on her coat. They got into the car and started off. Only then did she think of asking particulars. "An attack, Joel?"

He nodded.

"When?"

"Last night."

"Where?"

"In the store."

"Alone?"

He nodded again.

"Is that all you know?"

"I know Flora woke up in the night and saw his bed hadn't been slept in. She went over to the store and found him. Then she got Will Conary and he got the doctor from Cherryfield right away."

From Cherryfield. In a flash it came to her. She knew now why Joel had taken Luther there.

"You knew he was sick, Joel?"

"I knew he had a bad heart."

And for months she had been feeling sorry for herself, getting upset over nothing. While Luther . . . "Why didn't you tell me?"

"He made me promise not to."

"Did Flora know?"

"Nobody did."

She thought back over the summer, searching her mind for a clue. His visits had been less frequent, yet he had seemed cheerful when he came—in fact, now that she thought of it, more cheerful than she had ever known him to be. He was even cheerful about business. "We can weather it, Joel and me," he had said, "with a bit a luck thrown in." She remembered that Flora had complained about his appetite. She remembered, too, that he had moved into the front bedroom. "These hot nights," he had said, "are hard on Flo."

"Are they going to take him to the hospital?"

He shook his head. "Too far," he said. It was almost as though he had said, "Too late."

Jesse had stood it as long as he could. The word hospital was new to him. "Where we going?" he asked loudly.

"To see Uncle Luther," Joel answered.

"Why are we going so fast?"

"Sssh," Laura said.

If anything happened to Luther. . . . Over and over, her mind whispered those words but could go no further. If anything happened to Luther. . . .

Luther had been her father, her brother, her friend. She thought of how good he had been to her when she was a child, hanging around the store—a nuisance, of course, though he would never have admitted it. She remembered how he had let her mix up the spools of thread, making them into rainbows. How he had let her have all the candy she wanted, enough for herself and her friends. How he had let her reach her hand into the big cabinet with glass-front drawers and take out a handful of prunes or sugar lumps whenever she pleased. How he had let her count the coins in the money drawer, making them into little piles. How he had let her help him display the Christmas stock. "You got good help, Luther," customers would say, and Luther would answer back, "A-yuh, the best." She remembered how proud he had been when she could add faster than he could.

They rode on without speaking, along the barrens, stripped now and trampled, cut by aisles of broken string. Once when Jesse started to speak, Joel hushed him and he whimpered.

"Don't be a cry baby," Joel said.

If anything happened to Luther. . . . She thought of the times he had taken her with him delivering, letting her hold the reins, slap the horse's back, even turn the wagon when she was no more than eight or nine. She thought of the things he had made her aware of—how frogs sounded like sleigh bells, how the ferns sprang up like tight-closed fists. She remembered how, above Flora's protests, he had given her brand-new wallpaper to cut up for May baskets. How he had bragged about her to the traveling men and stood her up on the counter so that she could recite a poem for them to hear. Luther had never said "Stop that," or "What did I tell you?" The most he had ever said was, "I don't believe I'd do that if I was you."

If anything happened to him. . . .

Joel and Jesse loved her. Flora and Doris loved her too, in their way. But Luther believed in her, gave her credit for something special, something of value, something of her own.

She thought of his visits with her there in the kitchen, sitting, legs crossed or feet on the ledge of the cookstove, noticing everything—the jars of jelly on the window sill; Joel's shirts ironed and hung up for airing; Jesse's pants that she had patched—finding something to praise. She thought of the things he had given them—dishes, furniture, paint—"Just clutterin' up the store," he would always say. She thought of the little lunches they had had together, and how he always passed things first to her (something Joel never did except at Flora's). How, as she drank her Moxie, he kept filling up her glass. She remembered how he listened to every little thing she told him —leaning forward, never moving his eyes from her face. How he had asked her advice about lines to carry at the store, her opinion about things he had read in the paper. . . .

They drove past the church, past the green, over the bridge, past the store.

"Why is the store door shut?" Jesse asked.

Laura put her hand over his mouth.

If anything happened. . . . If anything did. . . .

It was on the steps of the store that he had offered to send her on to college. It was as though she could feel his hand, that big, rough hand, again on her own.

Tears came to her eyes. She blew her nose sharply. Jesse reddened and stared down at his feet. He had never seen his mother crying. It shocked him deeply.

"Crying's not going to get us anywhere," Joel said. The words were blunt, but he spoke them kindly.

When they drove into the yard at Luther's, they saw another car parked there. It was Harry's.

Before Joel came to a full stop, Laura got out and started for the house. Ed saw her coming and opened the door for her. For the first time she could remember, his face was completely serious.

Laura did not see Luther at once, for the doctor was still there. She sat in the kitchen with Beauty, heavy on her lap. She did not pet her; it seemed shocking that Beauty should be sleeping so indifferently when Luther, who had broken his own sleep at all hours to get up and let her out and in, was—she stopped herself—was seriously sick upstairs.

She sat numbly. Some things just could not be. There was a God, wasn't there? A merciful God, so the Bible said. A God who looked after the people who did His work. And who had done His work better than Luther? She thought again of how kind he was, how obliging to everyone, how he gave credit to those who could not pay. God took the good, people said. Well, she didn't believe it. If He took Luther, she would never have anything to do with Him again. She would never teach Jesse to, either. But He wouldn't take Luther. Luther was the strongest man she knew. The doctor would leave him some medicine. Tell him to be careful. They would all wait on him hand and foot. . . .

Harry came into the kitchen. Seeing him there in the door way, she was surprised by the strength of her feeling for him. He seemed exactly like a brother then.

"What did the doctor say?"

He shook his head.

"How long?" she whispered.

"Not very."

Then it was true. She couldn't deny it any longer.

She sat very still for a minute. Then she pushed Beauty to the floor. It took all her strength to do it.

"When can I see him?"

"Right away."

Luther was in the spare room. Flora was not there when they entered. The doctor was talking to her in the hall. It was the first time she had left Luther since she found him, slumped over his books, at the store. Coming in through the back door, Laura caught a glimpse of her in the mirror, still dressed in her bathrobe, which she had been wearing when she saw his bed empty. Her hair, braided, hung heavily down her back. Her face was haggard.

Luther's bed had been moved closer to the window. Wrapped in a blanket, he was propped up on two pillows. His face was blue. He was breathing hard, and there was sweat on his forehead.

"Here's Laurie, Pa," Harry said.

Laura had been determined to be calm, offhand, even, but at the sight of him all her resolution left her. She fell on her knees by the bed and buried her face in the blanket.

Very slowly Luther opened his eyes. With great effort he lifted one of his big, rough hands and laid it over hers.

Then he stopped breathing.

124

As long as Luther was living, Flora had shown real self-possession, but with his death she went to pieces completely. She shut herself in her room—their room—sobbed hysterically, and would answer no questions. "I don't know. Don't ask me anything," she kept saying. "Nothing makes any difference now."

For years she had made the family decisions. Now, for a time, the rest of them were completely at a loss. What about the casket? The funeral? The lot? "I guess it's up to me," Harry finally said. He looked older already. "You girls take over here."

Doris answered the door with more dignity than anyone had ever given her credit for, taking the messages for Flora. "If there's anything, anything . . ." At odd moments, she cleaned the house as thoroughly as Flora herself would have done it. She even remembered to feed Beauty.

Laura stayed in the kitchen, ironing and cooking. Luther is dead, she kept telling herself, trying to make the stark fact sink in. Then, because it wouldn't sink in, she would force herself to go quietly up the back stairs, open the door of the spare room, and see him lying there, like a statue that had fallen. Then she would come back to the kitchen again and, tears blurring her eyes, go on measuring out sugar and flour.

All that afternoon Flora would not leave her room. She wouldn't touch any food, though she had eaten nothing since the night before. Harry or some of the girls had to be always with her. She would not rest. Instead, she talked constantly about Luther. About their meeting. It had been at a box supper no more than a week after Luther had come to town. He had been standing outside the Grange Hall when she went in, carrying her box. It had been a shoe box—Mama had always wanted her to have a box bigger than anyone else's—and it had

had chicken legs and ham sandwiches and hard-boiled eggs and cheese sticks and angel food and chocolate cookies, besides, of course, pickles and olives. It had been wrapped in red tissue and decorated with sprigs of syringa. When it was put up, the auctioneer hadn't even asked for a bid when Luther shouted "Five dollars." It was the highest bid ever made at a box social in Millboro. He had walked home with her, of course, and told her that very night that someday he would own the store. Mama had never believed he would. Yet he had always been so good to Mama. Doris would remember. . . .

About Harry's birth. How he had insisted on staying right by her, though the doctor tried to put him out. How he had timed the pains and made her grab hold of his hands and pull. How, during the last stages, he had stood at the foot of the bed and sworn a solemn oath that he would never let her go through it again. How later she had begged him to change his mind, but he wouldn't listen. This was something she had never told before.

About the drownings and how he had tended to everything as if he had been a real son.

"If only Mama could have appreciated him," she said again and again.

"If only Mama could have known."

She talked about the awful, horrible night. She had waked up, she said, and had a premonition. Then over and over she told the details. How she had gone to Luther's room and seen his bed empty. How she had run over to the store, just as she was, and found him, barely conscious, doubled up on top of his books. When she tried to move him, he had vomited. Then she had lost her head completely and instead of calling the doctor herself she had rushed across the street and waked up Will Conary, who had come right over. Will had called the doctor and done the things he told him to—loosened Luther's collar and belt, raised his head so he could breathe better, and then wrapped him in one of the blankets from the storeroom. Will's wife had brought over a hot-water bottle. Probably Will had told her to. Flora wasn't sure. She had been shaking so much, she wasn't sure of anything. Then the doctor had come—how long after, she had no idea—and given him medicine. Digitalis, she guessed, and morphine. By the time it took effect, Will had rounded up two men (Joe Candage or maybe his brother and Ethan Grindle) and they had put together some kind of a stretcher and taken him home. He was back in his bed before he knew her. "Where's my Flo?" he had said. Those were the first words he had spoken. "Where's my Flo?" Over and over she told it, looking back to keep from looking ahead.

"You've got to eat," Doris told her. "You've got to keep your strength." Finally, she agreed to a cup to tea. "That Orange Pekoe kind," she said. "The kind that Luther liked."

Joel kept the store open. Luther wouldn't want anyone to be inconvenienced on his account, Harry had said. People kept coming in, less to trade than to talk, unwilling to accept the news until they heard it firsthand.

Couldn't believe my ears when they told me.

No, sir. I jest can't take it in.

Things that had bothered Joel earlier did not bother him now. He could willingly tell the same story over and over. How Flora had found Luther. Got help. Taken him home. How the doctor had come. What he had said. He could answer the same questions freely, again and again. Yes, Harry was there. Came the minute he heard. Yes, his father had known him. He had known everybody to the last. Yes, Flora was taking it hard. No, there was nothing folks could do—right then, anyhow. He could even talk to the summer people without constraint.

All the afternoon it was the same story.

Salt of the earth, Luther.

A-yuh, when they made him they broke the mold.

Joel had always liked and respected Luther. Now he had a new feeling, a pride in being associated with him. His grudges were forgotten. So were the mortifications the job had brought —the apron he had to wear when he cut up meat; the back doors of summer cottages; the way customers passed him by, waiting for Luther. He felt a little proud of himself, too, for all during the summer, ever since he had known, he had done everything he could to lighten Luther's load. He had swept and lifted and helped with the unloading. Instead of eating his lunch outside as he always had, feeling, as he told himself, a need to get out of the place, he'd eaten on the counter, still handling the trade while Luther took a nap on the old sofa upstairs.

He'd kept Luther's secret, too.

But now he could tell. And when Laura knew everything, she'd think better of him than she had.

Ed raked the lawn and took care of things at the house, keeping Jesse with him all of the time. Jesse knew that his Uncle Luther was dead. His mother had told him, but he wasn't sure what "dead" was, and he hadn't asked any questions, for his mother was crying, and he had wanted to get as far away from her as he could. When he had found a bird or a rabbit that was stiff and cold, that was dead, too. It had gone to sleep, his mother had told him, and wouldn't wake up. But Uncle Luther wasn't like a bird or a rabbit. He'd better find these things out, he thought, from Uncle Ed.

"What happens when you die, Uncle Ed?"

Ed, cutting around a flower bed, looked up at him. "What's your mother say?" he asked cautiously.

"She says you go to sleep with Jesus."

"Must be so then," Ed said, resuming his work.

Jesse squatted beside him. "Does Jesus go to sleep too?"

"Couldn't say fer sure," Ed answered. "Yer'll have to ask yer mother 'bout that."

Jesse began to pick one blade of grass after another and lay them carefully across his palm. "Uncle Ed."

"A-yuh."

"How can Uncle Luther be with Jesus and still be upstairs in his room?"

Ed whistled a little before he spoke. "Maybe Jesus ain't got a place ready fer him yet," he finally said.

Jesse watched him closely. "What place is he going to put him, Uncle Ed?" When birds and rabbits died, you put them in a hole in the ground. He couldn't believe anyone would do that to Uncle Luther. Besides, Aunt Flora would never let them.

"Couldn't say about that neither." Ed wiped his face with his bandana and looked toward the house, hoping for rescue. None came.

"Are you going to die someday, Uncle Ed?"

Ed's shears stopped. It was as if he had been confronted with an entirely new idea. "Say," he said, "how would yer like ter stop askin' questions and go out in my bo't?"

Jesse jumped up, tossing away the grasses. "I'd like that fine," he said. He was sorry that Uncle Luther was dead, but there were nice things about it too.

In the evening Flora's sobs subsided, but not her despair. When Doris made her bed, she got up and sat in the rocker by the window. The shade was still down. She would not have it raised.

"Would you let me brush out your hair, Flo?" Laura asked. She asked it hesitantly, for none of the sisters ever touched each other except by accident or necessity.

"That would be good," Flora said.

Eagerly, almost gratefully, Laura undid the heavy braid, loosened the hair, and brushed it gently.

129

Flora closed her swollen eyelids. Her neck relaxed. "Mama used to brush my hair like that," she said.

Doris came over to the window. "I'm going to relax your legs, Flo," she said, and waited. When no protest came, she got down on her knees, lifted one of the heavy legs she had ridiculed so often, and rubbed it gently, even the foot.

The room was quiet. So was the whole neighborhood. No one mowed his lawn. No one honked a horn in passing. Once the telephone rang and they heard Harry answer it. Once there was a knock on the door and they heard him talking with the Reverend Bigelow. Then they heard him open the back door to let Beauty out.

They went on brushing, rubbing, stopping to get Flora a sip of water, a dry handkerchief, an aspirin, a shawl. Brush, rub . . . rub, brush . . . a cold cloth for her temples.

Finally she spoke.

"I want Ed to have Luther's pearl stickpin and Joel to have his signet ring. They are good boys, both of them."

"They'll take good care of them."

"They'll be real honored, Flo."

At what must have been around nine o'clock, they persuaded her to get into bed. Then each of them took a chair by the window.

Almost at once she dozed, then caught herself suddenly. "Don't go," she said. "Don't leave me."

"We won't."

"We'll stay right here, Flo."

They were not three sisters. They were three women then.

9

With the passing of summer, things suddenly got worse. By the last of September almost everyone in Millboro had cancelled his subscription to the Bangor paper. Those who hadn't, flinched at what they read. BREAD LINES IN PORTLAND . . . MILL CLOSES IN ELLSWORTH . . . COUNTY POORHOUSE FILLED . . . POTATOES ROTTING IN THE GROUND IN AROOSTOOK. NOT WORTH THE PICKING . . . FREIGHT CARS IDLE ON SIDINGS.

People turned more and more to barter (a pint of clams, shucked, for a dozen eggs). That meant even less business at the stores. Sociability slackened. Women had to think twice before donating a chocolate cake or a custard pie for a church supper. Besides, with tickets costing thirty-five cents, how many could afford to come?

Rag bags were rummaged, and clothing once relegated to the Missionary barrel was retrieved. Telephones were taken out. Some of those who had electric lights went back to kerosene. The clam flats were never empty. Men who had dories fished in the bay; men who didn't fished from the wharf or along the streams. Smelts were pickled in greater numbers than ever before. Now and then there was a shot in the woods, but those who heard it asked no questions.

Most people stayed close to home, keeping their eye on their orchards and their woodpiles. Those who were normally generous with their Baldwins and their Pippins shared none of them this year. There were no pumpkins saved for Halloween; there was no trash set aside for bonfires. Everything that would burn at all was piled away. A good many shut off their dining rooms and their sitting rooms, or moved right into their kitchens, going to bed at sundown to save on wood and light.

Half the congregation stayed away from church, unwilling to let the collection plate pass by without putting something in it, yet having no dimes and nickels to spare. The library closed for the lack of fuel. There was talk of closing the schools at Christmas, for to pay teachers you had to collect taxes, and if you couldn't collect them. . . . Harry stopped giving credit at the store.

Harry wasn't a businessman any more than he had been a student in school, but it didn't take him long to discover that for the past six months Luther had been carrying half the town. At the same time, he had been paying his own bills by selling investments for a fraction of their cost. He could keep the place going, Harry figured, if he ran it himself, but he couldn't keep Joel.

He told him on a Saturday night in late October. "Gee, Joel," he began, red-faced and stammering, "I hate to tell you. I hate to somethin' awful."

"You don't have to tell me," Joel said. "I know."

For weeks he had seen it coming, seen people buying half a pound, half a pint, even half a yeast cake, then leaving quickly for fear Harry might mention their bills. Now things were about as bad as they could be. Since Harry had stopped giving credit, sometimes there weren't a dozen customers a day, and most of those wanted only corn meal or salt pork or molasses.

"You're goin' to have an extry week's pay," Harry told him, laying out the bills.

"Not a dollar," Joel said. "Not one red cent."

Driving over the roads already frozen into ruts, Joel stared ahead into the darkness. Once losing a job was nothing to him.

132

He had lost two of them in the woods—one because the foreman had it in for him, another because he refused to do work he figured was beneath him. Both times he had made out all right. He'd just drifted around until his money was gone and then found another place to his liking. But times were different now. Besides, he had a family on his hands and—he remembered this chillingly—no money to fall back on. Their cash was almost gone. It had bought the car. (Laura wouldn't listen to buying it on installments.) He could put it up for sale, of course, but who could buy it? And, living way out there on the barrens, how could he take a job without it even if one turned up?

When he had lost his other jobs, he hadn't had to explain to anyone. Now he had to face Laura. How would she act when he told her? Would she cry? Looking back, he could remember only twice that she had cried—when Flora had told her she couldn't go to Normal and on the day Luther died. Or would she complain? She seldom complained, but then, what had she ever had to complain about? All her life she had had things plenty easy. She'd lived in a good house. She'd had good clothes, and she had never had to ask anyone for money. Luther had seen to that. Her teachers were always holding her up as an example at school. She'd had a job that fell into her lap, and she'd kept it as long as she wanted to. Ever since they were married she had always had her own way.

But how would he tell her? How would he start? He rejected one approach after another. They were all too weak, he decided. The thing to do was put up a good front. That would keep her from getting upset, at least from making a scene. He would face her boldly. "Brace yourself," he would say. Then he would be prepared to move in either direction. If she cried —and he found himself hoping she would—he would try to calm her. He dwelt for a moment here—her head on his shoulder, his hand smoothing her hair. "It's not as bad as all that," he would say. Then abruptly he faced the other possibility. If she complained, he would ask her who made him take the job in the first place. That would stop her short.

Once the talk was over (he didn't believe in tackling more than one thing at a time), he would figure what to do next. He began to rehearse his approach.

Brace yourself, now.

When he opened the door of the kitchen, Laura was standing at the stove, taking up the beans. The brown bread, the pickled beets, and the cabbage salad were already on the table.

"Supper's ready," she said.

Since Luther's death, she had talked less than usual and almost never asked questions. In a way this was a relief to Joel, yet it bothered him too, for there were things he sometimes wanted to tell, like the way he had taken the load off Luther, once he knew. But she had never asked, never mentioned Luther at all. He couldn't come right out with it. That was unthinkable.

He washed and sat down at the table.

"Come on, Jesse," Laura called.

Jesse was the one who did the talking now. "You know what?" he began as soon as his chair was pushed up.

No one answered.

He spoke louder. "You know what?"

"What?" Laura asked absently.

He hesitated, for he still had no idea of what he wanted to say. Then his face cleared. "I heard a whippoorwill," he said.

"That's good."

They ate the rest of the meal in silence. When it was over, Laura turned on the radio and took Jesse upstairs. It was a news program, but Joel did not hear it. It was his own news he was concerned about. He sat on at the table, waiting for her to return.

Brace yourself, now. . . .

134

It's not as bad as it might be. . . .
Who made me take the job, I want to know. . . .

When he heard her steps on the stairs, he went to the radio and turned it off. He was ready, he thought, for either possibility.

"Don't turn it off," she said in the doorway. "There'll be music in a minute. Jesse's listening."

He had lost his job, and it was Jesse she thought about. " 'Twon't hurt him to wait," he said stiffly. He raised his voice. "I don't want to hear a word out of you, Jesse."

"I didn't say anything, Pa."

"Well, see that you don't."

He had been all ready to start. Now he'd been put off the track. He went to the sink, pumped some water in the dipper and drank it. Then he turned to face her. She was clearing the table with quick, sure motions. Watching her competence always confused him, made him feel useless and in the way. Whatever he did, she could always do better and twice as fast besides. Nothing ever fazed her. But this, he had told himself, half-hoping, might. Still, the thought of her bracing herself seemed a little extreme, and he decided to modify his approach.

"I've got some news," he said.

She was lifting the tea kettle when he spoke, and she set it down suddenly. "Who, Joel?"

"Who what?"

"Who's sick?"

"No one's sick," he said, exasperated. "I've lost my job, that's all." He waited, calmer now that it was out, ready to move in either direction. If she scolded . . . if she cried. . . .

She did neither. She merely sat there, letting the words sink in. They came as a surprise to her, for since Luther's death she had been dulled to the things about her. She could not show her grief as Flora did, for she could see how hard it was on people. But she felt it keenly. Along with her grief there was guilt that she should have been thinking of her own problems while he, knowing what might lie ahead, had never been more cheerful. And through the grief and guilt had run a question. Why Luther? Why then? Why her father? Why her mother? Day after day she walked to the little graveyard. Here. Gone. Why?

She could not talk with anyone about it. She couldn't talk to Joel because he had always resented her feelings for Luther. She couldn't talk with Flora, for when she was there she tried her best to turn Flora's mind to other things. She couldn't bring herself to talk with the Reverend Bigelow. In fact, when she met him she found herself treating him coldly, as though he were somehow to blame. No one could talk seriously with Doris and Ed. For the first time in her life she had seen no purpose in living. Now here was an immediate one. Her face lighted.

"Don't look so worried, Joel," she said. "There's nothing to worry about. Wait." She went to the cupboard, took down the sugar bowl that was their bank, and shook it almost gaily.

He watched her without speaking while she counted out the bills and coins.

Ten. Twenty. Thirty. Thirty-five. Forty. Ten. Five. One. Two.

"Forty-two dollars and seventeen cents," she said. "That's not bad at all. We'll manage fine."

None of the things he had planned to say would work now. He could neither comfort nor chide. He felt jolted, off balance. He had to hit somewhere.

"Well, *you* won't starve at least," he said, his voice cutting. "*You've* got that money in Bangor."

Her face changed again—this time to anger.

"Joel Closson, do you know what you're saying? That is Jesse's money. It's for his education. If you think for one minute—"

"I don't think anything at all," he said.

136

By late October, the gulls had gone and the red on the vines had deepened. Except for the noise of the crows flying solemnly overhead and now and then the bark of a rifle, the barrens were still.

Joel spent much of his time hunting, staying out regardless of the cold, until Laura rang the bell on the shed. Two strokes meant "Dinner in half an hour." Three strokes meant "I want you now. Come in." He came back, always shivering, usually empty-handed. But with the food Laura had put up, they made out well enough. She had always known ways to be economical and now she was learning new ones. She substituted molasses for sugar. She saved tea leaves and coffee grounds, using them twice. She put the soap above the stove to dry out, in this way making it last longer. She blocked the front door and stuffed rags in the cracks. She shut off the sitting room and put away the oilstove, opening the bedroom door only at night.

For days on end no one passed but the mail. Then, one morning early in November, Harry came out alone, just before breakfast. He looked very tired and his usually high color had faded.

"Ma wants to see you, Laura," he said. "I'll bring you back at noon."

Laura quickly closed the door to the bedroom where Joel was still sleeping. For some time after Luther's death, Joel had been very kind to Flora and very patient, but now his patience was wearing thin. Flora still kept the shades down all day. She had not dressed—at least she had not put on her corset—since the funeral. Nothing took up her mind except a monument for Luther. Who would carve it. What it would say. Her name was to be upon it along with his, for actually she was dead too, she told them, or she might as well be. She needed straight talk, Joel said, and threatened to give it.

"Pour yourself a cup of coffee," Laura said, "while I leave a note for Joel." Then she turned to Jesse. "Get your things on. We're going in to see Aunt Flora."

Jesse kept his eyes on his oatmeal. "I don't want to go," he said. He dreaded staying at Aunt Flora's now, for she cried a great deal, which made him angry.

"Then stay with Pa."

Jesse looked thoughtful. If Pa was going to talk nice to him, he wanted to stay home, but if he wasn't, he didn't. You never could be sure about Pa. He decided not to take the chance. "I don't want to stay with Pa," he said.

Harry spoke quickly. "I'll keep him with me. I'd like the company."

Laura turned to Jesse. "Hurry then," she urged. "Grab your sweater." She finished her note and laid it on the table. She wanted to get out without waking Joel, afraid of what he might say when he knew where she was going.

"Can I put your radio on at the store, Harry?" Jesse asked as soon as they started out. Their own radio was a battery set, and its use was limited to the news and perhaps ten or fifteen minutes of music a day.

"Sure thing," Harry said.

"How long—"

"You keep quiet now," Laura interrupted, "and let me talk to Harry. Do you hear?"

"A-yuh." When his mother spoke sharply to him, he felt all right, but when his father did, he felt sick to his stomach for hours and hours.

Laura turned to Harry. "Does your mother have something special on her mind?" It couldn't be the W.C.T.U. again, for Flora was concerned now only with herself and her grief. She wouldn't try puzzles; she wouldn't even see the neighbors when they called. In fact, she saw no one at all but the family and the minister. It couldn't be about the business. Though for years Flora had been attempting to find out how much money Luther had, she had no interest in it now. "Talk to Harry," she would say when any questions about business came up. "Ask him." She had shown no concern whatever when he had tried to tell her how bad things were.

Harry started to speak and then gave up. His stammer was back now, markedly.

"I thought it might be about the monument," Laura went on quickly. He was worried about the monument, she knew, for Flora was determined to have the most expensive one she could buy. She was talking about one that cost five hundred dollars.

He shook his head. "She'd better tell you herself," he said.

Flora was still in bed when Laura arrived—she stayed there now most of the time. She lay propped up on the pillows, her hair carelessly braided. Hearing Laura come in, she looked up with injured eyes. "Well, you came," she said.

"Of course I came."

"After I sent for you."

Laura felt exasperated. After all, she had come in every day as long as Joel was working. She had sat in the semidark house and listened while Flora talked, saying the same things over and over. But on Luther's account she must be patient. "I would have come before if I could." She took off the scarf she had worn over her head, stuffed it in her pocket, and hung her coat over her chair. "We're not using the car, you know."

"Well, you were bound and determined to live in that place."

Laura ignored the barb. "Besides," she went on, "I knew Doris was near."

Flora tossed her head and set her mouth tightly.

So it was Doris.

Determined to head the story off as long as she could, Laura picked up the paper from the foot of the bed—she and Joel did not take a paper now—and glanced over the headlines that she could just make out in the dimness. "Such trouble," she said pointedly. "Everywhere. Here's a man turned robber to feed his children. Here's a riot in a bread line. Think of it, a riot in the state of Maine. Here's about a whole family of children who can't go to school because they have no shoes. Here's—"

Flora interrupted her. "You sit there and talk about people having trouble to *me*, a widow," she said coldly.

If Luther knew. . . .

Laura laid the paper down. "Harry said you wanted to tell me something."

"I do." Flora sat bolt upright and paused to make what she had to say impressive. "Do you know what they've done?"

So Ed was in it too.

"What?" Laura asked, resigned to listen.

"They've mortgaged the place."

In spite of her determination to feel nothing, Laura was a little shocked. A mortgage was a last resort in Millboro. You didn't get one until you were destitute, until every other door was closed. Even when it was paid off, the stigma of it stayed. "Where did they get it?" she asked. Not that it made a difference, but she felt the need of a little time.

"At the Ellsworth Bank."

So that was why they had been going to the bank that day. And she had been green enough . . . No wonder they had laughed.

"Doris had the gall to come right out and tell me. 'We've mortgaged the place,' she said. Just like that, she said it. 'We've mortgaged the place, Flora.' Just like she was saying, 'We went fishing today.'"

Laura sat silent. Even in her moments of deepest discouragement, she had never considered a mortgage.

"Maybe they had to, Flora."

"Had to." Flora's voice grew bitter. "Just think of the money they've wasted. Bingo. Dances. Ball games."

"That's all in the past," Laura reminded her. "They can't have anything now. Ed's got no work and winter's coming."

Flora blew her nose. "I'm surprised at you, Laura," she said severely, "defending a spendthrift."

They were right back where they had been.

10

With November the weather grew damp and cold. Rain flattened the ferns and stripped the leaves from the birches. It worsened Joel's back, and he went hunting less often. With so many hunters out, there was little game left anyway. Cooped up in the kitchen, he grew restless and impatient. He read (only a few pages at a time) from Luther's Western magazines that Harry had given him, played a little solitaire. But most of the time he was moving from house to shed, room to room, chair to chair. His appetite slackened. He would begin a meal, then abruptly push away his plate. At night he made love less and less frequently. Sometimes he could not when he tried.

Laura planned to keep Jesse outside all she could. They walked hand in hand over the barrens, watching for birds, mostly finches and sparrows that came for the last of the seeds; gathering weeds, now washed colorless; rolling great balls out of the battered, broken lengths of string; watching the hawks making their slow circles; or just listening to the wind as it crackled in the dead bushes.

One day when the crows were abundant, one flock following another, she taught him the rhyme:

One crow sorrow,
Two crow joy,
Three crow letter,
Four crow boy.
Five crow silver,
Six crow gold,
Seven crow secret
Never to be told.

"Is it true, Mama?" he asked.

"No, no, of course not. It's just a game," she told him. "Just a game people have played for years and years."

Sometimes they stopped under the shelter of a big boulder and looked out over the shriveled landscape. A moor must be like this, Laura thought, and she told Jesse the story of the Secret Garden, which she had so loved in her childhood. Sometimes they walked to the little graveyard, and while Jesse traced the letters on the stones with his fingers, Laura sat on the crumbling wall. Had they, David and Hannah, gone through times like this? she wondered.

On the day before Thanksgiving the weather cleared, becoming warm and windless. After an early dinner, they started in town to buy provisions. Dried fish. Flour. Pickled eggs. Lard. Canned milk. Potatoes. "That will be $2.61," Laura had said, looking over the figures she had made on the back of an old paper bag. "We won't need to buy anything else until Christmas." After the confinement of the house, the long silences, they all felt a stimulation.

"Who are we going to see?" Jesse asked.

"The family," Laura told him.

There had been no talk of a family gathering on Thanksgiving. Without Luther, it was unthinkable this year. Besides, there was that trouble between Flora and Doris, which Laura hadn't told Joel about. Once she had told him everything.

142

"What's in the bag?" Jesse demanded.

"Just some jelly and a bottle of dandelion wine for Aunt Flora."

"Do we have to stay there?"

Joel slapped him on the knee. "You're a boy after my own heart, Jess," he said heartily.

Surprised by the attention from his father, Jesse expanded. "My birthday's coming soon, ain't it, Pa?"

"Not 'ain't,' Jesse," Laura said. " 'Isn't'."

"Uncle Ed says ain't."

Joel grinned a little.

"Well, Uncle Ed is wrong about that."

"You know what he's going to get me?"

Nothing, I hope, Laura thought quickly. Nothing that costs money. She must take care of that. She must talk to Ed today.

"I promised not to tell."

"Then don't," Laura said. When she got Jesse alone, she would explain things to him. She would make him understand why he mustn't expect presents this year.

Jesse turned to his father. "You guess, Pa, because if you guessed—"

Laura interrupted him. "No one is going to guess, Jesse. You hear what I say."

Subdued again, Jesse gave his attention to the crows. "One crow sorrow," he whispered. "Two crow joy . . ."

They parked outside the store, and Laura gave Joel the list and, with it, $2.75. "There'll be fourteen cents change," she reminded him. Then she turned to Jesse. "Come with me, Jesse," she said, reaching for his hand. Joel would never ask Harry if he was likely to need him again. He was too proud for that, but, given a chance, Harry might say something, and she wanted nothing, no one, to stand in the way.

"All right, Ma." Now that Uncle Luther had gone away, he

didn't like to stay in the store any longer. It gave him a queer feeling he had never had before. He had found that out the day he had stayed with Harry. He had thought at first that he was hungry, but when Harry offered him candy, cookies, crackers —anything he wanted—he couldn't eat a bite. Now, facing the steps, he took his mother's hand willingly.

It was good to see people again, even the loafers on the steps at Peasley's. Everyone they met seemed cheerful. "Nice to see you in," Mrs. Lester Gott said, shifting her can of kerosene from one hand to the other. "What a H-A-N-D-S-O-M-E boy Jesse is. S-M-A-R-T, too, I hear tell." Will Whitten stopped them on the bridge to talk. "Joel workin' anywhere?" And, when she shook her head, he added, "Allus darkest jest before dawn." Ethel Buzzell came to her front door, seeing them pass. "Nice day, ain't it?" she called. "Kinder keeps the spirits up."

Jesse wanted to go down to the shore. He begged to go there whenever they were in town, and she often took him, but only when someone drove them. To go on foot would be to pass Joel's father's house, and she feared an accidental meeting. So far that had been avoided, at least a meeting face to face. But what would happen when it came? When Jesse began hearing things, asking questions? . . .

But today he had begged harder than ever, and because she was afraid he wouldn't have much of a Thanksgiving, Laura had given in. Once there, he looked for minnows in the pools. He picked up driftwood. He crawled over the boats that had been drawn up for the winter. On their way back, just when they had almost passed it, Joel's father came out of the shed. He was wearing a winter undershirt, not a very clean one, and he hadn't shaved for days. He looked startled, and this time his start was genuine.

"Good morning," Laura said pleasantly but without slowing down.

"Mornin'," he answered, turning to go back in.

But Jesse would not be hurried. "What's your name?" he asked, stopping.

Laura's heart seemed to stop too. The first question had come. When he heard the name, what would the next question be?

Joel's father lowered his eyes, then raised them and looked, not at Jesse at all, but directly at Laura.

"My name's Mr. Jim," he said.

Within a week cold came suddenly, a real cold that meant winter. Following the warm spell, it meant croup weather too. Croup had always been chronic with Jesse. Once, when he was less than a year old, Laura had found him black in the face and struggling from the mucous in his throat. Since then she had been terrified of its return.

After one look at the thermometer, she made up his bed in the sitting room on the sofa. With the doors open, heat came in through the hall—enough, at least, to take off the chill.

"Are you warm enough, Jesse?" she kept asking after he was settled.

"Yes, Ma," he answered, pleased to be downstairs.

But that night she woke suddenly to the noisy, rasping sound she so dreaded. She jumped up and ran barefooted into the sitting room. "Jesse," she cried. "Jesse."

He was still too much asleep to answer, but she picked him up, bedding and all, and, staggering from her load, took him into their room.

"Joel. Joel. Wake up." She felt a fury that men should sleep —could sleep—so heavily.

"Why? What?"

"It's Jesse. It's the croup. Go build up the fire."

She laid Jesse on her side of the bed, put both pillows behind him, and drew the covers tight.

145

Only half-knowing what was going on, Joel started to dress.

"Don't dress," she told him. "Just get the fire going so I can give him some niter."

In half an hour the place was warm again and Jesse was breathing more easily. But the next day Laura did not like the way he looked or the sound of his cough. "Let's bring the sofa out in the kitchen," she said, "where I can keep an eye on him all the time." In the afternoon he seemed very hot. She took his temperature and found it was almost 102°.

"We'll have to have the doctor, Joel," she said.

The doctor came, not once, but twice. That took six dollars. And there was the medicine.

When Jesse was on his feet again, Laura took down the sugar bowl and soberly counted the money inside. Twenty-nine dollars and sixteen cents.

11

Jesse's birthday was just ahead. There would be a cake (eggless) with candles (left over from last year), a present from Laura (a scrapbook that she had made from old magazines in the shed), and one from Joel (a bow and arrow). But there would be no others. Flora would not remember anyway, and on the day they were in town she herself had been careful to settle the matter with Doris and Ed. Then she had tried to settle it with Jesse.

"You understand, Jesse?"

"Uncle Ed will bring me something," he assured her.

"Not this year, Jesse."

"He promised."

146

"But I've just told you—"

"He'll come," he said.

And he did come, in the middle of the afternoon, honking up the road, with Doris beside him, through the first snowfall. Butch was not with them, for he hated snow and could not be persuaded to come out in it.

Jesse, who had long since tired of the scrapbook and who had shown no interest at all in the bow and arrow, was waiting at the window. "Here he is," he called, rushing toward the kitchen door.

"You stay inside," Laura told him. He still was pale and coughed badly. "You hear me, Jesse."

Looking over Jesse's head, she saw Ed get down, go to the back of the truck, and take out a large box. After all she had told him. . . . After all she had said. . . . She was exasperated, yet at the same time touched.

Doris got out, hatless, wearing trousers and a mackinaw, and bounded up the steps. The minute she reached the door, Jesse had it open wide.

"Hello," he cried, jumping in his excitement. "Hello. Hello."

Laura hurried to close the door behind them.

At once they began singing:

> "Happy Birthday to you,
> Happy Birthday to you,
> Happy Birthday, dear Jesse,
> Happy Birthday to you!"

Jesse turned to Laura. "I told you," he shrilled. "I knew they'd come."

"Oh, you two," Laura said. "Here, let me take your things." Doris took off her glasses, drew a bandana from the pocket of her mackinaw and wiped off the steam. Then she looked down at the braided rug. "We sure tracked in," she said. She wore sneakers, though the snow was ankle deep.

"Never mind that."

Ed set the present on the table. "Where's Joel," he asked.

"Piling wood in the shed. He'll be right in."

Jesse's eyes were on the present. "Did you get 'em, Uncle Ed?"

"What do yer think?" Ed asked, closing both fists and making a gesture of boxing.

"I think you did," Jesse said, his eyes still on the table. "Can I open it now?"

"Don't you want to wait for your father?" Doris asked. She had taken off her sneakers and set them on the ledge of the oven. There was a big hole in the toe of one stocking.

Laura flushed a little. Joel knew they were there. He had heard them come—he couldn't help it. He had seen Ed carrying the package in. He must have heard the singing. She opened the door. "Yoo-hoo. Joel." Then she turned to the stove and pushed the kettle forward.

"Oh, Ed," she said, looking worried. "I do hope you haven't spent any money—" They had never mentioned the mortgage to her nor she to them. But on an old house like that they couldn't have got much cash, and the winter was only beginning.

Ed pinched her affectionately on the cheek, avoiding her question. "D'yer tell, Jess?" he asked.

"No, I didn't tell. Did I, Ma?"

"No," Laura said, with a quick look at the shed. "You didn't tell."

Doris took the towel off the roller and began to dry her hair. "We sure had a time finding 'em," she said.

"Where'd you have to go?" Laura asked anxiously. Just gas . . .

"Bangor."

"Bangor," Laura echoed, dismayed. "You didn't go way to Bangor!"

"Sure did," Ed said cheerfully. "Jesse don't have a birthday every day, do yer, Jesse?"

148

Jesse had not even heard him. "Have we got to wait for Pa?" he asked, fidgeting with the string.

Laura threw a sweater over his shoulders, then went to the door again. "Joel. Come on." She held the door open. "Hurry. We're waiting."

He came, taking his time, while snow sifted in and the wind blew the outer wrappings from the table.

"Hi, Dot," he said. "Hi, Ed."

"Hi, yourself," Doris said.

"Roads bad?"

"Goin' to be worse," Ed said.

"Look, Pa," Jesse squealed. "See what I got!"

Laura spoke quickly. "He was waiting for you before he opened it," she said.

"Well, I'm here." He made no move to join them at the table.

Ed and Jesse kept taking off layer after layer of wrapping while Laura looked on and Doris sat in the rocker, swinging her foot, her big toe working.

"How can they breathe, Uncle Ed?"

"They can breathe all right. I fixed 'em."

Paper. Excelsior. More paper. More excelsior. Finally it was revealed.

A bowl with two goldfish swimming in it. One was all gold. One had black gills and a touch of black beneath his chin.

Jesse stared at them in ecstatic silence.

"What yer wanted, warn't it?" Ed asked.

Jesse nodded.

"Oh, you two," Laura said again, this time almost crying. "I can't do anything with you." She turned to Joel. "They went all the way to Bangor for them," she told him with a prompting glance that he took pains to avoid.

"That so?" he answered.

149

When the cake was eaten, Ed and Joel started outside with a shovel in case the truck wouldn't start. Doris lingered, pulling on her sneakers, which had stiffened from the heat. "What's eating Joel?" she asked. All during the party he had sat glumly, speaking only when he was spoken to.

"He's discouraged, I guess."

"Humm," Doris said, "I thought maybe he'd heard some of the talk."

"What talk now?" Much as she hated to ask, she had to know.

"About you-know-who."

Laura looked significantly at Jesse, who was watching his fish, tapping the bowl quietly to keep them moving.

"Some of the young fellows tried to make a deal with—"

"Sssh."

Doris lowered her voice. "They figured he'd need some help over the holidays, working that whole stretch alone with business heavy."

"Sssh."

"Well, you wanted to know. Anyway"—her voice was now a whisper—"he wouldn't. Said it was no business for young fellers to get into. And they tipped off the Coast Guard." She rose and put on her mackinaw. "Now, don't go feeding 'em any beans and brown bread," she said to Jesse, pinching his ear.

Three days later the Bangor station broadcast the news that the company in which Laura had invested Jesse's money had closed its doors. She and Joel were sitting at the breakfast table when they heard it. At first she told herself that she had not heard it right; that her mind was too confused these days to be counted on; that two blows could not possibly come so close together. Then a look at Joel's face showed her it was true.

150

Showed her, too, that he was scared. That meant she couldn't be. "When these times are over . . ." she began, speaking with effort. Suddenly a great tiredness overwhelmed her. She could not have finished even had she known what she wanted to say. It was a tiredness such as she had never known before. It gripped her neck and pressed her shoulders. It crept sluggishly down into her arms and legs.

Joel said nothing, but got up almost at once and went outside. She just kept on sitting there, staring at her hands, without making a motion. Jesse had to call four times before she could answer.

As the days passed every move became an effort for her. She got the meals: rolled oats, cornbread, pea soup, baked beans, potatoes and pork scraps, boiled dinner, bread and molasses, apple sauce, baked apple. After the dishes were done, she lay down in the bedroom where, by lying just so, she could look out the porthole window seeing only a tiny patch of leaden sky or one crow at a time, flying over. Jesse, sensing something wrong, was quiet too. Compared to the quiet within, the wind seemed louder than ever before.

Joel grew more edgy. He had counted on Laura's willingness to use some of that money as a last resort to get them through the winter. Now what? Harry would not need him. He had known that all the time. He talked very little, and when he talked, his words were biting.

"We need more wood, Joel."

"I'm not blind."

"Is there anything special you would like for supper?"

"Roast beef, please."

He didn't read any longer. Most of his time he spent playing solitaire or stretched out on the sofa, which they kept now in the kitchen, staring at the ceiling.

No one came.

With the increasing cold, Jesse started to cough again; this meant more medicine. When it was paid for, the sugar bowl held only eleven dollars.

Eleven dollars with which to face a winter. Eleven dollars, and a woodshed already half empty.

12

Early in December Tom Pinkham stopped at the box and left them a letter from Flora. She wouldn't be able to have the family for Christmas this year, so she was enclosing ten dollars. It was all she could spare, they mustn't expect more.

Laura put the money on the mantel and handed the letter to Joel.

"Jesus Christ!" he said. "She's got her gall."

"She doesn't mean it that way, Joel," Laura said quickly. "Without Luther she's just lost her balance, that's all." Laura would have taken the money to give Jesse a Christmas, especially now that he seemed so white and frail. "But couldn't we just borrow it?" she asked.

"No we could not just borrow it," he answered, mocking her tone. "We borrow nothing from her." He seldom called Flora by name now—only "she" or "her."

Late that afternoon the first real snow fell. There was no wind—only a slow, steady sifting of white. Jesse stood enthralled at the bedroom window, now and then whispering softly to himself as he watched the world outside change form and color, then pressing his face against the pane to watch it disappear. When supper was ready, Laura had to call him twice.

"How soon is Christmas?" he asked the minute he sat down at the table.

"Haven't you just had a birthday?" Joel demanded.

"Yes, but I want Christmas too."

"Oh, you do, do you?"

"I want a tree."

"You'll get a tree," Joel said.

"I want singing." Always on Christmas they had sung together, gathered around the piano while Aunt Flora played.

"What's wrong with the radio?"

Jesse looked anxious. "Aren't we going in town for Christmas dinner?" Christmas dinner meant a special dinner. A dinner of at least five courses with himself sitting on the big dictionary so he could reach the table. With an enormous tree and presents galore and, best of all, Santa Claus, who never failed to come. Santa Claus was Uncle Luther, wasn't he? Then Uncle Luther would be coming again. That thought was a great comfort to him.

"Not this year," Laura said. "Aunt Flora isn't feeling very well."

Jesse's eyes filled. A tear crept down his cheek and he caught it on his tongue.

"Aren't we going to have any presents, Pa?" If there were no presents, there would be no Santa Claus. No Uncle Luther. And he had counted a lot on seeing Uncle Luther again.

"Haven't you had presents enough already?"

The tears quickened and spread.

Laura reached over and wiped them away with her napkin. "Eat your pudding," she said. "Christmas is a long way off." But he only dropped his spoon, covered his face with his hands, and began sobbing.

With a reproachful look at Joel, Laura picked Jesse up and carried him into the bedroom, where he slept now until their bedtime, when they moved him to the sofa. She gave him one of Joel's handkerchiefs, helped him undress, and lay quietly

153

beside him. She had never known him to cry so hard before. When he was finally asleep, she went into the kitchen, where Joel, having pushed aside the dishes, was playing solitaire on the table.

"Are you going to let your pride cheat that child out of a Christmas?" she demanded.

He did not answer, but went on playing deliberately. Queen upon Jack, six upon five . . .

"I spoke to you Joel."

"I heard you."

"Well, answer me then."

There was no sound but the singing of the kettle, the click of the clock, and the slap of the cards upon the table.

Ten upon Jack, nine upon ten . . .

With every move of a card, Laura's anger grew until she could control it no longer. "Shame on you, Joel Closson," she said bitterly. "To act like this. And after everything that's happened. To spoil our Christmas. Especially Jesse's."

Still he said nothing. His mouth was tight and sealed.

"Doris and Ed can take about the last cent they have and go to Bangor to give him a birthday. But because of your stupid pride you won't even touch the money Flora sent with the best will in the world. Sometimes I think you don't want him to be happy. Sometimes I think you don't love him at all."

For an instant his hand faltered. Then he laid down another card.

"You'll have your Christmas," he said.

Most of the next day Joel worked in the shed, every now and then starting the motor of the car. Laura thought nothing of it. He often did this in winter so the battery wouldn't run down. Her only thought was that, ashamed of the way he was acting, he was keeping out of sight.

After supper—the third meal that day he had eaten in silence —he lighted the lantern and went back outside. This time she

154

noticed that he was wearing his heaviest clothes, but she thought nothing of that, either, for the night was cold. She heard the car start, back, turn. Then she realized he was leaving.

"Where's Papa going?" Jesse asked.

"Oh, just on an errand."

With a quick glance through the window, she saw that he was headed toward town. Men can get away, she thought resentfully as she helped Jesse with his night clothes.

"Who's he going to see?"

"Aunt Flora." He had gone to take the money back; of this she had no doubt.

"Ain't we going to have any Christmas at all, Ma?" Jesse asked when she bent to kiss him good night.

"We'll take care of Christmas when the time comes. You go to sleep now."

Once he was settled and quiet, she turned down the lamp, pushed the rug against the door to keep out the drafts, lay on the sofa, and covered herself with a blanket.

Lying there, she thought what Christmas would mean this year. A tree decorated only with a few cut-out pieces of colored paper. Another vegetable dinner. A pudding. Canned milk for Jesse. Weak tea for her and Joel (the coffee had been gone for a week). No real presents—only something she could piece together.

And all because of Joel's pride.

She was angry and she was discouraged. But she was tired, too—she was always tired these days, it seemed—and in a little while she slept.

When she woke up, the room was cold. She looked at the clock and saw that it was almost ten.

Where was Joel?

She moved a soapstone from the ledge of the stove to one of the covers, then blew out the lamp and went to the window. There was a bright full moon, and by it she saw the barrens—

155

flat and white except for the dark of the ledges and the shadows cast by the bushes; still, except for an occasional flurry of snow carried along by the wind. As she watched, a fox appeared from behind the shed, crossed the road with complete confidence, and disappeared. The house snapped from the cold.

She shivered, but she would not use more wood, for she knew as well as Joel did how little was left in the shed.

What was keeping him?

She picked up the blanket, wrapped it about her, and went into the bedroom to check on Jesse. He was warm, but breathing heavily.

Back in the kitchen, she moved the sofa closer to the stove and lay down again. Had Joel quarreled with Flora? Had he really carried out his threat to tell her off?

Too restless to stay still, she got up, holding the blanket around her, lighted the lamp again, and sat down in the rocker, intending to read one of Luther's old magazines. But her fingers were too cold to hold it, her mind too jumpy to take anything in. If Joel had started trouble, with Harry so worried already . . .

She looked at the clock again. Ten thirty-five. Had he had an accident? It was a safe road, with neither curves nor deep ditches. Almost no one traveled it, so a collision wasn't likely. If a tire went flat, he would have left the car and walked. Perhaps he had. Perhaps he was on the road now, almost home.

She went to look out.

Nothing. No one.

Frost was forming on the window. The floors were icy. The pump might freeze tonight, she thought, and began to work its handle. She pumped until she was exhausted. Then she opened the stove and put in another stick—a small one. She mustn't let the fire go out, for he would be chilled to the bone when he came. When it started up, she went back to the rocker and, warmed by the exercise and the heat, dozed again.

It was Jesse's breathing that woke her, the kind of breathing that threatened croup. She woke him up enough to give him medicine, and then looked at the clock.

Twenty minutes to twelve.

It couldn't be.

She turned up the lamp to be sure. Twenty minutes to twelve.

Something had happened.

Again she looked out. The frost had thickened on the windows. The moon, high and pale, looked frosted too, lighting up the empty road. Perhaps somewhere on that road . . .

She would put on her things and start. She reached for her coat that hung on the hook near the doorway and the shawl she wore over her head when she went into the yard. Just as she bent for her overshoes, Jesse coughed roughly.

If he had an attack . . . if he called her. . . . She remembered attacks when there had been blue around his mouth, even on his fingernails, bright blue like the veins in his wrists. Weak with dread, she sat down on the couch to do the only thing she could do—wait.

A little after twelve the lamp began to sputter. It was running out of kerosene. She went to the mantel to get another and saw Flora's letter, the ten-dollar bill still in it. Then he hadn't gone to see Flora.

He had gone away. He had left them.

She had an instant of panic. Then it passed. Joel would never leave them. Besides, he had made her a promise. "You'll have your Christmas," he had told her. He might deliberately provoke her, he might say harsh things, but he would never break a promise. He had planned something for them. He wouldn't borrow from Flora, but he would borrow from someone else. Yet who? Who else in Millboro had money to spare?

As clearly as though someone had spoken the words, the answer came. His father. Could Joel have gone to him? It seemed impossible. Yet she had goaded, taunted. . . .

She set the lamp unsteadily down on the table. It flickered and went out. The moon was brighter now and she could see everything in the kitchen—the stove and table, casting monstrous shadows; the clear silhouette of the tea kettle on the wall; the pine cones on the paper; Luther's calendar—she could even make out the date; the spot of ketchup over Jesse's place at the table. . . . If he had gone there, why had he waited until night to go? Why wasn't he back?

She went again to the window. While she was standing there, looking at the road, at his tracks almost filled in by shifting snow, she finally knew. Joel wouldn't borrow from his father. But, desperate as she had made him, he might earn.

She felt a slow, creeping numbness that she tried to hold onto, for as long as it was there she could not think at all. But it dissolved in spite of her, turning into a confusion of guilt and anger and shame. She buried her face in her hands and sank down on the sofa again, shaking all over.

Joel breaking the law . . .

She knew how the whole thing worked. She had heard stories. The big boats came from Canada and anchored outside the three-mile limit so the Coast Guard couldn't touch them. Then the motorboats went out and, following signals, brought the liquor ashore, where trucks were waiting to take it to Boston and New York. Often the federal agents were waiting too.

She felt a rage against his father. Refusing to take other fellows because it was a bad business, but taking his own son. And she had defended him. Invited him for supper. Even schemed a reconciliation. How she had been taken in, thinking him kind, gentle, protective when he hadn't told Jesse his name. She would never speak to him again, never let Jesse.

Then, with a sharp pain in her stomach, she remembered that the Coast Guard had been tipped off.

If it should be tonight. . . .

The moon was bright. On the water the visibility would be perfect. She pressed her stomach against another cramp and closed her eyes. A motorboat with two men in it, making full speed for some dark cove. A Coast Guard boat—bigger, faster —in pursuit. A boat that carried guns. If they shot across the bow. . . . If the motorboat veered, overturned . . .

She began to tremble. Joel was no swimmer, even in calm water. And in this cold, with that heavy clothing . . . Or if they were overtaken, caught. If they had to face trial. . . . It would mean Atlanta. Ruin for Joel. Disgrace for Jesse.

She was shaking so hard that the blanket fell from her shoulders.

It was after four o'clock when she saw headlights. At the sight of them she lighted a lamp, put more wood in the stove, and drew the kettle forward. She should have felt relief, but she did not. She no longer felt anything.

She heard the car door close, the sound of his feet on the steps, the kitchen door open. Then he stood in the room.

At the sight of him, his shaking body, the tiny icicles in his hair, his frozen mittens fumbling at the buttons of his mackinaw, only one feeling came back—anger.

She stared at him without speaking while he took off his mittens, put one hand in his pocket, drew out a bill and laid it on the table. By the light of the lamp, she could see it was twenty dollars.

"Go and buy out the town," he said. His teeth were chattering so she could hardly understand him.

Her eyes still on the bill, she spoke coldly. "Joel Closson," she said, "if you got this money the way I think you did, I'll never spend it. I'd rather see it burn."

He shrugged his shoulders, took the cover from the stove, then the bill from the table.

"Suit yourself," he said, and dropped it in.

PART THREE

1935

1

It was spring again.

Laura Closson sat on the stone step of the graveyard, looking about her. For more than an hour she had been tramping over the soggy ground inspecting their land, half of which had been burned the year before. She had changed a good deal. Her skin had grown thicker and darker. Her eyes seemed darker too, because of the circles beneath them. A few strands of gray showed up in her hair. Sometimes, looking at herself in the mirror, she was surprised that she had any youth left at all. For these past five years had been hard ones.

As soon as Joel had got in bed that awful night, he had come down with chills. Nothing warmed him—not the hot, reckless fire in the cookstove; not the ginger tea she had made him; not the soapstone she had put at his feet; not her own body pressed against his. Before sunrise the chills had given way to burning fever. By morning he did not even know her. It had taken all of her strength to hold him down. "Let me go," he kept shouting, not to her, she knew, but to someone he took her to be. "Quit holding me." Over and over. "Let me go, I say! Let me go. Or you'll be sorry." She could not get the doctor, for that was before she had learned to drive the car. So in the morning, when he had at last fallen asleep, she had stood knee-deep in the snow waiting for Tom Pinkham, her eyes alternately on the road and on the bedroom window. It had been noon before the doctor came. "You've got a long battle," he had told her. And it had been—a battle never really won.

But for Joel's father, she could never have managed. He had come out as soon as he had heard, bringing some clothes wrapped in an old gray bathrobe and a carton of provisions. "I figgered yer'd need some help," he told her.

She did need help. Ed had come, but she had kept him in the kitchen, afraid of what he might hear. Harry had come and stayed one night, but she wouldn't let him come again, knowing that he already had his hands full with Flora and the store.

Yet, badly as she had needed help, she was particular where it came from. She didn't want help from a lawbreaker, from a man who would risk his own son's ruin. So she had only stared at him coldly until he started to leave, setting the groceries on the step. "Take them with you," she told him. Hungry though they might be, she would take nothing bought with his money. Even the sight of his stricken face had not moved her.

He had known what she was thinking. "The money's from my bo't," he said huskily. "I sold it ter a feller on 'Tit Manan fer three hunnerd dollars."

She had stared at him, astonished. Three hundred dollars for a boat worth three thousand!

"I wunt need it no more," he had added, almost in a whisper. "I'm through with that fer good."

She had been moved then in spite of herself.

Seeing her hesitation, he had spoken again, quickly. "I wunt git in yer way," he promised. "I'll go any time yer say the word."

"All right," she had said. "Come in."

He had stayed all winter, sleeping in the cold upstairs bedroom. At five every morning he was in the kitchen in his stocking feet, building the fire so that when she got up at six the place was warm, the coffee made, his breakfast eaten, the sheets, put in to soak the night before, rinsed and out on the line. Most of the day he worked in the shed, chopping wood or doing odd jobs at a bench he had set up there, but staying always within call. He got his own supper and ate it early; then, even in the coldest weather, he went to his room upstairs. "No need a me stayin' here underfoot," he would say when she suggested he would be more comfortable in the kitchen. At least twice in the night he would come down, his old gray bathrobe over his winter underwear in which he slept, to turn Joel or to lift him. During all those weeks Joel had given him no sign of recognition. He might have been a stranger.

Jesse knew who he was now and, after his first surprise, took his presence as a matter of course. All day he followed him around asking him questions about the sea.

Did you ever get shipwrecked, Mr. Jim?

Was your boat ever grounded?

He showed Jesse how to use tools, too, and together they made a desk with pigeonholes for Jesse's collections. Listening to his quiet voice, seeing his patience, Laura had gradually come to forgive him, reasoning that there were things—there must be things—she did not know and perhaps never would.

As soon as Joel was on his feet, his father had moved back to town and got a WPA job, working on the new school in Cherryfield. But all during the summer he came out often, knowing almost uncannily when there was work to be done, doing it, and then slipping quietly away. Half the time Laura did not

165

even see him come or go, yet the kerosene barrel never ran dry, the woodpile never got low, the potato bin was never empty. When Jesse started to go to school, he was waiting in his old car every morning to take him there, and he brought him back at night. Even after all this, Joel had little or nothing to say to him beyond "a-yuh" or "no" to a direct question.

In the spring of the second year, when Joel was up and around and could keep an eye on Jesse, Laura had worked in the sardine factory. A boat would come in, the whistle would blow, and either Harry or Ed would come out for her. She would grab her white cap and her oilcloth apron, put on her biggest shoes, for she worked best standing, and hurry away. She had worked there off and on three seasons, and what she earned, together with what they raised, had almost kept them going. When they needed more, she borrowed from Joel's father, keeping strict accounts on the kitchen calendar.

Until recently she had been full of hope. It was only a matter of time, she had told herself, time and patience. It wasn't as if Joel had lost opportunities to get ahead, for there were no opportunities then for anyone. If he was never really cheerful (after all, a man half crippled from exposure doesn't have much to be cheerful about), he was never really despondent either.

Time went reasonably fast for him. He played games with her and Jesse. He tried to draw and did a fair job of it. He read the papers Harry brought on Wednesday afternoons, excused by Flora, who until then had considered Harry's free time completely at her disposal. On fine days he walked, haltingly, over the barrens. Hunters dropped in and stayed to talk awhile. Doris and Ed came out whenever they had gas for the truck. People who took the back road to Ellsworth stopped long enough to swap hard-luck stories. There was a neighbor now— Mr. Pettigrew, who had sold his place in Larrabee and made one of the rakers' shacks into a presentable cottage. He couldn't think of a better place to spend his last days, he said. Like Jesse, Joel enjoyed his company.

There were days on a stretch when they all forgot how bad things were. There were nights when Joel tried to make love and sometimes succeeded. But now, suddenly, he seemed to have completely lost heart. And just when things were picking up all over.

The radio was encouraging. Employment had increased. Maine—even Millboro—was already feeling the effects of it. Most of the cottages were going to open. The town looked better. Work on the roads had begun. The school bus was running. Peasley's, out of bankruptcy, was open for business, and the pool table, its veneer peeling from long exposure to dampness, was once again in use. The blueberry crop showed promise.

Joel knew these things; yet, instead of rising, his spirits were dropping all the time. "Stop trying," he would say when Laura wanted to massage his hands—hands that, crippled as they were, still stirred her. One day in March, when he had refused to take his medicine, she pleaded with him.

"We can't give up now, Joel, just when things are getting so much better for everybody."

"Everybody but me," he answered bitterly, and she knew then what had brought on the sudden change.

After that he refused to play games with them, but played solitaire instead on the kitchen table, handling the cards awkwardly, all the time keeping up a low monotonous whistle.

Hour after hour. Day after day. Shuffle. One, two, three, four, five, six, seven . . . one, two, three . . .

He became more impatient with Jesse, especially for faults that were his own.

You're as slow as cold molasses, boy.

God, Jess, you're as clumsy as a cow.

The things he drew now were full of violence and torment.

A ferocious hawk seizing a terrified rabbit. A snake greedily swallowing a piteous bird. Laura kept them away from Jesse.

If only she had Luther to talk to.

For a long time after Luther's death, she had not been able to see him clearly. Now she could. Luther mowing the lawn, wearing his old straw hat, fringed with wear around the edges. Luther holding Beauty, stroking each of her paws in turn between his big fingers. Luther putting up orders, adding an extra apple or two for good measure, bending forward to listen, his blue eyes fixed on the speaker's face. Luther sitting quietly at his old battered desk with its little high, ink-stained drawer where he kept his pens and his quill toothpick, the blotter doodled with brands from his Western stories, the spindle piercing an untidy sheaf of bills and memorandums. Luther in her bedroom just before the wedding, wearing the blue tie she had given him, asking her promise. If *they's ever any trouble.* . . . And she had thought then she knew what trouble was.

She heard the school bus coming. Jesse would be on it. She always tried to be outside when he came because then she learned something of what had gone on during the day. Once he was in the house, she could get little or nothing out of him.

She waved in case he should be looking, smoothed down her hair and started back.

2

Shading her eyes, she saw him get up and move forward, holding his dinner pail. Always old for his age, he had matured since his father's illness, and the willfulness of his babyhood had

168

all but disappeared. Everybody liked Jesse. His teachers liked him because he did his lessons. The girls liked him because he had good manners. The boys liked him because, slight though he was, he could outrun them all. His years on the barrens had given him an endurance they didn't have, and his long practice with a butterfly net made him a star catcher in the field. Yet organized games were still distasteful to him, and unless he was really needed to make up a team, he didn't play.

Doris, Ed, and Harry all thought there had never been another boy like Jesse. Joel's father looked for him instantly whenever he came. *Where's Jess? Where's the boy terday?* Flora always asked about him, which, considering her absorption in herself, was a compliment. Laura relied on him. She relied on him for chores, for news of what was going on, for conversation at the table. Just for someone to look at when she talked. Joel hated to have her look at him while he struggled with his knife and fork. He was reluctant to get up while she was in the bedroom, and he blew out the lamp before he undressed at night. Most of all, she relied on Jesse for hope. Jesse would never fail her. Somehow, though she did not see how, he was going to be educated.

The bus slowed and stopped. Jesse stepped out, swinging his dinner pail. He was slight, like his father, but with his slightness he had a kind of grace. His short pants, which he still wore though he begged for long ones, showed off his straight legs, and the green sweater Laura had knit him fitted snugly over his widening shoulders.

"Hello, son."

" 'Lo, Ma."

He waited a moment. Then, sure that the bus was out of sight, he hurried toward her and seized her hand. "Guess what?"

"I couldn't."

"Well, guess anyhow."

"Give me a hint then."

His dark eyes brightened. "Someone in our school has won the Science Award." This was an award the new superintendent had offered in an essay contest open to all the elementary pupils in his district. Jesse's essay had been on the habits of crows. He had worked hours, days upon it.

In spite of the confidence she felt Laura tried to look thoughtful. "Gladys Coffin."

"Nope."

"Esther Conary."

"Nope."

"Jesse Closson?" she asked, unable to hold back any longer.

He nodded shyly.

"Wonderful, Jesse!" she said, pressing his hand. And only a few minutes before she had been depressed. "Where is it? Let me see."

He opened the cover of his geography and revealed it—*Certificate of Merit awarded to Jesse Closson.* . . .

It was as though she had never known pride, real pride, before. The feeling she had at the announcement of her own Valedictory had been pale and weak compared to this. She picked up the certificate and studied it. "Why, Jesse, I was never so proud of anything in all my life." She would frame it. It could go where the Coliseum had hung so long above the mantel. She read it again, smiling, and placed it carefully back inside the cover. Then she seized his hand and swung it.

"Are you going to tell Mr. Jim?" he asked.

"I certainly am."

"Uncle Ed?"

"The first time I see him." Ed, though completely contented with his own limitations, was full of plans for Jesse's future. "Goin' ter be a millionaire, Jess is," he would say. "Goin' ter buy one of them here cottages. Goin' ter buy a big bo't too, an' I'm goin' ter run it fer him."

170

"Harry?"

"Certainly."

His voice changed a little. "Are you going to tell Pa?" He got mad at his father; he was ashamed of him sometimes; but he admired him just the same. He didn't know why, but he did.

"Of course I'm going to tell him."

"Now?" It was easy to get praise from the rest of the family, but it was his father's praise he wanted most, and he had tried in every way he knew to get it. He did his chores. He got all A's at school. He would have worked on the barrens if they had bought him a rake and let him. But the praise never came.

"You tell him," Laura said. Joel had always thought she was too proud of Jesse. Here was evidence, indisputable. Joel would have to be proud too. It might be a turning point for him, give him a new lease on life. After all, he was Jesse's father. "Go on," she urged, reaching for his dinner pail. "Run."

He grinned and started ahead.

She walked slowly up the drive, giving them plenty of time. When she reached the steps, she looked in the window and saw Joel playing cards as usual at the kitchen table. He had grown to look considerably older, for though his hair had not grayed, his skin had. He was thin and his stoop made him seem smaller than he was. Jesse was standing beside him—proud, anxious, eager.

Just as she came to the door, Jesse was opening the cover of his geography. "Look, Pa," he said. "I've got something to show you. Look."

Joel looked. Then, his face expressionless, he turned back to his cards again. "So what?" he said.

They ate supper in silence. No one ate much. As soon as they got up from the table Laura picked up Jesse's geography, which he had laid on the shelf. "Take your award over and show it to Mr. Pettigrew," she said. He hesitated. The excitement was gone now. He wasn't sure he wanted to show it to anyone. "Come on," she said. "Hurry off."

When the dishes were done, she got out Joel's big boots and started to put them on.

"Haven't you worked enough today?" Joel asked, watching. He meant by his concern to show that he was sorry for the way he had acted. She knew it, but she did not soften. This time he had gone too far.

"I'm used to work," she said, picking up her mackinaw. She said it coolly but without self-pity. She had felt self-pity once, but it had died when Luther did. Besides, she liked work. Over the years it had been her salvation.

Not that it had always been easy for her. In the factory, she had stood all day and picked the fish from the conveyor belt. First she had snipped off their heads and tails, which she threw into a square hole in the bench leading to a chute below. Next, she had packed them—first, head ends, then tail ends, then reversing the order. At the start she had done only a hundred cans an hour, for, like all the new girls, she often cut herself or got a bone in her finger, but gradually, when fish were abundant, she had been able to work up to two hundred. She hated the noise and the smell that she could never wash from her fingers. But there had been people to talk to, laughter, things going on all the time. When the berries were ripe, she would have raked had she not been afraid it would upset Joel. He had stood it less than a day, she remembered.

"Couldn't the work wait?"

The work could, but she couldn't. She couldn't stand staying in the house with him any longer. It was bad enough for him to snap at Jesse the way he had been doing. But to say a thing like that!

Actually, nothing needed to be done outside. But she had to find something, some way to exhaust the sudden energy her anger brought. Now that the mill wasn't running, they banked not with sawdust but with evergreen boughs. These should stay on another week at least. But she had to do something that required violence. So she began to pull them off. She had forgotten her gloves, and she would not go back in for them. Pitch clung to her hands and stiffened them. But she was barely conscious of it.

Shame on him, she thought. Shame. Shame.

Dried spills cut into her palms and jabbed painfully under her nails. They went up her sleeves, into her shoes, from her hands to her hair, then down the neck of her mackinaw, prickling and scratching. Yet she kept on yanking, dragging off one brittle bough after another and piling them behind the shed where Joel's father could burn them someday when it rained.

When one side of the house was all but cleared, she looked unintentionally toward the window where, through the gathering dusk, she saw a white, wretched face, watching her.

Her love, less electric, more fluctuating than once it had been, was still strong enough to dissolve her anger.

I must be more patient, she thought.

3

The next day, while Laura was doing up the dishes and Joel was playing cards as usual, they heard a car coming. "It's Doris and Ed," Laura said, looking out. The truck was twelve years old now. One fender was gone completely; the tailgate was supported by haywire; the running board had almost rusted away. One side was its original black, though stained and scratched; the other was a bright green where Ed had started to paint the body and then abandoned the project. It ran, it seemed, by miracle. As it came closer, Laura could see Butch too. He lay decrepit across the entire seat, his head on Ed's knee, while Doris sat on a box in the back.

Joel swept the cards into the drawer. "Oh, damn," he said. He got up, took his mackinaw from a hook in the entry, and headed toward the back door. He didn't want to hear any more about how well things were going, how jobs were opening up left and right. Ed's high spirits had always irked him. The prospect of facing them now was more than he could bear.

"Wait, Joel."

"Not me."

"They'll feel hurt."

"Let them." His hand was already on the knob.

"But they'll see you."

"I'll wait in the shed."

The door of the shed had barely closed behind him before the truck turned into the yard.

Except that the roots of her hair were visibly darkened with tea, Doris had not changed at all. Nor had Ed. He had on a new plaid waistcoat—something no other man in Millboro would have worn—and Doris, a beret that matched it. They didn't seem at all like people burdened with a mortgage.

Greeting them, Laura felt a kind of admiration. "Sporty," she said, touching the plaid. She would not tell them yet about Jesse. The wound must heal a little.

Ed laughed and winked at Doris. "Birds of a feather," he said. They went into the kitchen where he deposited Butch upon the sofa. Doris sat down by the table and took off her glasses, as she always did when she faced a mirror. "Joel round?" Ed asked.

"No. He's outside. He'll be sorry."

"Guess I'll hunt him up while yer two chew the rag."

"Oh, have a cup of tea with us," Laura urged, hurrying to move the kettle forward. She must hold him if she could.

174

He dismissed the tea with a gesture and started out. Butch made an attempt to get on his feet and follow, but the effort was too much. Ed picked him up and put him on the sofa again, scratching his obese, almost hairless belly.

"Come on. Change your mind," Laura pleaded. But his hand was already on the doorknob.

"Don't be long," Doris called after him. "We're on the run, remember."

Laura set out two cups and saucers. "How's Flora?" she asked. Flora still dressed in black, still talked constantly about Luther. A number of people had suggested, cautiously, that she might relieve Harry sometimes in the store, but they got nowhere. She had given up all her clubs, all her causes, having no time for them now, she claimed. Yet, when she wasn't getting herself little lunches, she only sat idle and, as a result, had become massive. Her one activity was her Sunday-school class, which was shrinking in numbers week by week.

"Guess what she's up to now?"

"I couldn't."

"You know Annie Pettingill." Annie Pettingill was Flora's devoteé, the one girl in her Sunday-school class who had stayed with her from the first. She lived on a farm near 'Tit Manan with six brothers and sisters. "Flora's going to take her in."

"As a hired girl?"

Doris laughed cynically. "So she says. But it's as clear as the nose on your face that she's got other plans."

Laura carefully measured out the tea in the pot and poured the water over it. "You don't mean Harry?"

"Who else?"

"I wouldn't be too sure," Laura said. There had been a real change in Harry. His high boyish color had faded. His chest had filled out and his shoulders broadened. Away from home, his speech was almost normal. He had a warmth, too, that he had never had before—a warmth and an understanding. Harry had heard Joel in his delirium, yet he had never asked a question. To anyone who questioned him, he had given the same story. Joel's car had gone bad on the road. He had to spend the night there.

"Bet you twenty dollars."

"Haven't got it." Laura filled the cups, then glanced uneasily out the window. Ed was safely away from the shed and headed toward the graveyard.

With the mention of money, Doris remembered why she had come. "You know that undeveloped land down the road a piece? On the left-hand side? Where you take the road to Sullivan?"

Laura nodded.

"Well, I can tell you on the Q.T. that it'll go for taxes. Two hundred dollars would take it. If 'twas developed, 'twould be worth a lot. I thought maybe you'd want to know."

Laura looked thoughtful. If only they could buy it. The barrens were in her blood now—the colors, the silence, the far-off hills, the shadows of the big clouds racing. She quickened before a storm just the way the birds did. Besides, she was practical. Undeveloped land in the long run meant money. But there was no use thinking of it.

"Thanks, Doris, but we haven't anything ahead."

"How about Joel's father?"

"We've borrowed too much from him already." He had never considered the money a loan, she knew. He would never even have given her the slips from the store unless she had threatened to get duplicates from Harry.

" 'Twouldn't hurt to ask."

Laura shook her head. They couldn't take any more. Joel would never stand for it. She knew the mortification he had already suffered. Twice when she had come into the kitchen unexpectedly she had caught him adding up the figures she had put on the calendar.

"Well, keep it in mind."

"I will." She refilled Doris's cup. "What's the news in town?"

For half an hour Doris told it while Laura tried to keep from looking outside. Then the door opened and Ed came back in. "Must of been quite a walk Joel was takin'," he said. "I covered the hull place. Couldn't be he was duckin' me, could it?"

Laura gave him a pleading look. She couldn't lie to Ed. "He doesn't mean it, Ed. He's different now." That was what she had impressed upon Jesse. "You must make allowances for Pa," she had told him. "Pa's gone through a lot."

"Sure," Ed said, patting her arm. "Sure thing."

Doris shrugged her shoulders, got up, and put on her glasses. "If he was my husband, I'd take him to a head doctor," she said.

4

Laura woke early, smelling smoke. Someone was burning his land. She got up and looked out the window. It was a clear morning and so still that she could not tell which way the wind was blowing. She reached for her clothes and began to dress.

Hearing her, Joel stirred, opened his eyes, and looked at the clock. It was twenty minutes to six. "What's the big idea?" he asked.

"I'm going to get your father," she told him. "He'll help us burn."

Joel sat up, frowning, and moved his shoulders to loosen the stiffness in them. "We can manage ourselves," he said. "We don't need him."

"But Joel—"

"Joel what?" he asked irritably, moving to the edge of the bed.

"Burning's dangerous, and with just us two—"

"What's the trouble with Jesse?"

"He can't stay out of school."

"It's Saturday, isn't it?"

It was. She had forgotten. But Jesse wasn't quite nine. She hesitated, holding a shoe.

"He's supposed to be so smart."

She let that pass. "But even with us three—" She had always been nervous about fires. She never relaxed during a burn, no matter how distant, and she got up two or three times a night to look out the window when one was over. She even worried about matches, keeping them in a tin box, and never allowed the draft of the cookstove to be kept wide open.

"In a couple of hours," Joel said, "there'll be men all over the place."

She put on her shoes slowly. Aside from the danger of fire, there were other things to consider. For their first burn, Joel's father had drawn the pipe, setting the backfire. It was a hard job dragging it over the ruts and hummocks, too hard a job for Joel. Yet, for the sake of his pride, she didn't dare suggest that she herself do it. She went to the window again. The smoke in the distance was rising slowly, drifting to the north. That meant a south wind, which was what they needed. Yet . . .

"Your father offered," she said.

"What of it?" Normally he got up slowly, glum and grimacing, but now he was out of bed and reaching for his underwear. He had been acting badly, he knew. He ought to have praised Jesse. He meant to, but something cut him off. It wasn't so much the boy's being smart, smarter than he was that did it, as the sight of him running, swinging his arms, having good news to bring. It made him more conscious than he had ever been before of his own fingers that he could never

178

straighten, his own burning feet that no shoes could fit, his own lack of accomplishment. Here was a chance to redeem himself with both Laura and Jesse. He wanted very much to be in their favor again.

"Go call the boy," he said.

Laura hesitated.

It wasn't the thing to do, she was sure. Yet here was Joel wanting to work, believing he could. He had not shown this much initiative in years.

She went to the foot of the stairs. "Jesse, wake up. We're going to burn for berries today."

She delayed breakfast as long as she could, reluctant to begin until there were men in the area, and did the dishes, giving the sink a special scrubbing. " 'Twill be quicker getting dinner if the kitchen's straightened up," she argued when they told her to hurry. Then she went from window to window, stuffing paper in the cracks. That done, she took a long time tying a bandana around her head and putting on one of Joel's old shirts and a pair of his trousers. True, they had only six acres to burn, but it was the land the trees grew on. And any fire was dangerous.

Joel and Jesse were waiting on the steps. "Your mother's scared to burn," Joel said with a nudge.

Jesse laughed delightedly. His father had never nudged him before. It seemed such an intimate, grown-up thing that he forgot the wound he was bearing.

"She's afraid we'll burn up the graveyard."

They both laughed together.

Listening, Laura felt a little piqued. You bring up a boy alone, she thought. You give him all your time. You wash for him, cook for him, take care of him when he's sick. You answer his questions. Then just let—"Who's pulling the pipe?" she asked abruptly.

179

"Who do you think?"

The pique was still there. Let him pull, she thought. Let him try. "It's in the shed," she told him. "So are the rags and kerosene."

She turned to Jesse. "Get things together," she said.

He brought out the brooms and pails. She filled the pails from the well, then covered the brooms with burlap bags and drenched them.

Joel came out with the pipe and headed toward the back of the field. "Come on," he shouted. Jesse, carrying the shovels, followed him.

"Shouldn't we start the backfire around the house?" Laura called.

"No," Joel called back over his shoulder. "It's the trees we have to watch."

"But your father—last time . . ."

Joel turned and faced her. "Who's doing this? You or me?"

"All right," she said. "Go ahead." After all, he should understand fires, she tried to tell herself, remembering that he had worked in the woods. He had told her about fires—surface fires, duff fires, crown fires, spot fires. What was a blueberry burn compared to them?

Jesse dropped the shovels at the foot of the field, then came back to help her with the pails of water.

"Listen, Jesse," she said, "and I'll tell you how—"

"I know how." He did know, for year after year he had watched the big burns on the barrens, watched the flames licking the bushes, watched the men keeping guard, shovels in their hands and tanks on their backs while, from a safe distance, he had breathed in the pungent smoke. He wished he had a tank instead of just a pail of water.

"You and I will follow Pa to put out—"

"I know, Ma. You don't have to tell me."

By the time they had carried all the brooms and pails to the foot of the field, Joel had lit the wick and was already moving.

180

The fire did not start easily. Tiny, matchlike flames sprang up here and there, gutted and died.

"The hay's too wet," Joel shouted.

"Let's wait awhile," she said, relieved. The smoke from the early-morning fire was spreading, but so far no other one had begun. She could hear only their own voices.

But Joel persisted, and after a few yards the wick touched a bed of dried twigs. A flame appeared, wavered, and grew. Another followed. Then another, creeping into the hay. Black smoke streamed up. Watching it, Laura saw that the wind was shifting and her eye went anxiously toward the little pine trees.

"The wind, Joel," she called.

She saw him put his finger in his mouth, then hold it up before him.

"The wind's all right," he shouted back.

The flame, steady now, crept out and spread. Joel went on. Laura and Jesse waited, brooms raised and ready.

Where Joel was, the hay seemed drier. Flames moved quickly, darting in every direction. The smoke was thick, and looking up from her beating, Laura saw that it almost obscured the house. She listened again for voices and could hear none.

"Don't go so fast, Joel," she called. "We can't keep up."

He did not answer. The fact that he was moving fast, that he could do what he had tried to do, had gone to his head. He was running things. He was boss. He was giving the orders here. He had started the fire and he could control it. When his father came, ready to do the job, it would all be done.

We don't need your help. We're on our feet, see. We won't have to eat your food any longer. We won't have to burn the wood you fit."

"Joel."

You're going to get that money back. Every cent of it. Every red—

"Joel."

"I hear you."

"Answer, then. And don't go so fast."

A surge of flame came toward her, and she beat it out. The wind was certainly changing. It was stronger, too. Once the backfire was out, there would be no more burning that day, she determined. She would put her foot down.

"Are you getting all of it, Jesse?"

"Sure, Ma."

"Even the sparks?"

"I guess so." It was hot work. The wet brooms were heavy, and the burlap, loosening, had made them ungainly. He took off his sweater and tied it around his waist.

The smoke grew thicker, smarting their eyes. Laura wiped her sleeve across her forehead, and it came away blackened. Jesse started to cough.

"Joel," Laura shouted, without daring to look up, "you'll have to slow down."

Ahead—too far ahead—the whole edge of the field was burning, a low, struggling sheet of flame. The smoke thickened. It filled Jesse's throat and made him strangle.

"Get away, Jesse. Go into the house."

But he did not go. He felt that by siding with his father, he had gone back on his mother somehow, and he would not leave her, no matter what. Instead, he covered his mouth with one hand and kept on beating with the other. But the beating was not effective now. More sparks snapped into flames.

Laura worked faster. She must get them all.

Beat.

Wet.

Beat—Beat—

But she couldn't get them all.

They kept coming to life again, slipping away, growing. If she emptied her pails, she would have no water to soak the brooms in. She couldn't leave to go back to the well.

"Joel. Wait."

No, we don't need any help from you. Not a thing any longer. So stay away. See.

"Joel. Stop."

He kept right on moving. They had thought he couldn't do it. Well, he could. His legs were working. So were his arms and fingers. They thought he was a cripple. A good-for-nothing. Finished. But he wasn't. He was running. Flying, almost— spreading fire. Let them put it out. Let them worry. Let *them* catch up with *him* for a change.

"Stop, Joel. Stop, I tell you. *Stop.*"

There was alarm in her voice now, and he heard it. He turned, looked, and, seeing the spreading fire, he dropped the pipe, turned back, and seized a broom from Jesse. Together he and Laura beat out the flames.

When they were out, Laura straightened and wiped her sleeve across her eyes. "We're through," she said. They ought never to have started. She should have put her foot down. Joel was exhausted. His face was streaked with smoke and twisted with pain. She could hear Jesse cough, but the smoke was so thick she could not see him.

But she saw something else.

Joel had dropped the pipe, but he had not put it out. Now a new fire had started and was moving rapidly with the wind toward the shed.

Seizing her broom and pail, Laura ran toward it. Joel started after her.

A flying spark touched the pile of dried boughs from the banking and it burst into flame.

Laura reached it first and drenched it with the water that was left in her pail. The flame faded, sizzled, then started up again.

All the things Joel knew about fire left him. Surrounded by it, he stood still for an instant in panic, then stripped off his jacket and began to beat the low, creeping flames, only fanning them higher.

183

"Jesse," Laura screamed. "Jesse."

He was there, choking, carrying two pails of water. "Go ring the big bell," she told him. "Go. Hurry. Fast."

5

The fire had done no real damage, for two men, hearing the bell, had come running with their tanks. The steps had been a little charred, and some sparks blown to the roof of the shed had burned a small hole there. But to Joel it was another humiliation. He grew more depressed.

All the latter part of April rain fell, keeping him inside. He played cards from breakfast until bedtime. He had always played carelessly; now he barely looked at the cards he held. One. Two. Three. Four. Five. Six. Seven . . . One. Two. Three. . . .

Red Jack on black Queen.

Black Queen on red King . . .

Laura had come to hate the foolish, empty faces, even the colors red and black, wherever she saw them.

The dampness had worsened his rheumatism so that he could not tie his shoelaces, and because he would not allow anyone to help him, he went about with them flapping.

Shuffle. Slap, swinging his foot . . .

Shuffle. Slap. Flap. Flap.

And always the whistle.

And she had once thought she had no nerves, Laura remembered.

At meals he seldom spoke except to criticize the food. When callers came, he left the room openly making no secret now of his departure. The only one he stayed to see was Harry. Joel respected Harry, and well he might. For five years now Harry had been struggling alone to keep the business going, doing the delivering himself after the store was closed at night, then getting up before five every morning so that he could sweep out and get the place in order by seven. He had taken no salary. On Wednesday afternoons he drove his mother somewhere or worked under her direction on the cemetery lot, or came out to see Joel. Yet he was always patient, always kind. Joel talked almost like his old self with Harry. But with everyone else who came he was sharp and bitter. He shaved irregularly, went to bed early, slept little, and rose late. The only time he spoke pleasantly to Jesse was when he had something he wanted Laura to hear.

Nag, nag, Jesse. That's a woman for you.

Give up, boy. You may as well.

As Laura listened, her patience thinned sometimes to the point where she was ready to shout an answer. *What about the rest of us? What kind of life are you making for us?* Then she would see his hands, remember again their touch on her breast, and soften.

She welcomed spring cleaning. If only she could redo the whole place. Paint had peeled from the floor of the kitchen, especially near the thresholds and in the path of the rocker. Steam had loosened the paper, making blisters around the stove and sink. In the bedroom, the pink morning glories were almost indistinguishable from the blue. In the sitting room, rain seeping in had left long irregular stains beneath the sills. Joel's father wanted to redecorate for her, even paint the outside of the house. But she dared not allow it.

Even after all they had gone through together, Laura knew little more about Joel's father than she had known before. Pressed by Jesse, he would talk now and then about his experiences at sea.

But he never spoke of anything personal, and the core of the

185

trouble between him and Joel was as much of a mystery as ever. Once or twice Laura had started to question him, but his reserve, though not hostile, was as impenetrable as Joel's. In town his past had been generally forgotten. Prohibition was only a memory, a source of old jokes beginning to wear thin.

One day early in May he came out to bring them some fish. He had changed a good deal in the last five years. His paunch was gone, and so was the hair he had combed so carefully across his bald spot. His hands, once soft from lack of manual labor, were as hard now as those of any man in Millboro. Joel waited until his car was in the dooryard, then, sure that he was seen, started off over the barrens.

Laura met him at the door. "Hello, Mr. Closson," she said, wiping her hands on her apron.

"Brought yer some fish." He held out a long limp package wrapped in newspaper.

"Why, thanks."

"Jest cod."

"We like it as well as haddock. Come in. Let me get you a cup of tea." She knew he would refuse. Except when Jesse was there, he never sat down. He might lean against the pump occasionally, or linger in the entry, but that was all.

"Had one jest before I left."

"But have another with me."

"No, no. Don't bother."

You've bothered enough for us, she wanted to answer, but she knew it would embarrass him, maybe scare him away.

"Can't you even stop?" Days seemed long now, yet for Jesse's own sake she was relieved that he could be in school.

"Jest long enough ter split up some wood. Might 'swell, now I'm here."

They went outside, and he worked without speaking while she made a pretense of cleaning up the garden. "Mr. Closson," she finally said, her voice troubled, "what can I do about Joel?"

186

A change came over his face, but he gave no other sign of hearing.

"I'm at my wit's end."

Eyes averted from her, he picked up another stick. "I'm ter blame," he said in a low voice. He split the stick and tiered it. Then he drove the ax in the block. "I hadn't oughter of took him that night," he said, looking off in the direction Joel had gone. "I was set agin it. But he threw somethin' up in my face. Yer see, I stopped him once from doin' somethin'. Somethin' awful important ter him." His voice changed abruptly. "Think likely this will last yer till I git out agin?" he asked.

Hanging the clean curtains in the sitting room, Laura heard a car coming and, looking out, saw Harry turn into the drive. This was Tuesday. That meant he had closed the store. Before he had parked or even stopped completely, Flora opened the door and started to get out. At first Laura could hardly believe it was Flora, for over her head, in place of the usual black felt hat with its heavy veil, was a small brown shawl that had hung for years in the kitchen entry. The coat had hung there too, Laura remembered. That meant they had left in a hurry.

"It's Flora," she called to Joel.

"Jesus," he said disgustedly, and started outside.

Laura hurried to the front door. Flora was the only caller who used it. "Well, hello," she called while Harry was helping his mother alight. It took all his strength just to steady her.

"Nice day, Laura," Harry said over his shoulder.

Concentrating on her descent, Flora gave no greeting. Inside, she sank in the big leather chair, breathing heavily.

"You all right now, Ma?" Harry asked.

She nodded and began to unbutton her coat.

Laura stood, waiting to take it. "Joel's around. He'll want to see you," she said to Harry. What was it? she wondered. It must be important if they closed up the store.

"I'll hunt him up," Harry said, striding out through the kitchen.

Laura took Flora's coat and laid it on the sofa. By that time, though she had not entirely recovered her breath, Flora began speaking. "You'll never guess. You'll never believe . . ." She covered her face with her hands, her voice fading.

"Believe what? What is it, Flora?"

"What *she's* done now."

Laura relaxed a little. What had Doris done? What could she have done with so little money?

Flora's features, so long dulled with grief, became alive with anger. "She's let it go."

"Let what go, Flora?"

Flora looked impatient. "The house," she said. "What else? And she didn't even tell me. When Annie went by this morning, she saw the sign. I've had a premonition—"

"You mean—" Laura said, still not understanding.

"The 'For Sale' sign the bank put up," Flora said irritably. "Can't you understand? She mortgaged the place and deliberately let it go. The Leighton place. Our home." She wiped her eyes roughly and her voice grew hard again. "I always knew something like this would happen when she married that foreigner. That Catholic."

Laura said nothing. About the house, she cared little. What really concerned her was the fact that Doris and Ed did not have the money to prevent foreclosure. She thought of their extravagance, their waste. But most of all she thought of their generosity, of the presents they had given Jesse. A year ago Christmas it had been a printing press, last Christmas, a microscope. She had tried to refuse it. She had insisted that if Doris would not return it, she herself would. But Ed had been disappointed. And Jesse had wanted it so much. Still, she ought to have insisted. She ought to have realized then.

"Our house," Flora repeated with such vehemence that the

shawl she wore over her head fell back on her shoulders. "Our house. Mama's home."

"But it was their house, Flora. You sold it to them."

"For next to nothing," Flora said bitterly.

"But it was your price. You agreed."

This was something Flora preferred to ignore. "And think how they let it go. You know as well as I do. You have seen it. No paint. The shutters falling off. The step broken down. And heaven only knows what's happened inside. She's never let me upstairs."

Keeping-Flora-From-Going-Upstairs was a game Doris had played with relish for years. It meant keeping the front door locked, the hall filled with furniture, and the use of a good deal of agility besides. Actually, things upstairs were in no worse a state than those down, but the procedure gratified Doris's desire both to frustrate Flora and be mysterious as well.

"To think that the Leighton place . . ." No one had ever called it the Levesque place. It took several generations to change the name of a place in Millboro. "I remember Grammie Blodgett thinking no place could ever be good enough for Mama. But she liked the Leighton place. If she and Mama could ever know . . ." She began to bring up the past. Grandfather Leighton had cut the timber from the back pasture and sawed it in his own mill. Grammie Leighton had picked out the parlor furniture at Jordan Marsh's and brought it home on the *Mildred Mae*. Grammie herself had made braided rugs for every room in the house. Mama had brought all of the Blodgett china. The price hadn't really included the china. Doris understood that perfectly well at the time.

Laura interrupted her. "But if they didn't have the money to keep it," she said, thinking not of the Leightons and the Blodgetts but of Doris and Ed.

Flora blew her nose. "They've been throwing money away left and right. Everybody knows it. Besides, they could have saved it if they had had a mind to. They could have sold the truck."

"But it isn't worth anything, Flora. It's a wonder it runs at all."

"Or if they'd even come and told me," Flora went on. "But going behind my back. . . ."

"But you've been so upset, Flora."

"They should have come anyway. Now, the public disgrace of it. A mortgage was bad enough. But letting the place go. . . . If Mama knew. . . ." She blew her nose again vigorously.

"People don't think about those things the way they used to," Laura said lamely.

"I do. Mama would." Tears filled Flora's eyes and rolled down her fat cheeks. "There's only one thing to do," she went on, speaking with difficulty. "I'm going to the bank and buy it back."

"But can you afford to, Flora?"

"I'll use Luther's insurance money." Luther was one of the few men in Millboro who carried insurance. "You know what he used to say."

Laura nodded. He carried it, he used to say, so that if he went first, Flora would have peace of mind.

Flora reached in her purse and took out another handkerchief. Her hands were so puffed that her wedding ring appeared imbedded in her flesh. The doctor had warned her that it must be filed off, but she had refused to listen. "I'd never have any peace of mind seeing Mama's place go to a stranger."

"But what about Doris and Ed? You wouldn't put them out?" Laura asked anxiously.

"No, I wouldn't," Flora granted. "Though I ought to, goodness knows. They can stay if, after I get the place fixed up, they will keep it that way." She rose and adjusted her head shawl. "At least the house will still be in the family."

They walked in silence through the hall.

Her hand on the latch of the screen door, Flora spoke again. "I should have expected you to have more feeling about this, Laura," she said severely.

Laura colored. "I do have feeling, Flora, but you took me by surprise." Reassured about Doris and Ed, her mind had moved to Joel and Harry. She could hear no voices. It couldn't be that he had run away from Harry. It couldn't. But if he had. . . .

Harry appeared from around the side of the house, nonchalantly whittling.

"Where's Joel?" Flora demanded.

"Guess he didn't know I was here," Harry said quickly. He closed the blade of his knife and hurried to open the door of the car. "Say hello for me, Laurie."

Flora gave a cluck of disgust. "Why you were bound and determined to marry a fellow like that," she said, turning again to Laura as she lifted a portly foot to the running board, "is beyond my understanding."

6

Every day after the first of June Laura inspected the blueberry vines that would bear. They were sturdy and heavily budded. By the middle of the month the buds had become blossoms. Bees were everywhere.

"If we can avoid fruit flies," Laura said to Jesse, "we should have a real good crop." She had heard a great deal about fruit flies and the damage they caused. The year before they moved to the barrens, so people told her, there had been a heavy infestation, and fifty thousand bushels of berries had been abandoned there. Recently she and Jesse had been reading the bulletins from the state agricultural department, studying how to control such pests.

"Don't kill any ants or spiders," Jesse warned her. "They kill the flies."

But Laura had heard of another control. One of the bulletins had told about a spray of calcium arsenate being tried. Why couldn't we try it too? she thought. It didn't cost much. She spoke to Joel about it.

"What would you think?" she asked.

"I never think," he answered.

The next time his father came out, she spoke to him, explaining the spray. "We ought to have a cart and horse to put it on, but on our little piece don't you suppose we could do it by hand?"

"A-yuh," he said. "We could do it easy."

They began just as the berries were ripening. Joel could have helped too, for the tanks they rented were light and portable. He could easily have managed one partially filled, going at his own speed, but he made no move and showed no interest. Jesse wanted to help, but he was not allowed to because of the poison in the spray.

They worked early in the morning while the wind was down and the dew still on the vines, stirring up a chipmunk or two, a few crows, and now and then a flurry of butterflies. They worked rapidly and without talking. Laura had come to feel at ease with Joel's father and to accept his silences. But since their talk about Joel, the silences had a tension in them, giving Laura a feeling all the time that he was about to tell her something. Once he paused in his work, and she paused, waiting while the muscles of his throat tightened and his lips moved as if they were seeking words to begin. But when the words came, they were commonplace.

"Good crop this year."

The next day he hardly spoke at all. Every sound seemed

louder to her. The birds' songs. The rustle of the vines against their feet. The click of the pump and the hiss of the spray. It seemed as though she could almost hear the beat of their wings as the crows passed over.

When they had reached the very end of the land, he turned and faced her. She waited while he shifted the strap of his tank from one shoulder to the other. Still he was silent, his eyes on the buckle.

"You wanted to say something, Mr. Closson?"

He started to move away. "Jest 'bout red leaf," he said quickly. "None here ter worry yer." Red leaf was what operators dreaded most, for a plant, once struck, spread the infection before it died.

But it was not about red leaf, she knew, that he had wanted to talk.

Summer went on—hot days, cool nights. Good weather for tourists. All along the coast, hotels registered guests and began looking for lobsters to feed them. A whisky dealer from Cleveland bought a piece of land on one of the coves, so recently a haven for rumrunners, and started to build a cottage, employing fourteen Millboro men. Harry's business picked up considerably.

In town sociability revived. The Sidewalk Society gave a cooked-food and candy sale. The W.C.T.U.—the wind taken out of their sails by repeal—had turned cultural and brought in a folk singer, selling tickets at twenty-five cents. Forty-two people turned out. Church attendance grew. Now and then a quarter would show up among the nickels and dimes on the collection plate. The sardine factory was running. Laura did not work there again, for she felt too uneasy about leaving Joel. Besides, the berries looked good, and with what she got from them, she could manage.

She had already arranged for the sale of their crop. At Mr. Pettigrew's suggestion, she had also seen the operator on the land adjoining theirs, who agreed to let her use his winnower and a few of his baskets and boxes after his crew laid off at four. She had bought three rakes, secondhand.

Joel was sitting as usual at the kitchen table when she told him her plans. "Doris and Ed will rake too." She waited. "Since we won't have to work in the sun, we ought to be able to stand it a few hours at a time," she went on, watching his face.

He said nothing.

"Jesse can carry the baskets and help us load the truck."

Scoop. Shuffle. One. Two. Three. Four. Five. Six. Seven. Whistle.

"I thought you could run the winnower."

One. Two. Three. S-S-S-S—

"Joel?"

"I heard you," he said without looking up.

On a morning in July when the berries were just beginning to ripen, Jesse sat alert and ready for action on one of the low, flat ledges. On his right was a crumpled strip of red and white oilcloth that had once covered the long shelf in the kitchen. On his left were two doughnuts grabbed from the jar in the cellarway. The morning fog had not quite lifted.

He was waiting for the gulls. A few gulls always came inland, but this year, with the berries large and plentiful from so much fog and rain, they had been coming in greater numbers, plundering the best patches. Whirligigs did little good. It was Mr. Pettigrew who had suggested the oilcloth. "Wave it hard an' high," he said. "They wunt take ter the noise nor the shine." So his mother had found this piece in the bottom of the rag bag and given him the responsibility of trying it out. It was his first real family responsibility, his first chance to show he was growing up.

The ledge where he sat was his favorite. He always stopped and sat there for a time when he was out hunting for flowers—

violets, lady's tobacco, dandelions, wild stawberry blossoms, all dwarfed and short-stemmed, but so rare that each one must be treasured. It was the place he came to watch the animals, keeping as still as a statue, just as the fawns did when they saw him. His favorites were the rabbits with their long quivering ears, the chipmunks with their tails held high and rigid, and the little field mice with their beady eyes, always busy. He had no use at all for their enemies, the foxes, though they made a handsome sight.

That ledge was his listening ledge. Sometimes he lay there listening to the grasshoppers among the vines and grasses. When he was small he had caught them between his hands and chanted a rhyme:

> Grandfather, Grandfather, Grandfather Gray,
> Give me some molasses and I'll let you away.

But his mother had never liked the idea of the molasses and scolded him when she saw it on his hands.

He listened to the birds there too—wrens, robins, sparrows —liking them best in the fall when they got together on their way south. They covered the dead trees then like apples or plums, and they sang in a chorus so loud that it almost hurt his ears. He listened to the wild geese, though never very long at a time, because they made him feel lonesome. But most of the time he listened to the crows. He'd listened to them so much that he often thought he knew their language and that they knew his. (He didn't dread seeing just one crow any longer, for Mr. Pettigrew had told him he had only to count ten before the crow was out of sight and in that way he could escape the sorrow.)

But he had never liked the gulls. They were trespassers. They didn't care a thing about the barrens, the way the other birds did. They just came for what they could get. He was glad he had a chance to drive them back where they belonged.

Scanning the sky, he found it empty, so he relaxed a bit and began to eat a doughnut. If he did a good job, Ma and Mr. Jim would be proud of him. Maybe even Pa. He could never stay mad at Pa, and he didn't know why. Pa wouldn't care if he did. Not a single thing he ever did suited Pa. Remembering, his face sobered. He laid the doughnut he was eating on the ledge with the other and wiped his fingers on his pants.

The fog had completely lifted. The sun was bright now and sending out warmth. There were cobwebs on the ground. That meant it would be a good day. He got up and looked at the sky again, turning squarely in each direction. North. East. South. West. Again he saw nothing, only blue space with mist and clouds mixing together. Maybe he was too early, he thought. He sat down, picked up his doughnut, and finished it.

Then from far off he heard a thin, shrill call. Looking toward the east, he saw three gulls coming, dipping and coasting, looking the situation over. He jumped up, grabbed the oilcloth, and stood ready to leap from ledge to ledge, remembering that he must avoid the vines as much as he could.

The gulls took their time. Curving, climbing, dropping.

He was ready for them.

They came closer.

"Git," he screamed, waving his banner. "Git out a here." It wasn't good English, but it was good enough for a gull. "Git. Git."

They swooped, fluttered, lighted quite near him, bold as brass.

"Git. You hear me. Git, I say."

Slowly they rose and drifted away.

It had been easy. There was nothing to it, really. No need to buy whirligigs while he was there. He began to eat the other doughnut.

Then all of a sudden they were back. Not just three. Four more had come from somewhere. He dropped his doughnut and got on his feet again. The sun had broken through now and glittered on his oilcloth.

"Git. Git. You hear me."

Ten at least. One brushed against his leg and grabbed what was left of his doughnut. "Git. Git, I say. Now git. Skidoo." They were lighting all around him. He leaped. He slipped, for the ledges were farther apart than he had realized. He waved. He screamed. "Git, you gulls. You hear me. Now git. Git. Go back where you belong."

But they didn't go back. They kept right on coming, settling in great churning rafts on the best patches, their screams drowning out his own. Now and then a rough wing would touch his shoulders, or his head, or his arm, tired now from jerking the heavy weight.

Yet he kept on. He was responsible. He wasn't a child any longer. He had said he would drive them off. He had promised his mother. He would show her. He would show Pa. Even if he was a little scared.

"Git. Git." He leaped faster and faster. He threshed with both his arms. But they kept coming. Sometimes just the wind from their wings all but knocked him over. They screamed. He screamed. Now and then a crow would join in noisily. *Ca-ah. Ca-ah.*

But he wouldn't give up. "Git. Git. You hear me. Git. Skidoo." He waved until the cramp in his arm was so great that he almost dropped the oilcloth. Then all at once they rose together and flew away, making a big white bristling cloud.

Hot and exhausted, but triumphant, he sat down to wait for more.

On the first day of August when the berries were dead ripe, hanging in great pendant clusters, Doris and Ed arrived late in the afternoon, ready for raking, and went on ahead to make a bed for Butch under one of the little pines. Jesse had already gone for the baskets. Laura went inside to call Joel, who had disappeared upstairs.

"Ready?" she called from the hallway.

He did not answer.

"Ready, Joel?"

"Ready for what?"

"For winnowing."

"What's that got to do with me?"

"But you said—"

"*You* said," he reminded her.

She stood a moment, flushed with anger. The work at the winnower was easy. Anyone could do it. He wouldn't even have to lift the baskets, for Jesse could do that for him. All he would have to do was pour and wait. "All right," she said. She picked up the rakes and went outside.

On the adjoining land, only an operator and a few isolated rakers, delaying to fill a final basket, were in sight. Near the winnower a great block of flat boxes, evenly filled, was waiting the truck's return.

"Where's Joel?" Doris asked. She was bending over a patch of berries, dressed in a pair of Ed's trousers, rolled up at the knee, and, like Ed himself, in a T-shirt bearing the insignia of the local ball team. Her mouth was blue already.

"Not coming."

"Not coming?" Doris echoed and looked at Ed, who was juggling two of the baskets.

A look passed between them. Simultaneously they shrugged their shoulders.

Flushing, Laura handed each of them a rake. "Jesse can do it," she said.

As she worked, Laura felt her tensions lessen. The sun was warm on her shoulders; there was just enough breeze to keep the bugs away. The rhythm itself was soothing. Bend, rake, straighten, with a look at the hills or at Jesse standing proudly at the winnower. Bend, rake, straighten, and all the time company—talk, jokes, laughter. (How long had it been since she had laughed? she wondered.) To be sure, there was an ache in the back of her knees and between her shoulders, but what of it? It was their own land she was raking. The berries were their own. She herself had sprayed them.

She began to figure what she would buy when the money came in. Shoes for Joel and Jesse. Maybe, if the crop was as good as it looked, long trousers for Jesse's birthday. Wood. Kerosene. Sugar. Molasses. Eggs to pickle. Beef to corn. Whatever was left would be put aside for Jesse's education.

She thought of him at college. On the campus, wearing a sweater with the numbers '42. (She had figured that out by the time he was three.) In the library, where there would be at least a thousand books to choose from. She saw him in the long line at graduation. Saw his diploma: *Jesse Closson, magna cum laude*. She would frame it, of course, and hang it above his science award in the sitting room. She saw him with an office in Bangor. *Jesse Closson M.D.* On the faculty at the university in Orono. *Professor Jesse Closson*. In Ellsworth, *Jesse Closson County Agricultural Agent*. That pleased her most. "I ought to know blueberries," he could say at county meetings. "I learned the business before I was nine."

Every time she filled her basket and took it to the winnower, threaded with grass and peppered with bunchberries, she stood smiling at his side. "Pretty smart, aren't we?"

"Pretty smart, Ma," he shouted above the roar of the fan and the scolding of gulls overhead.

One hundred bushels this year. Two hundred next. And with the rest of the land burned in the fall . . .

Here was a new venture. A new beginning.

Joel watched them from the window of the water closet. He had been dreading the raking. He didn't know which he had dreaded more, being in it or being out. They had expected him to run a machine, but when it came to machines he had a jinx on him. Just let him as much as lay his hand on one and it stopped working. Then somebody else would come along, do just what he had done, and it would start up, making a fool of him.

So now he was out.

He didn't want to look at them, and yet he looked. There she was, working first with one hand and then the other, keeping right at it, talking, laughing, just as if he didn't exist. There was Jesse at the winnower, quick, steady, never spilling a berry.

He didn't want to listen, yet he had to.

"Two bushels for Ma. One for Doris. Come on, Uncle Ed."

"Look here, Mr. Big Business. Ain't yer never heard a labor laws? I'm a-goin' ter sick the sheriff on yer."

Laughter.

Then Ed's high voice in a song:

> "Dis was de story of boy an' girl
> Dat's love each oder above de worl'
> But it's not easy job for mak' l'amour
> W'en de girl she's rich an' de boy he's poor. . . ."

More laughter. Laura had even laid down her rake to applaud. Once *he* had been a singer, Joel remembered. Once people had listened to *him*.

The misery that was chronic with him sharpened. *Failure. Burden.* He looked down at his hands, his twisted joints, his drawn-up fingers.

Suddenly the smell of the lye can in the corner struck him sharply. He groped for the door and went outside.

At seven o'clock the wind went down and the bugs grew vicious. It was time to lay off, Laura decided. While the rest of them loaded the truck, she sent Jesse in to get a fire going. It was hard to think of supper then.

She watched them off. Blue hands. Blue mouths. Blue stains

on their knees. Even Butch showed blue, his pink belly stained from the patch where he had been lying.

"By. Thanks. By."

"Ta-ta."

"See you tomorrow."

She stood for a minute or two looking over the land—the land that was going to get them back on their feet again. Then she started up the steps.

As soon as she opened the door, she knew something had happened. Joel and Jesse were there in the kitchen, standing with their backs to her. She stood a moment, silent.

Then, "Hello," she said.

Neither answered.

She waited and then spoke again. "Jesse."

"A-yuh."

"I'm talking to you."

"I hear."

"Look at me, then."

He turned slowly and, as he did, she saw a rising red mark across his face.

"What's that?" she asked sharply.

"What's what?"

"That mark on your face."

His eyes evaded hers. "From the winnower. The belt kicked," he said.

It was a lie, and she knew it. She stood silent, waiting for Joel to speak, but he said nothing.

Her voice sharpened. "Get yourself washed, Jesse. It's suppertime."

"I don't want any supper."

"Then go up to your room," she told him.

Sitting on the edge of his bed, Jesse undressed slowly. He was still hot, and his clothes stuck to him. First he took off his pants and laid them over a chair, very carefully, as though they were his best ones. Then his blouse. Then his underwear. He took his nightshirt from under his pillow and put it on. Then he sat for a minute or two, frowning at the blue stain under his fingernails. Next he took off his sneakers, stained, too, above the soles, set them neatly under the bed, and next, very slowly, he pulled off his stockings, examining each piece of beggar's lice that clung to them. As long as he had something to do, he didn't have to remember.

But when everything was done, when he had fooled around with his collection of feathers and looked over his butterflies, there was nothing else to do but lie down. Then it all came back.

He had come, making too much noise, he guessed, into the kitchen where the fire was going and the table set. He had never known his father to start supper before, and he wanted to say something to please him.

"Gee, Pa," he had said, splashing his face at the pump, "we did fine. We didn't even need you."

And then, while the water was still in his eyes, before he had even reached for the towel, he had felt the blow across his cheek.

He had been punished lots of times. He had been sent to his room; he had been deprived of pleasures; he had been slapped on his hands and on his bottom—hard. But he had never been slapped in the face before.

For a minute he had just stood there, smarting, too stunned to say a word. His father hadn't said a word either—just breathed heavily, as though the slap had worn him out. Then his mother had come in.

He began to hear voices from the kitchen, voices that rose and fell. Angry voices. His father and mother were fighting. The realization shocked him. Other kids had parents who fought, but they were roughnecks. Their fathers and mothers didn't amount to anything. But Ma and Pa . . .

He began to sweat again. Not the way he had at the winnower, on his forehead, under his arms, in his crotch. This was a sweat that came all over—a cold, funny sweat that had no smell. A sweat that made him shiver.

The voices grew louder. "Ssssh," he heard his mother say. "Ssssh." But in a minute the voices rose again.

He put his fingers in his ears. His cheek still smarted. So did his pride. All summer he had worked hard. He had done his chores; he had scared the gulls away; he had carried the baskets all the way to the winnower. Then he had stood there, lifting them high, spilling hardly a berry, keeping his eye on the wheel, the belt, his throat full of dust. Then he had carried the boxes all the way to the truck. Everyone else thought he had done fine. "Good boy, Jesse," his mother had said. His Uncle Ed had made all kinds of jokes about buying him and hiring him out. Yet his father . . .

His mother's voice rose high piercing his blocked ears.

"For the sake of our son . . ."

Then his father: "*Your* son, you mean."

Suddenly, though he hadn't had to go at all, the bed was wet around him.

7

Laura's berries did not bring her the amount she had expected, for the price had dropped because of a glutted market. She still might have worked in the cannery, but where once she had been unwilling to leave Joel alone, she was now unwilling to leave him and Jesse together. Actually, Jesse was not at home much of the time. Right after breakfast he would start off for

Mr. Pettigrew's, not coming back for dinner until his father had begun his nap. But she was taking no chances.

At supper neither spoke. At first Laura tried to ignore this, talking to each in turn.

"How's the soup, Jesse?"

"Gravy salt enough, Joel?"

Then to both of them together. "Some of the vines are turning. Did you see?" But Jesse now responded little more than Joel.

She had begun to see a change in Jesse. He put off his chores. He didn't wash without being reminded and then only half did it. Out of his father's hearing, he sometimes talked back. It must be his age, she told herself. But she did not like it. If she hadn't been afraid of stirring things up again, she would have taken him to task. It was a relief when school began.

And yet when he was gone she missed him terribly. Each day was the same. Right after breakfast Joel opened the table drawer and took out the cards.

One, two, three.

Black Queen on red King.

One, two, three . . . one, two, three. On and on, accompanied by the low tuneless whistle. Except for brief walks on the barrens, he kept at it hour after hour. And try as she did, she could not block her ears to it. Cooking, making the beds, doing the dishes, sweeping the floor, she heard it, and her fingers shook, dropping a plate, spilling salt or molasses. Sometimes the whistle would become a hiss through closed teeth, but that was the only variation. Her one sure respite was when he took his nap. She had the kitchen to herself then, and all that hour she sat in silence, facing the little window, trying to make out the hills.

Joel was out on the barrens when Jesse came home with his first rank card. Since Laura's hands were wet, she took it gingerly by a corner. She didn't want to blur it, for she was keeping all of his cards. Someday she was going to put them in a special scrapbook. As she took it, she was ready with her usual commendation. *Goodness, Jesse. All A's. That's wonderful.*

But this card didn't have all A's. A second look showed her not a single A on it. There was one B-, four C's, and a C-. She held it for a time, hardly believing; then she laid it on the mantel. Wiping her hands on her apron, she turned to face him.

He stood, eyes down, but defensive.

"How did this happen?" she said.

He shrugged his shoulders.

"Didn't you do your lessons?" In the past she had checked on him, following his progress. But this year she had been so sure he was responsible, so confident she could count on him to do as he should.

"Guess not."

"You guess not. Aren't you sure?"

"Well, I read them."

"How many times?"

"Dunno." He made a flippant face.

She wiped her hands again on her apron, then seized his chin the way she had done when he was very small. "Jesse Closson, you answer my questions. Did you do your lessons? Did you hand your papers in?"

He scowled. "Sometimes."

She released her hold. "Sometimes," she echoed in a tone of disgust. She looked at the card again. "What gave you that C- in Deportment?"

"Dunno."

She saw the tenseness in his face, and her tone softened. "Careful. Don't lie to me, Jesse. Now, what did you do that you shouldn't?"

There was a long silence.

"I'm waiting, Jesse."

Still he said nothing.

"Jesse, this is your last chance to tell me."

He wet his lips. "I sarsed the teacher," he said.

"You sarsed Miss Turner?"

" 'Swat she said."

Jesse talking back in school . . .

"How did that happen?"

He shrugged again. "Dunno."

She moved a step closer to him. "What did you say to her?"

No answer.

"What did you say to her, Jesse?"

Silence.

"Jesse, I'm going to know, if I have to ask Miss Turner. Now, tell me straight."

He wet his lips again.

"Go on."

"She said Mt. Washington was the highest peak in New England."

"And what did you say?"

He raised his eyes, half-scared, half-defiant. "I said, 'So what?' " he answered.

She slept badly that night for thinking about Jesse. He had talked back to her, yes. But to talk back to his teacher—to let his studies go . . . Even more disturbing than that were the words he had spoken. He had learned them from his father. What else would he learn?

While she was doing the breakfast dishes, she heard Tom Pinkham sound his horn. "Thought I'd better hand yer this letter myself," he explained when she got out to the road. "Looks like it might be important." He pointed to the return address. It was from the building and loan company in Bangor.

She stood for a minute just staring at it. She would not open it. She would send it back unclaimed. If there was more trouble, she did not want to know it. She could not bear another thing. But Tom had already started off. By the time she reached the front steps, she decided that nothing worse could happen to her than had happened already. So she sat down and tore open the envelope.

"We are pleased to inform you that we are honoring our obligations to our investors and that you may expect a check for $516 on October 10, plus interest. . . ."

Tears rushed to her eyes and poured down her cheeks. She did not try to wipe them away, though they blurred and magnified the words on the sheet as she read and reread it. For the first time she began to realize just how hard these years had been, how empty of hope. Until now she had lived one day at a time, never allowing herself to look ahead. Now everything had changed. If only she could have known. Only believed . . .

Joel was still sleeping. He stayed in bed later and later now, sometimes until almost ten o'clock. She must wake him up, let him know their debts could be paid. It couldn't fail to cheer him, perhaps even give him a new start.

She hurried into the kitchen and bathed her eyes. Then she started toward the bedroom. "Joel," she called from the doorway. He did not answer. "Joel. Good news." She sat down on the edge of the bed and touched his hand. "Listen."

He stirred and opened his eyes. "Listen to what?"

"This letter." She held it up. "Shall I read it to you?"

"I can still read," he said, reaching out his hand. As he read, his face showed nothing. When he finished, he handed it back without comment.

"Don't you want to know what I'm going to do with the money?"

"Not especially."

Careful, she told herself. Careful. "I'm going to pay our bills. Then, if you approve, I'm going to buy a piece of land on the Ellsworth road and develop it for berries."

She waited.

He said nothing, only pulled irritably at the covers.

She could feel her blood hot and rising. How could he act like this? He knew what it meant to her. He knew, if he had a sympathetic bone in his body, that she had suffered too. She would make one more try. Just one. "Don't you want to know which land?"

"No," he said listlessly. "It's nothing to me."

His hand was on the cover, the hand that had never failed to stir her. She looked deliberately at it now and felt nothing.

She got dinner early, then changed her dress and started to drive to town. Out on the road, with the cool, clear air on her face, her spirits rose again.

Five hundred and sixteen dollars.

Five hundred and sixteen dollars and interest, too!

She took her hand from the wheel to touch her pocketbook, where the letter lay. The money that was lost, gone, was safe again. She could pay Joel's father three hundred and still buy the land. It was good land. She knew it well. Since Doris had told her it could be bought, she had been there many times. Half of it was wooded (pulpwood was bringing a good price again), half was swampy, so it could be burned in the fall. Berries grew there now, and by the time Jesse was ready for college there would be enough of them to put him through.

If only no one had got in ahead of her. . . .

She couldn't know that until she could reach one of the Selectmen. Will Silsby peddled fish, so there was no telling where he would be. Roy Whalen worked in Cherryfield on the job with Joel's father. She'd better try for Joe Buzzell. But first she would stop at the store.

Harry was slicing some beef liver for Elsie Eaton. "Hi, Laurie," he said. "Be with you soon."

"No hurry."

But she was in a hurry and, in spite of herself she showed it. She opened the drawers of the spool cabinet one after another. Then she fidgeted with the scales.

If it was gone. If she'd lost her chance. . . .

Elsie Eaton left, lingering, sensing something in the air, and Harry closed the door behind her. "What's on your mind?" he asked, taking off his apron.

Laura gave him the letter, crumpled now from the heat of her hand.

He read it, beaming. "Gorry," he said. "I sure am tickled for you. What are you goin' to do with all that money?"

"Pay what I owe. Or most of it. Then I was thinking of buying a piece of land just past our place and raising more berries. What would you say to that?"

"I'd say 'Go ahead.' "

She felt relieved. "Haven't seen Joe Buzzell, have you?"

"He's lobstering." He went to the door and looked at the water. "Be back in about an hour, I'd say. Why don't you go over and see Ma while you wait?"

Flora was not at home. A note on the door revealed that she was over at the old place. She was spending most of her time there now, busy with pail and mop. "Such filth," she would say with poorly concealed relish. "Such clutter. If Mama knew." She didn't have time to eat between meals any longer, and as a result was beginning to take off weight. This, together with the fact that she wore her oldest clothes, none of which were black, made her seem almost like her old self.

Laura opened the front door that had been locked so long and stepped into the hall. "Flora," she called, confident she would find her upstairs.

Annie Pettingill answered, leaning over the bannister, her head tied up in a towel. It had been a month now since Annie had moved into Flora's house. She was a sallow, broad-faced girl, quiet and subservient with Flora, but, out of her sight, aggressive. Laura hardly knew her.

"Oh, it's you, Laura. Mrs. Sawyer's up in the attic, goin' through some things. Go ahead on up."

Laura found Flora sitting on a camp stool, her broad lap filled with family keepsakes. A picture of their mother as a bride. Of their mother and Flora taken together. Of the entire family, their father standing in the background; in front of him their mother and Flora on a small settee; then, sitting cross-legged, Laura, straight and serious, looking right at the camera and Doris, slouching, making up a face. A picture of Grandpa Leighton taken on the steps of the church he had built. One of Grandpa Blodgett (circled in ink) with the entire legislature. Flora's first curls. The white gloves Flora had worn at her Junior Exhibition . . .

Beside the camp stool Beauty, graying, her whiskers worn away, her nerves appeased by paregoric, lay drowsing in her basket. She was never left alone now for fear "something might happen." There was betting in town as to which would be the first to go, Beauty or Butch.

Flora read the letter calmly. "I'm not surprised," she said, gathering up the slipping keepsakes. "As long as three weeks ago I had a premonition."

Halfway down the road that led to the wharf, Laura saw Doris and Ed in their boat, heading in. Seeing her, Doris waved a string of flounders. Laura waved her letter back, then went down to the shore, where Butch, who hated water as much as snow, lay guarding a frying pan, a loaf of bread, a package of corn meal and a jar of butter that had already melted and seeped out, darkening the sand. A gull switched teasingly by him. His old jaw trembled; his old eyes feigned scorn. Laura bent to pat him and then thought better of it. Drenched with citronella to keep off the flies he was too lame to combat, he gave off a staggering mixture of smells.

"Whatcha got?" Doris yelled from a distance.

"Good news."

Ed gave the old engine all the speed he could. "Somebuddy leave yer a million?" he shouted.

"Not quite."

Before the boat had touched the shore, Doris jumped out, drenching her sneakers. Butch stirred, gave a croak, staggered a step or two, and then sank down again.

Doris rushed to him, falling on her knees and rubbing his face with hers. "Poor, poor baby," she said. "Poor sweet old thing."

Ed took his cap and swished off the flies that had braved the citronella. "Old sow," he said with a hearty pat. "Old ton o' blubber." Then they both reached for Laura's letter. Doris held it and Ed read over her shoulder.

Laura watched their faces, wondering how Doris would take it. If she was mean . . . If she tried to spoil it . . . "I'm going to buy the land if I can," she said. "The land you told me about."

"Good idea," Doris said without a trace of malice. She handed the letter to Ed, who was a slow reader. "You oughter of done it long ago when I first told you."

Ed had finally grasped what it was all about. He seized Laura, who held her breath against the mingled smell of fish and citronella. "Three cheers," he yelled. "Horray! Horray! Horray!"

Butch joined in with another croak, and they all laughed together.

"Don't tell yet," Laura said as the excitement began to subside. "It's a secret, remember."

They both promised. "We can keep secrets," Doris added airily. "We got one ourselves. Haven't we, Ed?"

"Yer damn tootin'," he said.

8

The papers were signed late in October. As soon as she got home from the Selectmen's office, Laura changed into her oldest clothes and hurried outside.

Until almost time for Jesse to come home she tramped over the new land, estimating again the number of trees and the area where the blueberries already grew. There was plenty of underbrush for burning; it would not be necessary to spread any hay. She observed the shape of every ledge—some bare and smooth, fitting the contour of the land; some steep and wrinkled, with dried moss in their crevasses; some in fantastic shapes (a springing beast, a giant egg, a sacrificial altar); some great, tilting boulders, barely balancing. She noticed every old wall; every stray, rotting fence rail; even the bayberry bushes, stripped now of their berries; the fat, bright rose hips; the blackberry vines and strawberry plants turned purple. She followed the brook for a time, clear and lively in its bed of gravel, and regarded with special pride the willow trees growing beside it. A few leaves still clung, gold and curling, to their branches; more lay, dark and sodden, in the brook's bed.

Land. Trees. Vines. Water. Rocks. All theirs.

Her back to the wind, she sat down on one of the highest boulders and looked out toward the barrens, drawing in the sharp fresh air.

Ever since she had lived on the barrens, she had tried to catch and identify the color of the blueberry vines in the autumn. But she had failed, for it was too elusive. Right now, she decided it was almost magenta. Not quite magenta, for there was still a touch of rose. From where she sat she could look on a vast expanse of foliage that the strong wind put into motion.

She studied the vines thoughtfully, sitting high on the boulder, like an island—mile after mile of it reaching to the horizon. And suddenly, prompted from somewhere deep in her memory, she knew, for a moment at least, what she saw.

What she saw then was "a wine-dark sea."

They would burn on Sunday.

Laura broke the news to Joel at breakfast. She dreaded doing it, for he had neither gone to look over the land nor shown the slightest interest in it. Besides, because of his blunder at the last burn, she realized that he would be upset when he knew. But she had to tell him. "Ed's coming out and so is Harry," she finished. Harry had offered to help, and she had agreed to let him, sensing that with Annie in the house he was glad to escape all he could. "Your father said he might drop around too."

He made no answer, but she saw his color rise.

"I thought maybe you'd like to have me drive you down," she said.

"What for?" he asked.

"We could watch for a while." If she did not help this time, he would feel less left out, she had decided.

"No, thanks," he said, frowning into his coffee. "Besides, I want the car."

He said it impulsively. He did not know why. All he knew was that he could not be there when they came. One he might elude, provided he got a head start, but not three, gloating over him, twitting him with their eyes. The memory of that day had never left him—the flames running ahead of him, the smoke blinding his eyes, the deafening sound of the bell. For weeks he had heard it vibrating in his head. At night it still woke him. CLANG. CLANG. CLANG. Besides, he felt a need of shocking Laura, of making her know that, useless as he was, he still had to be reckoned with. In shocking her, he had shocked himself too, for he had not driven in years.

"You think you ought?"

The alarm in her face pleased him.

"Why not?"

"Because—" She stopped.

"Because I'm crippled. Because everything I touch, I ruin."

"That's not true."

It did not sound to him as though she meant it. "Say it. Come on. Come right out—" Then he saw Jesse in the door, dressed in his oldest clothes. "Well, hello, Mr. Too-Big-for-His-Britches." It was the first time he had spoken directly to him since the blow.

"Hello, Pa."

"So you're going to burn."

"I'm going to help."

"I'm surprised that you don't do it alone. Anyone as smart as—"

"Joel," Laura said sharply.

He turned to her. "Where's the key?" He could see she was upset. It pleased him, made him feel stronger. "The car is mine, I believe, if nothing else is."

She pushed back her chair. "Tell me where you want to go, Joel, and I'll take you."

"Maybe I don't want you to know." He tried to look mysterious. "Where's the key? Give it to me." He held out his hand.

"If you'll just be reasonable. You haven't even a license."

In the mirror on the mantel he could see Jesse's face. It looked scared. "Then I'll get arrested. You and Jesse will have the fun of seeing me in jail."

She moved and stood deliberately in the doorway. "I'm not going to give you the key," she said quietly.

He turned to the cupboard, opened the door, and took the key from its hook. He had known where it was all the time. He had only wanted to make a demand.

214

Inside the shed, he stood shaking a little. He had said he was going to do it, and now he must. But could he remember? He opened the car door and with difficulty placed his right foot on the running board, his left hand on the wheel. Once he was in the seat, he told himself, it would all come back.

But it didn't come back, for his effort had exhausted him so that he could not think at all. For what seemed a long time he sat there, fumbling with the gear shift. Then he remembered the key and managed to get it in. Very slowly he lifted his left foot, put in the clutch pedal, and pushed, causing a hot pain in his calf. More slowly he lifted his right foot to the brake. This time the pain was worse. But he must do it. He had said he would, and he must. Once he had started, he might not have to use the brake or clutch at all. He would drive toward town, turn off on one of the old dirt roads, and stay there until the burning was over.

Now he would start. Wincing, he stretched his right leg again so that his foot could reach the starter button. Then, bracing himself for the pain that would come, he moved his left leg to the clutch again. He must go in reverse. But how? He sat still, waiting for his head to clear. Then, faintly, he heard a car coming. He had to get out of the yard at least before they came or they would catch him.

He let in the clutch and, stretching his right foot, pushed down on the accelerator. The car began to back. Before he could move his foot to the brake, a pain tore through his leg, running up his thigh, throwing him off balance. He yanked the wheel. Then he felt a jolt that knocked his wind out, and at the same time heard the sound of splintering wood and smashing glass.

That night Laura sat in the kitchen rocker, gazing at the wall where the little window had been. The house was quiet. Joel was upstairs in Jesse's room, where he had fled, moving the bureau against the door so no one could get in. He was not hurt or he could never have moved that heavy piece. Harry had tried to speak to him, but he had not answered. He had not touched the tray she had put outside.

Her eyes returned to the wall again. In some odd way that window had promised something. As long as it was there, with its view of the hills, life could never be completely drab. And now he had broken it—not deliberately, she allowed him that much—but stupidly, perversely. He knew what it had meant to her, and he had not even said he was sorry.

I cannot love him any longer, she told herself. I shall not try.

9

When Joel did not get up the next morning, Laura began to worry. Suppose, after all, the jolt had hurt him. Suppose his moving the bureau had been his final, desperate burst of strength. She had heard of such strength. But it was not an anxiety of love she felt. It was an anxiety that came from bondage.

At nine she took up a tray, knocked on the door, and called his name. He did not answer. "I'm leaving your breakfast," she said, and went downstairs.

After the work was done, she got out a roll of paper she had saved for ten years and began to cut it to the shape of the window. Joel's father had wanted to replace the glass. He would take a day off, he told her, and go to Ellsworth to have it cut. But she had refused to let him. "Just saw out a piece of board and block it in," she told him, feeling that a new window would be only a mockery now. And he had done it.

As she worked, she kept listening for sounds upstairs. If she didn't hear him by ten o'clock, she would go into town and call the doctor. Joel would be mad at her, for he had turned against the doctor long ago, and as likely as not he wouldn't let him in when he came. But she would call him anyway.

She spoiled the first two circles that she cut, for her fingers were shaking. She had been awake most of the night before, listening, as she was now, to silence and to the grating of the castors of the living-room sofa where Jesse lay. He hadn't slept either. What can he be thinking? she kept asking herself. How can all this be affecting him?

At a quarter to ten she heard Joel get out of bed and cross the floor. His steps were firm and steady. Then he was all right. He was just up there sulking. Still holding the scissors, half-open, she waited to know if he would go to the door for his breakfast. He didn't. He went straight back to bed.

All right, she thought. Let him go hungry.

At noon she took up another tray. "Your dinner, Joel." Downstairs, she listened again and heard nothing. Normally she went outside in the afternoon, but today a heavy fog saturated everything. From the front windows she could see only the road; from the back, only the garden where a few late pumpkins showed yellow through their withered vines. When the dishes were done, the bits of paper picked up, and the roll put away, she went into the bedroom to lie down.

Almost asleep, she heard him moving around again and sat upright. What was he doing? There was nothing he could do, really. There were a few old books in the room, but Joel didn't read. He did not even glance at the Bangor paper, to which Flora had subscribed for them at Christmas. Yet he was still walking, trying to tiptoe. "What are you looking for, Joel?" she almost called from the habit of years.

Then she heard the clink of china, and realized he was taking the water Jesse kept for brushing his teeth. She had forgotten that. With water, he could hold out for a while.

Well, let him, she thought.

But again she could not sleep.

Jesse came home quietly and did up his chores. He did not mention Joel nor did he appear to see the new circle of un faded paper that stared out against the old. At supper she would have had a chance to ask him about his schoolwork, something she was unwilling to do in Joel's hearing. But he ate quickly, avoiding her eyes. Right after supper he lighted the lantern and went out to the shed, just as he always did at night. He stayed for a very long time, and when he came in he went at once to bed. As soon as he was settled, she closed the door between the hall and sitting room. Then she went into the bed-room and closed that door too, taking pains that Joel should hear her do it. When he thinks we are asleep, she told herself, he will come down and get something to eat.

She slept little and lightly. But all she heard was the stir of the wind in the hackmatacks and the castors creaking on the uneven floor.

Jesse ate breakfast in silence, still avoiding her eyes. He sat, dawdling over his oatmeal, with both elbows on the table. There were circles under his eyes, and the pulse in his temple throbbed heavily. A good twenty minutes before it was time for the bus, he took his dinner pail and started outside.

Around ten o'clock Laura went for a walk, making sure that Joel should hear her close the door behind her. She did not want to go, for the air was still damp and she was very tired. But she realized that as long as she stayed in the house, Joel would not come down. Since the foliage was wet, she took the main road toward the village.

When she had gone less than a quarter of a mile, she saw a car coming. It slowed down, then stopped beside her. Lillian Carter, who lived on the Junction road, was driving, and with her was her youngest boy, holding a scarf over his mouth.

"I'm lookin' fer yer," she said, rolling down the window. Then, ignoring Laura's greeting, she turned to the boy. "Show her, Billy. Let her see."

Billy dropped his scarf, showing lips that were bruised and swollen.

"Open yer mouth."

He opened it and pointed with a grimy finger to his gum, still bleeding a little where a tooth was missing.

His mother leaned toward Laura. "Yer boy done that," she said, bearing the news with obvious satisfaction.

"Jesse?"

"That's right."

"But there's some mistake. It couldn't be." Jesse hitting someone! It was impossible.

"Well, 'twas."

Laura turned to the boy. "Are you sure it was Jesse?"

He nodded and began to sniffle.

"But what started it? What was the reason?"

His mother answered for him. "There warn't no reason. When the teacher asked him why he done it, yer know what he said? He said he jest felt like hittin' somebuddy." Her voice grew scornful. "Pickin' on a little boy, a first-grader. The bully."

Laura's eyes moved back to Billy's face. But what she saw was Jesse's face with the red mark on it that night in the kitchen. She stood waiting while the car turned; then, determined to have things out once and for all, she hurried home.

As she opened the front door, Joel was coming in the back. His hair was disheveled, his face unshaven. "What are you doing around here?" he demanded.

The irony of his words stopped her own for an instant. What was she doing in her own house, the house she herself had bought and paid for? The house she had papered, painted, scrubbed on her own hands and knees. Where she had waited —waited for Joel to get up, get off, come home, start something, finish it. The house where she had borne his child.

"Looking for you," she told him, coming into the kitchen. "I've got something to say and you are going to listen." She saw that he was carrying the slop jar. She had him at a disadvantage. That pleased her. "You've got to stop badgering Jesse."

He set the slop jar in the hall, then faced her, tense and defensive. "What do you mean, badgering?"

"You know what I mean," she answered coldly.

"I don't even know what you are talking about." His eyes, meeting the blocked-in window, shifted suddenly.

"Then I'll tell you." She paused until her breathing steadied. "Jesse hit Billy Carter. His mother came way out—"

"Aw, boys always fight," he interrupted.

"It wasn't a fight. Jesse walked right up and hit him."

"Well, what of it?"

"Billy Carter's only five."

He shrugged his shoulders. "That's got nothing to do with me."

"Jesse hit him right across the face." Her voice was full of meaning.

His color rose.

There was a tense silence. They could hear the clock tick, the pump drip, the fire crackle. It was fully a minute before she spoke again. "If you can't be civil to him, you can at least let him alone," she said.

A sneer came over his face. "You're a good one to talk about leaving people alone. You've pushed me around for years."

She'd heard that hundreds of times. Times when she had insisted he do the things he ought to do, like taking his medicine or putting his rubbers on. Even things he really wanted to do, like going over to see Mr. Pettigrew. It seemed as though he forced her to push him and then gave her only blame.

"What's the use of bringing that up again?" she said wearily. "Right now the one to talk about is Jesse."

His breathing deepened. "There you go again. Jesse, Jesse. That's all you think about. Jesse."

"You'd better think a little about him too."

"Why should I?"

Her face flamed. A father saying that about a son. A son like Jesse. She thought of Jesse at the burn, the smoke half choking him, beating out the flames. Bringing the buckets of water, much too heavy for any boy. Ringing the bell. Jesse scaring off the gulls. At the winnower, doing the work of a full-grown man. A boy like that made into a bully by his own father. Her anger rose until she felt it swelling in her ears, her throat, even her fingers. It blurred her mind so that she forgot all about her promise to Joel. "You've always complained about your own father," she taunted.

He moved suddenly closer. His eyes, she saw, were blood-shot. His breath was bad from hunger. "You leave my father out of this," he shouted.

She knew she should stop, just as she should have stopped that day in the kitchen with Flora. But she couldn't. All her restraint was gone. So was her caution. "He's been ten times as good a father to you as you've been to Jesse," she shouted back.

Once the words were out, both of them stood pale and motionless. For a moment or two the room was loud with silence. Then Joel moved toward her and began to speak huskily. "Now, you listen to me. For once in your life you're going to pay attention to what I've got to say."

His look was so terrible that she grasped the back of a chair for support. She had never seen such a look before.

"I never wanted to work in your family's store. You knew that all the time." He moved still closer. There was sweat on his forehead. "But you fixed it. You and your family. You had things just the way you wanted them."

She had always been afraid this would come and she had thought she was ready for it. *Where else could you have made so good a living? Where else could you have found so considerate a boss?* She had rehearsed those words in her mind over and over. But now that the time had come to speak them, they dried in her throat. She had lost ground and she knew it.

His words kept coming. "You knew I hated it. But what difference did that make to you? You had what you wanted. Why should it matter about me? Just a nobody."

The clock began to strike ten. They both stared at it until it stopped. Then he went on, his voice low again but hoarse and terrible. "I never wanted any of the things you wanted. I never wanted this house."

She winced.

"I never even wanted to get married."

Her hands jumped to her ears.

He raised his voice so that she could not fail to hear every syllable. "Once you got me, it was nag, nag, nag, trying to make me amount to something. And when you couldn't do that, you had to start showing me how smart you were. You and your son." He stumbled toward the outer door, knocking against the broom on his way. "God damn it," he shouted over his shoulder, "why couldn't you have left me alone? Why couldn't you have let me go to hell in my own way?"

Very slowly she took her hands from her ears. He had left the door open behind him. Through it she saw him go into the shed, come out again with his gun and a box of cartridges, then hurry off, limping, across the barrens.

She picked up the broom, got a drink of water from the pump, then sank down in the rocker. She did not cry. She just sat hunched, staring at her hardened palms. Almost half her life gone. Given up. Thrown away on a man who had never even wanted her. A man she had pushed, nagged, made miserable.

. . . Well, why didn't he start? Why didn't he shoot off all his cartridges to show her how mad he was, to ease his rage? She listened, but she heard nothing. Only the clock. Quick, quick, quick . . .

Why did he tell her this now? Why hadn't he told her years ago, when she could have sent him away? Now there was no escape for either of them. She hunched her shoulders and pressed her elbows against the dizziness in her stomach. She would take care of him because someone had to. She would get his meals, clean his house, wash his clothes, make his bed. Their bed. The bed in which he had never wanted her to be. She would do these things because there was no one else to do them. No other reason.

The clock struck the half hour. She got up stiffly, took off her sweater, put on her apron, and started upstairs. The room was a mess. Jesse's old clothes, which he had left on a chair, had been swept to the floor. The water pitcher and the toothbrush glass were on the rug by the bed. The bed itself was tumbled.

Pulling at the quilts, she stopped again to listen. Why didn't he start? If he walked too far, he would come home exhausted. He hadn't worn his jacket, and there was still fog. Suppose he got sick again. As if she didn't have enough on her mind already. . . .

She finished the bed, went back down, and stood in the kitchen doorway. It was too damp for him to be outside. Where was he, anyway? The fog was low. If she went upstairs in the shed she could see above it.

Brushing away the cobwebs from the window of the shed, she looked out over the barrens. Half a mile or so to the east, she saw him sitting in a posture of wretchedness on one of the ledges. The sight of his slight, stooped figure against that wide expanse of withering landscape moved her in spite of herself.

His gun was across his knees. Why hadn't he fired it? Could it be that he wasn't mad any longer? That he hadn't meant the things he had said? That he had said them only because she had goaded him into it? Because she had brought up his father? Measured the two of them? She wanted to know. She had to. But what if she went out there and he sent her back? What if she went and the quarrel began all over again?

Then she thought of the bell. She could ring it three times, as she had often done as a signal. If he wasn't mad, if he hadn't meant what he said, he would come in. She would have saved face for him.

She hurried down the stairs and pulled the rusty chain. I WANT YOU. Then she hurried back up to the window again.

He was coming. He was on his way. He was running.

The relief. Oh, the relief of it. She felt her old love rush back, untinged, complete.

In the kitchen again, she opened the draft of the stove and pushed the kettle forward. He would be half-starved. She went to the breadbox for the bread, then to the cellarway for the corned beef and doughnuts. Then she opened the cupboard door and reached for the can of tea.

Before she could open it, she heard a single shot—loud, nearby. For an instant she stood motionless clutching the can. Then she set it carefully down on the shelf and went outside. The fog had lifted. She could see clearly now for half a mile. Yet the shot . . .

She began to run in the direction from which it had come. Across the spongy sod of the garden, through the drenched vines and stripped bushes and the rough brown stalks of golden rod. Over the tearing blackberry hoops, the shriveled ferns, the fallen seed pods . . .

She found him lying on his face, one arm beneath him, the other flung out, almost touching his rifle, his left foot caught in the half-burned root of the tree on which he had tripped.

Two days later he was buried beside David in the little

graveyard. Flora had been upset about the arrangements, for she had offered a place in the Leighton lot.

"I can't figure what you're thinking of, Laura," she had argued. "Letting him lie out there beside a stranger."

"He won't be lying beside a stranger," Laura had answered. Then, looking squarely at Flora's puzzled, disapproving face, "This is the way it's going to be."

And it was.

The afternoon was warm and so clear that the hills showed up in sharp outline. The wind was down. The crows were quiet. Laura had asked that there be only a committal service with the family at the grave. They stood there together, Flora, exhausted from the walk, supported by Doris and Ed; Laura, bareheaded, in a bright blue dress that Joel had liked, with Jesse beside her, wearing, by his own request, the long pants she had bought and put away for his birthday; Joel's father, his face strained and pale, his eyes on his hat that he held and kept turning, the clean edges of his winter underwear showing below his cuffs. Harry—quiet, kind—in charge of everything.

When he gave the signal, the Reverend Bigelow, evenly and without the slightest hesitation, read the psalm Laura had chosen:

> The earth is the Lord's and the fullness thereof,
> The world and they that dwell therein. . . .

Only Flora cried.

"How's Laura Closson taking it?" people kept asking. Nobody knew, for she showed nothing. When people came, she was as composed as she ever had been, moving the kettle forward and asking about their families.

"I don't see how she manages," they whispered out of her hearing.

Days she managed well enough. There was the regular work

of course—as much as ever, for Joel's father had moved in, coming promptly as before, his belongings again wrapped in his old bathrobe. There were Joel's things to take care of. His clothes must be sponged and pressed for the Missionary barrel, for, poor and practical though she was, she could not bring herself to cut them over for Jesse. His fountain pen and his watch, which had never run right since the night on the water, must go to Harry, his fishing equipment to Ed. Luther's ring would be put aside for Jesse. Joel had never worn it, for, even tightened with string, it was too big for his biggest finger and too heavy for his hand.

Then there were the things to destroy. This took a long time, for each one had to be deliberated, His comb? His brush? His wallet? His belt? His razor? His magazines?

Yes, magazines must go. But first she must look them all over. She must handle them because he had handled them. She must turn every page, for it might possibly be that he had left some drawing in them, or even just some sketch in a margin.

His cards?

No, she would keep his cards, the cards she despised, to remind her of her guilt.

Not that she needed to be reminded. Night after night, as she lay in their bed that had never seemed big or cold before, she listened to Jesse, turning on the sofa. What would this do to him, this thing she had started? What scars would he bear? He had gone with Harry and Ed to bring his father home. She had forbidden him to go, but he had gone anyway, and he had come back carrying his father's cap and his rifle. He had sat beside her with his father—a boy not yet nine—until the undertaker arrived. He had watched them off through the kitchen window; then he had vomited in the sink. How much should she ever tell him? How much did he already know?

When at last he was quiet, she heard again every word of the quarrel.

226

Nag. Push.

That's all you think about. Jesse.

I never wanted to work in your family's store.

And then, over and over, the terrible words, the words that nothing, not even the remembrance that he had come back, that he had been running, could ever completely drown out.

I never even wanted to get married. . . .

Never wanted their home. Never wanted their garden. Never wanted their walks on the barrens. The food she had cooked him. Never wanted her touch. . . .

Turn. Toss. Trying to figure.

Where had she first gone wrong? Should she have just left him alone? Hidden her competence? Stood by and watched him fail? Didn't the Bible condemn the man who hid his talent under a bushel? Or was it different for women? If it was, then why were they given talents? And, most baffling of all, the same old question: How could you need a thing, rely on it, and then resent the one who gave it?

Then questions gave way to remorse, burning, cramping, sickening. If only she had been more patient, more understanding. If only she had left things as they were. Hadn't started the quarrel . . . If only she hadn't brought his father into it. . . .

When she could not lie still any longer, she got up and lighted the lamp on the bureau, careful not to see herself in the mirror, for she could not bear the sight of her own face; then went into the kitchen and sat down in the rocker.

If only . . .

If only . . .

Back and forth.

Back and forth.

If only . . .

If only . . .

Then the rockers took it up.

If only . . .

If only . . .
If only . . .

10

Flora wanted to have the entire family for dinner on Thanksgiving. "I've got good help now," she explained, "with Annie." That was true, for Annie had the kind of energy that once had been Flora's. She was up early. She cooked, she cleaned, she ran the errands. She knew exactly how to ingratiate herself with Flora—admiring Beauty, waiting on her, cleaning up cheerfully when she didn't get her out in time; prompting stories of the Leightons and especially of Luther; bringing back news every time she crossed the green.

But she hadn't made any progress with Harry. He was pleasant to her. He complimented her cooking. He drove her to see her family whenever Flora arranged it. Now and then he joined the two of them in a hand of Flinch or Donkey. But that was all. Two things especially piqued Annie. No matter how she and Flora schemed it, he managed never to sit beside her in church (sitting together in church was an announcement of courtship in Millboro), and he refused her offer of helping him afternoons in the store.

But if Annie was discouraged, Flora was not. Harry was slower than some, she told herself. Once he got used to seeing Annie with the family, he would break down gradually. It was with this in mind that she had planned the dinner on Thanksgiving. "You can bring Jim Closson with you," she told Laura. Ever since he had sold his boat, Flora had been civil, even pleasant, to Jim Closson. But this was the first time she had included him with the family.

"Not this year, Flora."

"But if you don't come you'll spoil everything."

"Not this year," Laura repeated. "Christmas, maybe."

The weather cleared for Thanksgiving after a week of wind and rain that flattened the weeds and stripped the last of the foliage. Everything was drenched and disheveled. The land seemed less even now, the ledges larger. Puddles showed up in ruts and hollows.

Right after breakfast Jesse filled the woodbox, taking pains, as he always did now, to lay the sticks evenly. Joel's father finished the banking. Then the two of them began tiering wood in the shed. At ten-thirty Laura called them inside.

"No more work today," she said.

They cleaned up, went into the sitting room to keep from getting under foot, and looked at shells under the microscope until Laura called them for dinner.

It was a good dinner—chicken, squash, and potatoes from their own garden, biscuits, apple jelly, mince pie. But no one had an appetite.

"Squash, Mr. Closson?"

"No, thank yer, Laura."

"Oh, try a little."

"Well, jest a mite," he said, wanting to please.

"How about you, Jesse?" Once she had despaired of ever filling him up. Now, even though it was Thanksgiving, he had barely touched the little she had put on his plate. "Those are good biscuits."

"I know, Ma."

"Then try one."

He shook his head.

"We have to eat, Jesse."

He reached for one and spread it. Then, abruptly, he pushed

away his plate. It was just no use. He couldn't eat. He'd be sick if he did. He took a sip of water.

Laura saw but said nothing.

The clock struck once and her hand, holding her fork, faltered. Whatever hour it struck, for her it struck ten. *I never wanted to work in your family's store. I never even wanted to get married. . . .*

Joel's father, who sat facing the window, pulled aside the curtain and looked out. "Car comin'," he said. "Looks like it's slowin' down a bit."

It was Doris and Ed. They had come to take Jesse out in their boat.

"Should I go, Ma?" He wanted to go, and yet he didn't want to. He wanted to go because he wanted to forget for a little while the sight of the shoe Harry had taken from his father's foot, the weight of the cap, the horror of the rifle he had carried. He wanted to forget his father lying flat on the bed and the blood—it seemed funny there was so little of it—staining the blanket. He didn't want to go because if he went, he might not be bearing his share like a man. More than anything in the world he wanted to do that. Lying on the sofa at night, he had sworn a solemn vow. Though he hadn't been able to make his father proud of him, he would make his mother proud. He would remember that vow always. He would say it over to himself the first thing every morning. *Remember your vow. Remember your vow. . . .* "Should I go, Ma?" he repeated.

Laura hesitated. It would be cold on the water. Jesse caught cold easily. He wasn't eating. He looked run-down.

"Aw, let him," Ed urged. "Sun's comin' out. Besides, 'twill be his last chance."

Still Laura waited. It was so late in the season. Most of the boats had been drawn up for a month. She looked at Joel's father, but he was looking at his plate. As hard as she had tried, she had never been able to make him feel at ease with company. "There's always next year," she said.

Doris and Ed exchanged a look. There were secret sounds and gestures.

Another scheme. The new one. She must act interested. Laura laid down her napkin.

"Come on. One of you tell," she said.

Ed cleared his throat as though about to begin a performance. "We've sold the bo't," he said.

"Sold the boat!" Laura repeated. All summer Ed had been doing fairly well. They might have saved the house, she often thought, if they had waited. "But why in the world?" It was impossible to think of Ed without his boat, just as it was impossible to think of him without Butch or even Doris.

"You'll see," Doris said importantly. "Just wait. You'll see."

"How long must we wait?" Laura asked, looking at Jesse. Jesse had never tired of their schemes and secrets. Yet now he showed no interest, asked no questions. And this was obviously one of the most important schemes of all.

"A couple of weeks, maybe." Then, disappointed by the lack of response, Doris snapped her fingers briskly. "Well, can he go or can't he?"

Laura studied Jesse's face more closely. "As soon as he cleans his plate," she said.

After they had gone, Joel's father suggested that he and Laura look over the new land. They had not been there since the burn. They started off leisurely, not talking much, pointing now and then to things they saw on the way. A toad crossing their path; a woodchuck hole; the bones of a bird that an owl had regurgitated; a blackberry hoop the frost had spared; a flock of cedar waxwings plundering a mountain ash.

The burn had been a good one—even, just the right depth, with only here and there a hollow missed. They had better look over the woods too, they decided.

Just inside the first grove, they came upon the remains of a campfire. "I wonder who's been here," Laura said uneasily.

Since the burn of the spring, she had been more nervous than ever about fires. Scattering the soggy, blackened sticks with her foot, she saw something glitter. Joel's father saw it too, and bent to pick it up. It was one of the spoons he had given them.

Laura hurried to tell him the story about the Indians and how they had run away, betraying her kindness. "They must have camped here that night," she said. Then, looking at his face, she saw he was shaken. "I'm sorry about the spoon. I hoped you would never know."

"Losin' it don't matter," he answered hoarsely. "It's findin' it ser sudden-like." He put the spoon back on the campfire and turned to walk on. "No," he said as she hesitated, "leave it lay."

She followed him, keeping up with his rolling walk. There was a turbulence in their silence now. He was going to talk to her. She could feel the words mounting.

In a few minutes they struck a path, and he waited for her to go ahead of him. Then, when she could not see his face, he began. "There's somethin' more I oughter tell yer. One thing special."

He paused, but she did not speak for fear of interrupting what he had at last determined to reveal. It was fully a minute before he spoke again, his words low and halting. "Joel's mother took on on account a my sailin', an when Emmie come I give it up an started workin' in a mill at the Junction. But I warn't contented there. I was used ter quiet an bein' out in the open air, an the sound a them saws grated my nerves somethin' awful."

Joel would have understood that, she thought.

He slowed his steps, and she slowed hers, careful not to miss a word.

"Things warn't goin' good in the family. Even after I'd give up the sea, she kep tellin' how fer years I had deserted 'em. How I hadn't ever give a straw what happened ter 'em. T'warn't true, but the boy believed it. He'd heard it all his life.

232

He wouldn't have northin' ter do with me, which was natural." A noisy flock of crows flew over, and he waited for it to pass. Then he went on, his voice thinning. "T'aint easy ter live like that. Shoved aside. Hearin' yer words twisted. I kep tellin' myself if I brought 'em presents enough, like them spoons"—he turned and looked back—"things would go better when I come home. But they never did. Every time I come, I felt more like I was a stranger."

The path had dwindled. They were in the open now, surrounded by ledges. True to Ed's prediction, the sun was beginning to come out. "Let's sit down for a while," she said.

They settled on the nearest ledge. A pair of goldfinches lighted on a nearby spruce tree, but neither of them noticed.

"You were sailing again," Laura prompted.

"That's right," he said. "But 'twarn't fer long. My mind wouldn't rest. So I decided ter go back an try seinin'. I figgered that would give me enough time home ter fix up the place. Maybe put in a bathroom. That was somethin' she said she wanted bad. But once I gut there, things was worse'n ever. 'Twarn't all her fault. Yer see, I like things shipshape. Northin' makes me ser cranky as things layin' round. She didn't like housekeepin'. She liked ter play cards. Sometimes her and Joel would keep at it all day an half the night."

One. Two. Three . . . Laura drew her knees up and pressed them to her.

He did not notice. "I got along good with Emmie though. She was a lot like Jesse in her ways. When things gut bad at home, we used ter walk along the shore." His voice slowed and stopped.

"Then what?" Laura asked resolutely, determined to hear everything.

"Well, I give up seining' fer lobsterin'. I had the bo't. The hotels was after lobsters. But it turned out she didn't want a bathroom. She wanted the money in the bank. So I give her all

I made. Still she warn't satisfied. Then along come this other thing." He took a bandanna from the pocket of his mackinaw and wiped the sweat from his face.

"Why don't you smoke?" she asked him. She could never persuade him to smoke inside.

"Sure 'twon't bother yer none?"

"Sure."

He reached into another pocket. Before he could find the pipe, a rifle cracked in the distance.

Both of them stiffened.

Laura was the first to recover. "You'd given up lobstering," she said evenly.

He drew out his pipe, struck a match, and held it unsteadily to the bowl. After a few hard puffs, he went on. "Well, as I told yer, this other thing come along. It had real money in it. An somethin' else. I reckon you'd call it adventure." He looked at her shyly. "Yer wouldn't think it, seein' me now, but I've allus kinder craved adventure. I had a taste a it when I was sailin' an I was missin' it bad." His face sobered again. "She knew. But she didn't let on. Fer two years she took the money and asked no questions. Then one night she come inter the kitchen when I was lacin' my boots an said she had a public car comin' ter take her an Emmie ter the evenin' train. Said 'twarn't fittin' fer Emmie ter stay round a man like me." He knocked his pipe against the ledge and put it in his pocket.

"Go on. Please."

He took a long breath. "I'm no talker, as I guess everybuddy knows. But that night I talked plenty. I'd give up the hull thing, I told her. I'd git myself a job agin in the mill at the Junction. But it didn't do no good. She jest turned her back on me an went upstairs ter git Emmie. Emmie didn't know what 'twas all about. She was little then, ter say northin' a bein' half asleep. When the car pulled up, I tried ter talk some more. Not jest on my account, but fer Joel. I knew how tied he was ter her. But she didn't pay no attention. She went ter the bureau an took out the bank book. Then she pulled Emmie along an went out, slammin' the door behind them."

Laura winced and pulled her knees tighter. Joel, standing shaking in the kitchen. *I heard a door slam.* She covered her face with her hands.

He stopped talking and lowered his eyes.

"Go on, go on," she urged, her words muffled by her fingers.

He wiped his face again with his bandanna. "Joel heard an started down. He caught right on ter what was happenin' an began hollerin' that he could bring her back. That she would listen ter him. I knew 'twarn't no use, like I said. 'Twas January, ten below. He was in his nightshirt an barefooted besides. So I grabbed him and held onter him till the car gut a start."

Words came back, words spoken, shouted, the night of the fever. *Let me go. Let me go. Quit holding me. Let me go.* She closed her eyes tight behind her fingers.

He was speaking again, more slowly. "I dunno if I done right or wrong. Jest that it seemed right at the time. But he swore he'd hold it agin me fer the rest of his life. An he did." He paused. When he spoke again his voice was lower, almost a whisper. "I more'n held him. Maybe I lost my head. Maybe 'twas old grudges. Anyhow, I bruised him bad."

So that was it. That was the reason for the week he had been in hiding. Joel alone, nursing his bitterness and his bruises. Tears wet her palms and slipped through her fingers.

For a little while they both were silent. Then Laura took her hands from her face and sat erect. At last she understood everything. With that understanding had come relief. It was as if a burn had passed and the new green was coming through, softening the sere. "Did you ever hear from her?" she asked quietly.

He nodded. "In 'bout a year she wrote. Said a real man had took 'em in." He reached for his pipe again and lighted it. "I never told Joel."

"I'm glad."

"They'd started up a business. Things was goin' bad an they was goin' ter lose it without they had some money ter put in. So I kep sendin'." He felt her quick glance. "On Emmie's account," he added.

"How long did you send?"

"Till I give up . . ." He flushed and faltered. "Till I sold the bo't," he said.

Then you took us on, Laura thought warmly.

There was another silence. In it she watched his face, old though he was hardly more than fifty. Old and lonely. "Do you know where Emmie is now?" she asked.

"Portland. Workin' at Porteous Mitchell. I seen her once when I was walkin' by. It give me a real start."

"Didn't you go in?"

"No, no. She don't know northin' bout the past. Like as not, she thinks hard on me. She's a real nice-lookin' girl, Emmie. I don't want ter git in her way."

"But don't you think you ought to write her about Joel?"

The muscles of his throat moved, but he did not answer.

"Could I write to her? Could I tell her the whole story?"

He faced her eagerly. "Would yer?" he asked.

11

On the first Sunday in December the secret was revealed. When the church door opened, the first members of the congregation to file out stood dumbfounded. It couldn't be, but it was—a bright red house moving slowly around the green.

"Look!"

"Come!"

"Come see!"

The church emptied rapidly and, handshakes forgotten, people already dazed by the sunlight, stared. They crowded the steps, blocking the doorway. They lined the sidewalks and the edge of the green. Children waiting for Sunday School to start came pouring out of the vestry.

"Quick!"

"Hur*eee!*"

Yes, it was true. A house was moving.

Miss Marie Hodgkins left her switchboard to stand on her front steps, a coat thrown over her shoulders. Mrs. Nellie Eaton's head appeared among the display of hats in her parlor window.

A house moving . . .

A horn sounded and Ed's long arm appeared, waving from the cab of his truck. Then, from the house itself, through a real window, Butch's ugly, dismal face.

"It's an ark," one of the Sunday-school children screamed.

"A nark!"

"A nark!" the others echoed.

There was general laughter.

"It's a trailer," someone shouted.

Sunday behavior was forgotten as children and grownups alike elbowed for a better view. It was the first trailer ever seen in Millboro.

"What's it for?"

"Where'll they keep it?"

Loafers from Peasley's steps hurried across, mixing their sheepskins and mackinaws with the sedate Sunday attire. Here was something unexpected, and on a cold Sunday morning, too.

"Gut any sails fer her, Ed?" Joe Wessel shouted.

"How'll she float?"

Ed drew up abreast of the spectators. A window lowered and Doris, a red ribbon in her hair, stuck out her head with an air of innocence. "What's all the excitement?" she demanded.

More laughter. You could always count on their being up to something, Doris and Ed.

Flora had remained after the service as usual to comment favorably upon the sermon. Now, pushing through the doorway, she stood motionless, trying to take in what she saw. "Another of their jokes," she scolded in an undertone to Laura, who was beside her. "Making a spectacle of themselves, and on a Sunday too." She blinked and stared again. "What is it, anyway?"

"A trailer," Laura told her. She herself was taken aback. This was more of a surprise than she had expected.

"What's it for?"

"It's something to live in." Jesse had shown her a picture of one he had found in a magazine. But it hadn't been red.

"Who does it belong to?"

"To them, I guess."

"To *them?*" Flora echoed. She continued to stare while Doris wet her finger on her tongue and wiped away a smooch that had obscured Butch's view. "To *them?* Why, where in the world would they get the money to buy such a thing?"

Laura dreaded to tell her, but there seemed no way out. "Probably the money from Ed's boat," she said, lowering her voice. "I know he sold it."

Flora's own voice rose. "To buy that? That contraption, when they couldn't pay . . ."

"He couldn't have got much for it," Laura said quickly. "Probably just enough for a down payment."

Flora had no use for down payments. Her color, already high, mounted. "The disgrace of it," she began.

Laura looked around, fearful that they were being overheard, but all attention was on the trailer. People had moved closer. Some were even peering in.

238

"Whatcher goin' ter do with it, Dottie?" Will Silsbury shouted.

"Why, live in it, nut," she shouted back. "We're leavin'."

"Leavin'?"

"Leavin' Millboro?"

"A-yuh," Ed said. "Goin' back ter the place I come from."

"Oh, no, Ed."

"Can't spare yer."

" 'Sthat true, Dottie?"

"Sure is."

"Honest?"

"Honest to God."

Flora gripped Laura's arm. "Did you hear that? Did you hear what she said?"

Laura nodded.

"Well, do you believe it? Do you believe they would do such a thing?"

"It looks that way," Laura admitted. She had known for a long time that this secret was a big one; known, too, that Doris and Ed weren't likely to stay on with Flora as their landlord. But to go far away . . . Yet she mustn't show any misgivings before Flora.

Flora's grip tightened. Her anger changed to distress. "But what if they get sick? They don't know how to look after themselves, either one."

"They're never sick, Flora. You know that."

"But in that climate."

"They're young." For a long time now she had felt years older than Doris. As for Ed, sometimes he seemed hardly older than Jesse.

"But to start off on a thing like that. To break down among strangers."

"It's new. It's not going to break down, Flora," Laura said, careful to keep her eyes on the trailer and not on the truck. "Besides, Ed's good with machinery."

"But now in winter . . ."

Gene Pinkham's voice drowned out all others. "Whatcher goin' ter do when yet git there?"

"Run a café," Doris shouted.

"In that?"

Ed opened the door, slid back a wall, and revealed a tiny kitchen.

The crowd pressed closer.

"A-yuh," Ed said. "Goin' ter back her right up ter a lumber camp. Serve pie. Doughnuts. Hot rolls."

Flora's distress changed back to anger. Doris living like a gypsy. Cooking for lumberjacks. Canucks . . . All her life Doris had sassed her, mortified her, ridiculed her, even to her face. Doris had neglected the old place, mortgaged it, and then let it go without a thought as to what would happen to it. But to leave Millboro without so much as telling her ahead! To break up the family! Let it be talked about! She pushed her way through the crowd to where Harry was standing with Jesse. "Get me out of this," she said hoarsely. "Get me home."

They started off, Laura, Jesse, and Annie following. Flora's face was dead white and her breathing heavy. "Making fools of themselves. Making fools of the family. Leaving a good home they were lucky to have for some wild-goose chase." She paused to catch her breath. "That's what comes of her marrying a foreigner. A—"

Harry turned to Laura.

"You all go on ahead," he told her in a voice that might have been Luther's. "I want to talk to Ma."

12

Sitting by the window, Laura heard a car and saw Harry coming. He had come out every Wednesday since Joel's death. She went to the door to meet him.

"Oh, don't take your rubbers off," she said.

"Might's well. Didn't need to wear 'em. Winter's awful late this year."

"Bring them in, anyway."

He placed them carefully on the thin platform of zinc where the cookstove stood. Then he set the bag on the shelf. "Jest some samples," he said lightly. "Some new lines we're carryin'."

Three boxes of cookies and a can of apricots.

"You're much too good to us, Harry."

"Dunno what you're talkin' about," he said, pulling off his gloves and stuffing them in his pocket.

"Now give me your mackinaw and cap."

He handed them to her and she hung them in the hall. When she came back into the kitchen, he looked at her closely. "You look better, Laurie."

"I am better." Since Thanksgiving she had been able to sleep at night. And she was doing something she had never done in all her life before. She was taking a real nap in the afternoon. Sometimes when Jesse came he had to wake her. Now that she slept, Jesse was sleeping too. After supper he and his grandfather would work at the kitchen table until seven-thirty, constructing a ship in a bottle. By eight he was dead to the world. "No word, I suppose, from Doris and Ed?" she asked.

"Not yet," he said, spreading his hands over the steam of the kettle.

"When do you figure they'll be back?"

"Not till spring, most likely. There's snow to the north. They're going to stay put."

"How's your mother taking it?"

"Good. Ma's like that. Once she sees a thing's got to be, she takes it fine."

"I know," Laura said warmly. Since the day at the church when Harry had given his ultimatum, Flora had been a different person. She had seen the trailer off with dignity, its shelves stacked, at her instigation, with provisions from the store. When anyone asked what she thought about it, she answered that while it wouldn't suit her as a way to live, it suited them, and that was the point to consider. So that people wouldn't think she was ashamed to face them, she began to go to her meetings again. Already she was back on three committees. Now that she was feeling better, she said, she wouldn't really be needing Annie.

Laura drew out a chair. "Sit down, Harry. What can I get you? Pie? Cake? Sandwich?"

"Got any coffee."

"Of course."

"Good. A cup of that will sure hit the spot."

Harry never minded questions. As he drank his coffee, he told her who had been in and what they had had to say. How many had been at the Grange supper. How thick the ice was. Who had smelt tents on the bay. How his Christmas stock was moving. What his mother was doing. "She's got the old place cleaned out," he said, "from top to bottom."

"What will she do with it, Harry?"

"Don't s'pose you and Jesse would want to move into town?"

She shook her head.

" 'Swat I figgered."

Laura refilled his cup. "I had an idea she might be fixing it up for you, Harry."

He tipped back in his chair. "You didn't think I'd . . ."

He meant Annie. "No, Harry, I didn't. But there are other girls."

"Not here," he said.

"Will you always be here, Harry?"

"If Ma needs me, I will," he said earnestly.

They sat quietly for a time, Harry sipping his coffee. Finally he pushed his cup away and looked directly into her face. "You're not blamin' yourself any more, are you, Laurie?"

She did not answer.

"I've been thinking about Joel," he went on, speaking very slowly. "Joel meant a lot to me, especially when I was a kid."

"I know, Harry." Often now, walking, or working, or lying in bed, she remembered how things had been. Joel the leader then, Harry only the kid who tagged along, asking Joel's opinion, copying all his ways. Looking over his shoulder while he drew. Willing to put up with anything for a word of approval. Then everything had become topsy-turvy. Somehow . . . Somewhere . . .

"And I believe I've figgered things out."

"Yes, Harry?"

"I believe that what happened to Joel would have happened sometime, in one way or another. He was always clumsy, Joel."

Her first memory of him. Joel, a boy of five, with a fish-hook in his finger . . .

Harry picked up his unused spoon and began, very slowly, to draw a pattern on the tablecloth. "But 'twas more'n that," he said thoughtfully. "Remember the way he used to walk that rickety railing by the mill?"

243

Joel, stumbling, swaying, filling her with fright . . . She nodded, swallowing against the pressure in her throat.

"Seems like after his mother left he changed a lot. He got awful reckless. Take those accidents in the woods."

She started to speak, then stopped abruptly.

He laid down the spoon and studied the pattern he had drawn. "That night on the water." This was the first time Harry had ever indicated straight out that he knew. "And takin' out the car."

She covered her eyes with her hands.

Harry paused, then went on, speaking more gently. "Seems like somethin' in him was always headin' toward calamity. Almost like . . ." He hesitated. "Sounds crazy, I know, but almost like he wanted it that way. Does that make any sense to you, Laurie?"

She took her hands from her eyes and raised them for a moment to his face. But she said nothing.

There was another silence, a long one. In it they could hear the kettle's soft boil, the clock's tick, quieter now, almost soothing, and the sound of one crow, far off, calling to another. Finally Harry pushed aside his cup. "What's next, Laurie?" he asked.

She shook her head. She did not know. With Joel's father's board they could get along comfortably enough. In a year or two the land would pay for itself and show some profit. Beyond that she could not look.

"I was wonderin' if maybe you wouldn't want to go to the University in Orono," he said. "You could rent a place there. There'd be a better school for Jesse. Joel's father and me could take care of things here. You'd be back in the summer to look after the berries. 'Twould always be home." He waited. Still she was silent. He leaned forward and spoke again. "What are you thinkin' about, Laurie?"

Her mouth trembled. When she could speak, her words were whispered. "I'm so old. It's too late, Harry."

He put one of his hands, red now and hardened, over hers. Another time . . . another hand . . .

"It's never too late to start," he said.

On the Friday afternoon before Christmas, Laura sat reading by the kitchen window. She read a great deal now, and by spring, she often told herself, she would have worked her way to Miss Baker's highest shelf. Conscious that the room was darkening, she looked outside and saw the first snowflakes of the season beginning to fall.

She watched them for a minute or two, then replaced the straw she used as a bookmark and looked at the clock. It was time for Jesse, and she had promised him she would be ready when he came. They were going to cut their Christmas tree. She had dreaded Christmas. Lying awake those long, long nights, she had told herself she could never face it this year. But now she could think of it quietly, without emotion.

Emmie was coming. As soon as she had received Laura's letter, she had sent one in reply, carefully written on pale blue paper. Laura had shown it to Harry, just as she would have shown it to Luther.

Dear Laura, she had written. *I thank you for your letter. That is all I can say right now. Perhaps someday we can talk about it.*

I should like very much to come for Christmas. I can come the twenty-fourth on the afternoon train. I do not want to put you out, so I will come over on the mail. I should like to surprise my father.

She had enclosed a small colored photograph, showing a gentle, appealing face with big blue eyes and soft, close-cut brown hair. Harry had studied it carefully. "I liked Emmie when I was a kid," he said. "But I never expected she would be as pretty as this." Laura had planned to meet her at the Junction, but Harry was determined he was the one to go. "No tellin'

245

how bad the roads will be by then," he told her. Then, "Maybe I'd better take the picture with me," he added, "so as I'll know her when she gets off the train." (As if more than three passengers ever got off!) Now everything was planned. Emmie and her father would spend Christmas eve with Laura and Jesse. On Christmas day they would all go for dinner at Flora's.

She got up, went into the bedroom, and looked out. The bus was late, but this was not surprising, since it was the last day of school. That meant a Christmas party. It meant rank cards too. Concerning this she felt no apprehension. Ever since his father's death, Jesse had brought his books home and sat down at once with them at the kitchen table. On his own initiative he had sent away for bulletins on forestry and agriculture. That is what Joel would have done, she thought, had things been different long ago. She seldom mentioned Joel to him now. Let him forget, she thought. When he is old enough, I will tell him the whole story, and he will understand, as I do.

She went back into the kitchen and looked at the clock. Four-twenty. She put a stick of wood in the stove, opened the draft, waited until the fire had started up, then closed the draft again. By that time Jesse was opening the back door. His cheeks were red. Snow shone on his cap and mittens.

"Ready, Ma?" he said breathlessly, dumping his books on the table. "All ready to start?"

She turned toward the window. The snow was falling faster now. She knew how he hated to wait, just as she had, but they really ought to put it off until morning. Then she looked back at his eager, animated face.

"Ready," she said, reaching for her boots and mackinaw.

With Jesse carrying the ax, they crossed the road and took a short cut toward the woods. He had not stopped to show her his rank card, and when she asked about it, he dismissed her question lightly. "Just A's," he said. He went on to tell her

246

about the party at school—the cornballs, the candy, the presents exchanged; about the Nativity play put on by the sixth graders; who could be heard, who couldn't, who had to be prompted. How the herald angels had started trouble with the shepherds before the curtain could be tightly closed . . . About the tree, ready to be set up on the green; about the lights Harry was putting along the front of the store . . .

It had been months since she had heard him talk like this.

The flakes came faster now—big, soft, tumbling as they fell. Already the ledges were topped and the bushes lightly crowned. The paths had disappeared. It was like moving in a new world, freely, lightly.

At the edge of the woods they stopped and looked about them. All angles were softened. All disfigurements that the frost had left were blotted out. All scars on the landscape, healed. The branches of the spruce and hemlock—white above, green below—were still.

They stood for a time, silent in the white darkness. Then Jesse nudged her, smiling.

"Look, Ma," he said.

She looked, following his gesture, and saw two crows—slow, stately—beating their way across the sky.

About the Author

VIRGINIA CHASE was born in Blue Hill, Maine, not far from the "barrens" she so movingly describes in ONE CROW, TWO CROW. She attended the state university one year, taught a year as principal of a small Maine high school, then transferred to the University of Minnesota, from which she was graduated *magna cum laude*. She received her Master's degree from Wayne University.

Her teaching experience has been widely diversified. She has taught all ages, all races, all levels, completing her career at Smith College in 1950. Since then she has worked as a part-time lecturer in the adult program of Hartford College For Women. Aside from teaching, she has published five books, as well as articles and stories for leading magazines.

She and her husband have raised blueberries commercially on the Maine mountainside where they once picked them as children. They are also ardent amateur archaeologists. They have crawled through tombs and climbed ruins in Mexico, Greece, Italy, Ireland, and England, and spent one summer digging near Hadrian's wall.